From Red to Dust

By Ra Na-Ged

Prologue- A Warning

"Because of men's blood
And the violence of the land and the city
And all who dwell in it."
~ Habakkuk 2:8

There is a place out in the West where the land rushes red, a color of friction and vitality. When the shunting wind shoots across the wrinkled landscape, the red mist appears as the wrath which piques the face of God Himself.

To touch the red dust with your bare hands would allow you to experience its unexpected softness, as smooth as blood, but the specks are not agglutinative like red blood cells which stick to all surfaces they touch. The dirt of the land here persists in endless days and years, gracing humbled men's faces, but never succeeds in changing Man's dissatisfied soul.

A rider approaching the red mountains and hills for the first time would be confronted by a manifestation of a blooming rose surrounded by small woods in a sea of green, like the first flowers in the Garden of Eden, and the red contrasting with the lush Ponderosa pine trees and juniper bushes will make any horseman ask aloud to the Lord if he has been summoned back to the kingdom of heaven without realizing he has left this mortal realm behind. But the traveler is *not* dead yet; rather, he sees the valleys, creeks, and dry washes, perhaps for the first time in all of his days on Earth, not as a place to walk or break silence, but as an altar to the gloried power of the eternal universe. A man could build in the red lands, but he can never alter the underlying geological systems fabricated in providence.

The iron of the man's flowing blood is of the same iron found within the red dust particles that will blind him during the summer months of monsoon rains and shadowed haboobs, times when vengeful gales of wind further erode both man and the land alike, sparing neither injudicious creatures nor verdant vegetation. A drop of blood touching the land is the return of borrowed elements, and the bleeder must give back what he has purloined from the segmented bodies of the cosmos.

Local bands of Yavapai and Apache tribes used to tell the white men passing through the red lands on their way to the gold coasts of California that the Sky Father had judged the local soil and He must have found the ground to be righteous and just, to allow such a force of life that once flowed through the veins of extinct antediluvian Giants who roamed the mountains to be poured out and dried upon the flat rocks in such fashion, thus giving color to the land. Wouldn't every man or being be blessed to yield to such fates as this, his expended matter anointing all those bearing foot or hoof or root?

A curious white man would inevitably ask the Apache how God could bless a land with the blood from Giants, and the old and toothless tribal elders would question the stranger back, had not the coming of the Great White Fathers, Washington and Jackson and Lincoln *also* brought forth a crimson wave of 'Progress' to the lands of the Indian?

No white man from the East shores had a response to their question.

One pink-sky day, another white man of 'Progress' happened to pass through the red, lush area but this fellow had chosen a more dignified trade and title to use,'Scientist', and he told the Indians that he knew the real reason why the rocks were sunburst orange, much like the skies themselves after the passing of a hot, clear afternoon. He told the local villagers and natives that just as a piece of metal can rust, so too could the region's rocks.

'The rock formations of this land are made of sandstone and granite,' began the 'Scientist'. 'The minerals that form these stones contain iron, and when this metal is exposed to oxygen and water, iron oxide transforms soils and rocks and dusts into hypnotic coloring pigments. As iron oxide-rich water washes over exposed limestone, the faded blood orange spreads out the stains and mark of Cain, and the bright colors that we are breathing into our very lungs as I speak right now, gentlemen, is merely the result of weathering, erosion, and chemical reactions, over long periods of time, a-course! There are no such giants of the land; this is just a myth.'

The old natives stared back at the white man, leaving the 'Scientist' to conclude to himself, 'now, even an *Indian* could understand the basic mechanics of geology, no?'

On a cold autumnal night soon after the man's lecture to the grieved elders, when he was riding back to his work camp alone, the 'Scientist' was struck in the face with a wooden hammer tied to a stone-head, and the white man fell dead before he had plummeted to the ground.

The red seeping out from his nose and ears and mouth soon enjoined and mixed with the stained specks of dust the former man had studied and known so much about. The factual story of his rocks now seeped into the wetted Earth, and the bloodstones became seamlessly meshed with the legends of these mysterious red lands.

Chapter 1- Redview: Population- 1,200 Souls *~1880s A.D.~*

The town of Redview had originally been established by Union officers and soldiers in 1864, during the years of the American Civil War, when the United States Government attempted to build a supply outpost in the northern Arizona territories. The engineers of the Army Corps who had constructed the village named the would-be fort Grant's Pass, and while the name changed after more settlers arrived to form a true town, the original general store's foundation was the same skeleton and bone structure used today by Zeke's Fixtures and Wares clothing shop, one of the few garment and fabric stores within a twenty-five mile radius of the current town of Redview.

The Civil War had ended without much affecting the layout of the small outpost, as pacification was specifically required by the southern Arizona Apache tribes and the firm guiding hand of the Federal government allowed for further progress to sweep across those lands. Development of buildings was suspended by the neutralization of the Red Man, as the war drums were beaten throughout the hills, and the cannon and musket were all that could quell them.

In the year 1869, the first of the painted ladies would arrive at the still-named 'Fort Grant's Pass', and some of the indelicate and uncouth soldiers would muse aloud amongst themselves on how a new kind of 'redness' had come to the town covered in gritty crimson, a redness which could stain the white sheets shared by the entranced blue soldiers and put upon paid women, but this is not how the name of 'Redview' came to grace the town. Prostitutes were among the first prosperous residents of the upstart town, if just for the fleeting time they could keep their money from being spent on rogue, satin, and drink.

No, the new name would be obvious to any newcomer, as you witness the surrounding hills of red rocks, known only to the sun and rains and winds for countless eons, now started to become riddled with wooden structures painted white, but these buildings soon turned tear-streaked orange. From the bottom toes of a man's boots to the tips of the hair follicles atop of his head, the red specks were ubiquitous, and in the windy season of spring, a man's view was not only colored by this light dust, but he would grow accustomed to eating traces of the dirt that would fall into all of his meals, grinding the granular redness betwixt dull, yellowing teeth.

'Ashes to ashes,' the men who worked as ranch hands would joke to their party's cook. 'Dust to dust, come on, Chef, don't make us eat rust!'

Those first working painted ladies, as well as the more reserved and respectable women who would become future residents of Redview, soon discovered that they should not wear dresses or lace consisting of white. Nature may indeed be a mother, but she has never shown kindness to her local daughters striving to live a life of pure fashion sensibility in the land.

Redview continued to grow during the 1870s, as sheep farms and cattle ranches in the surrounding counties and towns started to dot central and northern Arizona. As more progress was made across the territory, all classes of men, and then women, came to these enterprising locations near the town. Navajo cattle ranchers and Mexican villagers from their poor pueblos formed an uneasy truce with the incoming pugilistic white men, and because the closest fort and railroad depots were in those days hundreds of miles away from town, Redview took on an appearance that absorbed all creeds; this was out of necessity, if not by the grace of providence's merciful design.

The initial wooden courthouse of Grant's Pass was lost to fire damage in 1873, but a new building was constructed using the orange and white sandstone rocks that can be seen in the structures of today, if you were to walk along Main Street. Hangings were kept to a minimum, at a mere seven lost souls per year. And the beautiful progress could not be abated.

With the coming of the 'Atlantic & Pacific Railroad' company into Flagstaff, north of Redview, in August of 1882, the town of the red dust attracted ever more rowdy and ambitious citizens of the world. As cotton, copper, citrus, and cattle markets developed vast trade networks across the face of the entire Arizona territories, so too did the 'Rose of Central Arizona', as the first mayor of Redview tried to nickname his town. The accumulation of saloons, dance halls, and gambling dens, particularly in the side streets linking off from Main Street, tended to lend the more appropriate sobriquet 'Scarlet Rose' for Redview, by both newcomers and long time residents of the area. The most honorable townsfolk tried to de-cowboy the way of life within the town's jurisdiction, with limited success. The town's jail had been built by donations from Redview's leading citizens, congregants of St. George's First Episcopalian Church, and members of St. Mary's Catholic Church. Although the jail contained a mere three cells, they were seldom vacant for long, but the brutal work of the land soon emptied the drunken rowdies back into the streets, leaving decent people to their own protective abilities, and the sanctity of their waxing righteousness.

The changing of the local sheriff and his accompanying deputies occurred with swift frequency, but Redview's current leading lawman, Sheriff Daggs, had been able to form and develop a type of personal understanding with the various factions of cliques and posses of ranchers, rustlers, cowboys and the rare honest man, although the good Christian folk of Redview spoke in hushed open whispers concerning the sheriff's inner moral fiber; much was left to be desired when considering the man's internal constitution.

'No matter,' some people would say. 'At least Sheriff Daggs hasn't run off yet, like all the rest of 'em boys a-fore him have done. Let the man collect a dirty dollar, every now and then.'

And these voices were correct.

To the east of Redview's jail, to the south down Main Street, and then by taking the offshoot path through Massie Lane, a person will find one's self in front of the most notorious saloon and whorehouse in Redview, The Eye of the Needle, which serves as a club headquarters, of sorts, to the shooting Neary Gang, led by the man from Galay, the infamous Boze Neary.

As a man walks through the saloon's inner swinging doorways, he would do well to ensure that the doors do not strike back at him, and throughout all the time whilst he is inside of an establishment where men sometimes do not come back through the moving door.

Chapter 2- The Eye of the Needle

"C'mon, Jake, goddamnit, pour us out another! Or leave the bottle," roared Frank Jones to the bartender, as the ranch hand stood next to his fellow disruptive friend at The Eye of the Needle bar. "I ain't gonna ask so kindly again!"

The men were in their early twenties, unpaid, and quite thirsty. The powdery redness of the area had settled permanently upon their dried-out tongues.

"Light a fire, Jake!" shouted the second young man, Ted Channing, and he hit both of his fists against the bar.

Both men were armed, as most patrons of the saloon tended to be, and the persistence in the men's ornery voices towards Jake, The Needle's long-suffering bartender, was also not in itself unusual. No, what was a mark against the ordinary was that these two sporadically employed ranch hands chose Boze Neary's own headquarters to complain about the gangleader.

The entirety of Redview was aware of The Eye of the Needle's ruthless reputation, but the prideful, rebellious heart of a drunken young man nursing a grudge knows of no means towards restraint, outside those of greater and compelled violence. 'Tis the way of the world.

"About time, you son of a bitch!" Frank Jones yanked the fresh whiskey bottle from Jake's outreached hands. "Now, in a little while, you let that damn mick know that Jones and Channing are here to collect payment for works rendered, and we ain't just some paddies off the coffin ships, either!"

The two youthful men at the bar toasted to themselves, celebrating their ability to be treated like men. The rest of the saloon's denizens went unnoticed by the petulant ranch hands, but the dozen or so other fellows drinking and playing cards at nearby tables in the Needle kept an eye and ear at the ready, watching for the arrival of the Irishman and his gang of cowboys; some whispered that they were already present in the building, waiting like the wolf. The sweaty-browed men rubbed at their temples and breathed in the tainted dust of the saloon and whorehouse, but they did not dare to exhale the fiery air, just yet, out of fear for the consequences for such impropriety.

"Like I told you fellars an hour ago when ya got here, the boss ain't in yet!" scowled Jake, a man in his mid-forties.

Frank Jones eyed the barman by incorporating the mimicked look of a threatened diamondback, before the young man took out his revolver, and he pointed the gun in the bartender's direction.

"You watch how ya talk to a man, boy," said Frank, the usual leading instigator of the two ranch hands.

"Hey, I don't need no gun for the likes of him; lookie here!" shouted Ted Channing, as he reached over the bar top and slapped Jake across his face with an open palm. "Now go wipe down the other side of the bar, would ya, old timer?"

The two brazen young men laughed while they became drunker and meaner.

Juvenile seconds would become prime minutes, and minutes wandered til they became wizened hours. The last rays of the splendid Arizona sun splashed along the soiled bartop through the Needle's sole, dirty front bay window, but the Neary Gang and its leaders had still yet to arrive.

Looking out the bay window during sunset, a person can witness the evening dusk flee the redness in a hurry, as a murderer tries to escape from the scene of his crime; but even darkness would be insufficient to hide all the acts that have come to pass in the days of men and stones, for there are eternal eyes that do not require light in order to see.

As the evening made its presence known, Frank and Ted had almost finished another whiskey bottle; while still simmering in the angry vaporous cauldrons of their own making, the young men had become sloppy and uncaring towards their personal safety, placing their scratched revolvers onto the bar, at a distance that was out of reach of the ranch hands' grasp.

Distracted by the confidence of ardent spirits and wasteful youth, neither man heard the quick approaching footsteps from above their heads, as a stout figure jaunted across the Needle's upper balcony, and the man made his way towards the top of the staircase, near the west end of the back of the bar.

The other patrons of the saloon watched in silence, and waited for the explosion.

The man strode up on sturdy legs on a frame of medium height, and being in his fifties, the salt of his sideburns and the lined crow's feet around his gold, gray eyes could attest to the man's age. Boze Neary, the man from Galway, in the western wilds of Ireland, looked down from the balcony's bannister at the slurring and guffawing former ranch hands of Neary's financial backer, Mr. William Ridge, or as he makes all of his employees refer to him as, 'Colonel' Ridge, although the vain man had never achieved that rank, even after a brief period of service in his home state militia when he was a far younger man. Mr. Ridge had fired Frank and Ted after various infractions related to insubordination under his employ while working his ranch property outside of town, but the two rowdies had refused to leave Redview without collecting back pay from the would-be 'colonel'. Ridge's refusal to pay them had rendered the men vindictive, thus causing the businessman to utilize the deadliest tool in his work belt to dispel the growing threat the contentious youth presented to his proper authority. The faux 'Colonel' Ridge's first instinct in both business and personal matters was to never aim to violence. However, if a man failed to understand reason as the 'colonel' saw matters to be, then other methods to obtain his ends were deployed both swift and most visceral in their use.

The current brutal but effective method came in the form of Boze Neary and his gang of outlaws, from which any success derived from the posse came at the expense of Ridge's respectability and the envy experienced by other, less dishonest cattlemen and nearby ranchers in central and northern Arizona. Just as a hammer helps the carpenter to build, so too can the tool smash the own thumb of the unwatching, impatient builder.

Boze Neary now stood one step down from the top of the Needle's staircase. Scanning the ground floor of the saloon for a moment, the gangleader next clapped his tanned, hairy hands together three consecutive times, helping to garner the drifting attention of the almost dead-drunk young interlopers.

Ted Channing's head rested upon the palm of his right hand, which was in turn supported by his forearm and elbow, and the limb bore the brunt of the combined weight of the drunkard's upper half, but he struggled to even slur his words out from a cotton-lined mouth.

Frank Jones, on the other hand, could not only still see straight out of his left eye, he was also able to recall, with some bleary vagueness, why he had come to the Eye of the Needle to begin with.

"Hey, you cheating bastard, Neary!" screamed the hoarse-sounding Frank. "We want our money! Right, Ted?"

Frank tapped his friend on the shoulder, but this resulted in Ted losing his balance, causing him to collapse onto the floor. Although the young ranch hand was quick to bounce back up, neither of them were witness to the silent saloon entrance of Neary's right-hand man, Jimmy Cotton, who was armed with a long Bowie knife, and he grabbed the top of Ted's hair and then glanced upwards to Boze, awaiting the boss's command. Neary nodded his approval once, and Jimmy Cotton slit Ted's throat. Jake dropped a glass cup from behind the bar, but every other man present inside of the saloon did not even dare to breathe, with the lone exception being Frank, who gasped in open-mouthed shock, as his friend's body gurgled out a loud death-rattle, the carotid artery being severed, thus gushing out a fresh collection for the town's redness, as the man's blood now served as further drops of paint coating a furious tapestry along the Needle's floor.

"Now, Mr. Jones, where to begin with you," said Neary, as he made two steps down the staircase. Only the most discerning of a linguist's ear could detect the faint sing-song, western Irish lilt in the old man's voice, and this was practiced by design, as the accent reappeared even thicker when Neary was inebriated; unlike the caricature depicted concerning his countrymen, Boze Neary restricted himself to a single day and night of drinking on the anniversary of the day his mother deserted him. "I believe Mr. Ridge had been quite forthright in his expectations of you boys. You were given advice, and then came the warnings. What do you have to say for yourself, Frankie?"

"Damn you to hell, paddy," Frank spat out a brown gob of spit as he tried to grab his loaded revolver on top of the bar.

"Jimmy, if you would, please." said Neary, as he took a few more steps down the staircase.

Jimmy Cotton used a closed fist to smash the left side of Frank's face, causing him to lose several teeth, before the ranch hand fell onto the floor.

"Help him to stand back up," said Neary, now standing a few steps from the bottom of the stairs, where he stopped to take out his own knife. "I know a lot about birds, Mr. Jones. Yes, a strange matter to confess to, at a time such as this, but it's true. Even as a young child, I loved to watch birds fly through the winter sky, heading to parts unknown to my youthful eyes, and invisible to all but my own deepest hopes and desires. But anyways, Frank, I'm afraid I have an indelicate observation that I must confess to you. Your great American bird, the emblem of this nation, the bald-headed eagle is a savage, dirty bird, a most dreadful creature which wreaks havoc amongst all of the other birds; it's a quite horrible beast, wouldn't you agree? Kinda like you?"

Boze Neary had completed his journey to the end of the staircase and he came within grabbing reach of the wounded Frank at the bar, where Jimmy continued to restrain the bloodied man.

"Did the two of you really think you would be safe from death because Ridge had said you would be? Well, you dirty bird, a dodo who refuses to fly away, you must now have your wings clipped."

Frank's eyes closed while Neary's gray ones watched his demonic craftwork, as his left hand plunged the knife up to the hilt of the blade into the heart of the now sober, dying young man. Frank fell forward towards Neary, but he let the body slide past his own, allowing the dead ranch hand to hit the floor again.

"Gentlemen," said Neary, looking around the saloon, from Jimmy Cotton to Jake the bartender and on to the random fellows seated around the rest of the Needle. "The less said about this matter to the 'colonel' and Sheriff Daggs, the better it will be for you."

After ordering the clean-up and disappearance of the bodies, Boze Neary, Jimmy Cotton, and several other members of the Neary Gang ventured out into the night, ready for the devil to try to find them before they found him.

Chapter 3- The Visit to Dr. Taig Ward's Ranch Home

Seated at the head of a long oaken table in the dining room was the ranch house's patriarch, 36-year-old Dr. Taig Ward, a self-made man. To his right was his 30-year-old wife, Nelcy. Their four children, Rachel, Michael, Stephen, and Elmira, sat on either side of the table. At the far other end of the dinner table sat the Honorable Judge Eugene Graves, with Mrs. Graves next to him.

The children were lost in conversation amongst themselves, but the adults were shorter on words, each considering the major rumor spreading around Redview. Mrs. Graves, Nelcy Ward, and Dr. Ward were of one mind in agreement that Boze Neary had murdered the Jones and Channings boys earlier in the month, with several witnesses offering first hand details concerning the double homicide inside of the Eye of the Needle saloon, where the Neary Gang honed their debaucherous schemes.

Standing alone, as was his typical temperament when considering urgent legal matters, the 63-year-old Judge Graves made no loud argument in Neary's defense, nor did he take any time to persuade the others with a specific line of reasoning for why he thought as he did, and left the measure at the lack of evidence.

"I'm sorry, Taig, but without any bodies, it seems just as likely those boys could have skipped town, headed to God knows where, but hey, at least they're not stirring up trouble around these parts right now, no?"

"Not if they're dead, Eugene!" wailed Mrs. Graves at her husband, who had never raised his voice towards her, but neither did he tend to show his wife affectionate emotion of any kind.

"Now, now, mother, please calm down," said Judge Graves. "I've discussed the idea with Sheriff Daggs, and he agrees with me. No bodies, no crime."

"I can't say that that surprises me, Judge," said Nelcy Ward, whose husband nodded in agreement. "Daggs has hardly the sense to know how to read and he can only spell his name. The man might be an old gunfighter, but he is not sophisticated enough to know how to be a policeman in a modern-day county."

"He *used* to be a fighter, maybe, but whether he now refuses to fight, or he forgot how, I think that only you, Judge, are the true arm of the law in Redview." said Taig, as he took a moment to immerse himself in deep thought once again.

Doctor Ward had left his birth state of Texas in his early twenties after becoming licensed to practice medicine, and the young man began traveling throughout the American southwest. After hearing rumors describing crumbled hills of red rocks, Taig arrived in Redview, where he fell in love with a girl and thus decided to build a practice in the town near to where his new wife, Nelcy, part of a 1st-generation white family, had been born, in the area known as the 'Scarlet Rose' to local inhabitants.

Many years of helping the people had allowed Taig to purchase his most prideful of possessions, the 200 acres of land and the bricked Spanish Colonial-style ranch house that had been brought over brick by sandstone brick from Sonora, Mexico, in order to be re-constructed on the doctor's expansive estate.

Taig Ward had come far from Texas, but his grandfather, Ronald Ward, had journeyed farther still; being born in Quincy, Massachusetts, Ronald Ward left New England behind for flatter pastures and dreams of cattle riches, as he hustled through the Great Plains of Kansas and Oklahoma, earning money hand-over-fist by practicing steel determination and losing it just as quick through his spendthrift habits. After a bad spell of luck while cattle rustling in Cimarron County, Oklahoma, the patriarch of the Ward clan drifted southwards into Texas.

The Ward spirit was known to roam.

Taig's father, Ronald Jr., was a honest man, unlike Ronald Sr. before him; he married an Irish immigrant named Sally, who insisted that she be allowed to christen their son with a Gaelic name, and she would do her best to beat the Ward craziness from out of her only son, Taig, if it was the last she ever did. Dr. Ward's paternal uncles and cousins were not so fortunate to have been whipped by a lady from Limerick, and the road came to an abrupt end for Grandfather Ward, as well. Ronald Sr. never met a liquor bottle that he did not surrender to. The old man had attempted many times to quit drinking, but the booze had never quit him. Ronald Ward Sr. died in the shallow waters of a sanitarium at the age of 67.

The other Ward boys, uncles, cousins and what-have-yous, all meandered throughout the western regions of the developing nation, and usually ended up for the worse. Nelcy was persistent in persuading Taig to return to prayer time after time, but the doctor could recall just one or two other Ward relatives who were able to stay on the right side of the law and run away from humanity's endless vices. Taig's own father, Ronald Jr., had been an exception.

Looking at his own two sons, Michael and Stephen, Taig had arranged for their military careers, as he believed the Academy would foster the boys' raw electric energy into proper outlets. Nelcy had thought her husband odd, for Dr. Ward possessed a peculiar dislike of the firearm. He did not detest their usefulness and, when he was younger, he had even been a passable shot under the direct tutelage of a particular uncle Ward and his son, but Taig knew that the way of the gun had an ability to destroy the shooter's soul, no matter if he survived the shoot-out or not. Although Dr. Ward had never been involved in a gunfight, he'd treated three men who'd been wounded and later died after, and he considered himself to be no idealist about pursuing glory. If some men's spirits were born towards that way, then let the Federal Army build him into a warrior. Taig holstered a revolver only when circumstances pressed him to.

'The only good renegade gunfighter is a dead one,' Taig had declared once inside of his own mind, as reason and logic had had a tendency to re-assert their domains against his weaker judgment, and in spite of all natural human impulse to do otherwise.

Ending his pause, the doctor looked to his older friend.

"Let me ask you a fair question, Judge, and I'll give you an honest moment's consideration for your benefit, but please allow me a dignified response by you, good sir. Would you entrust the lives of all those present, including your own, into the hands of Sheriff Daggs?" asked Taig, as all eyes, both adult and child, now turned to face Judge Graves to hear what he would say.

The judge sat as a stone with long white eyelashes, much as he had on the 17 occasions when he had sentenced and condemned men to die by a variety of methods, including hanging and by firing squad. Graves felt and understood the present company's discomfiture and disgust at his refusal to accept the common wisdom of the dinner table, but the judge also realized the most mitigating factor; there was simply no other gunfighter to relieve Sheriff Daggs of his duty, election or no election upcoming this fall season. Each and every man in the county who could be considered semi-qualified to wear the badge and serve as sheriff had been approached beforehand, and each, down to the last decent man, had firmly rejected the pleaded offer.

No one else at Ward's ranch house may have wanted to confess, but the judge understood he did them all a favor by keeping his concerns to himself, for now.

"Regardless, Judge, we all trust your heart is in the right place," added Nelcy, as she looked into the white-haired man's eyes. "But these murders are not the usual range war shoot-out. These were cold-blooded executions, with over ten witnesses, if you listen to Old Bill Murphy spout it out on Main Street when he is deep in his cups."

"Then what is to be done?" asked Judge Graves, pausing for effect, as he looked in a circular motion around the oaken table.

At that moment, Gunther, one of Dr. Ward's manservants announced to the dining room that a rider was approaching the home; a lone man, from the looks of things.

"Thank you, Gunther," Taig said to the older German man. "Let some of the ranch hands deal with the incoming messenger. Unless it is urgent, I intend on continuing to entertain my guests without interruption for the rest of the evening."

As the manservant left the dining room, Judge Graves signaled to Dr. Ward that he had eaten all that he could, and was now ready for post-dinner stogies and expensive drink.

"And shall coffee be served with your usual brandy and cigars, gentlemen?" asked Nelcy Ward. "Or perhaps a slice of blueberry pie? Mrs. Graves? I know the children and myself would be delighted to have some company in the parlor room."

"Indeed, yes!" replied Mrs. Graves.

"No," said the men in unison, as they stood up to take their leave from the children and womenfolk.

"Goodnight, Mrs. Graves. Children, remember your chores in the morning, so do not stay up too late," said Dr. Ward, as he walked over to his wife, and then kissed her. "And you, Mrs. Ward, I shall see later on tonight."

Taig Ward saw the look in his wife's eyes, a sorrowed face he'd seen at various times over the course of their 14 years of marriage. Taking a moment to offer Nelcy kind eyes in return, acknowledging that he would continue to attempt at convincing the judge in the Ward smoking room, the older law man's patience permitting, of course. But Dr. Ward had to try, and he further knew that his devoted wife believed that he was just the man to convince his longtime friend to act against the Neary Gang, at long last.

Nelcy nodded in agreement and then looked to the children to help the waiting staff bring in the dessert, as Judge Graves and Dr. Ward headed to the explicit sanctuary of the ranch home's smoking room.

Nelcy Ward, mother to now 2nd-generation Redviewians, had spoken last week about their prospects for selling ranch home and land and moving away from this land, perhaps venturing out to the coast.

'If our family cannot be protected here, then why risk all that is sacred in this life?' she'd asked her husband.

Although she had listened to each of his arguments, at the end of the day, both Nelcy and Taig concurred with each other that the Neary Gang would need to be removed from town if real law and order were to be instituted not only in Redview, but also throughout the entire county.

After cutting the tips from both of their cigars, Taig Ward steadied himself into a plush chair, and then he inhaled a deep breath of smoke, speculating on how the judge would react to his request.

"Does the cigar suit you? That's Virginian tobacco, that is." said the doctor.

Judge Graves nodded his head, before expelling a large burst of smoke from both of his nostrils and open mouth.

"Indeed, young man, it is most excellent."

Taig hesitated for a second, wanting to linger with his cigar a little longer, but the doctor felt a sense of urgency soon wash over him, as the gray smoke started to waft throughout the air.

"What if the two of us talked to Mr. Ridge, in the capacity of concerned citizens, and not throwing around rank or making any demands of him? I mean, I am practically the man's nearest neighbor, our ranch properties being so close to one another, and you, Judge, being an occasional poker buddy of his, I just do not understand why we cannot ask him what he intends to do about Boze Neary and his pack of wild wolves."

Dr. Ward paused to take another puff from off of his smoldering stogie.

Judge Graves' response came in the form of his own streaming burst of inner vespers, as the silence between the two friends grew louder.

"Alright, then, Judge," Taig attempted to reason again. "Sure, we've broached this subject in the past before, but if you're not willing to have a discussion with Ridge, then I suppose that leaves us with the Federal troopers. Do you really want to involve the Army in Redview's matters? I say none of this needs to end in bloodshed. If we can just talk to this wannabe military man, as two men talking to another honorable man, I remain utterly convinced that Ridge would be compelled to agree with us, and that he'd send Neary and his ilk back down south to Tombstone, where they can run wild in that crazy town, far away from the placid place the good founding peoples had deemed worthy enough to christen the name Redview."

At last being riled to his last nerve, and the brandy beginning to take effect, the judge's mind broke as the soft snow triggers an avalanche down the faces of the Rocky Mountains.

"Okay, Taig, let's *really* bring the matter to its conclusion, shall we? Have you ever been to a Ringling Brothers Circus? And have you seen the man called 'lion tamer'? This brave fool has a whip and wooden stool to control the feline beast. Now, of course, the carnival folk play up the dramatics of the whole affair, but continue to go along this path with me further, good doctor, and just consider this; if the lion were not to respond to the tamer's commands anymore, or if the sting from the cracking whip was unable to frighten the beast, how much longer would a man be able to control the lion, before the savage animal consumes him and everyone else in the vicinity?"

"Where I come from, Judge, two gentlemen can disagree and become physically violent towards one another, but that doesn't mean the shootings need to start." observed Dr. Ward.

"As is the same for where I come from, sir, but this is Redview we are talking about, and the time is now. No, Taig, our options are severely limited. The facts remain that, it would seem, good men tend to be cowards. The wolves and lions of this world, they hold no qualms concerning their awful actions, and the wolves take all that they can from the rest of us. No, I *do not* want the Army to be called into town, but we all must recognize that we have few good choices to choose from."

Before he could make a counterargument to his aged friend's claim, Taig's concentration was interrupted by a knock at the smoking room's door.

"Come in!" huffed Dr. Ward.

"Master Ward, I'm sorry to bother you, sir, but the new visitor we discussed earlier this evening says that he knows you, and he further wishes to speak with you," said Gunther.

"Is someone dying or need me to operate on them? So what if I know this man or not!"

"He says he is a relative of yours, a cousin from back in south Texas."

"Send him in." demanded Dr. Ward, as he watched a man a year older than himself enter the smoking room.

Taig recognized the clean-shaven face as being similar to his own, minus the doctor's kempt beard, and the fact that his cousin's hair hung low, just above his broad shoulders. But the man was odd, in that he neither wore a hat nor carried one in his possession, akin to the Indian style of habit.

Taig had not seen Owen Ward since they were both teenagers, when Owen was riding tag along with various hoodlums and outlaws, but before the young man had turned professional. Taig had not even considered becoming a doctor at the time, he was so much greener, then.

"Hello, Taig," smiled Owen in a closed-mouth and wry manner.

As the dusty man nodded, his dirty blonde hair cascading down his forehead and ears, Taig had a moment to glance over his long lost kinsman. Owen Ward wore a simple gray work shirt, brown work pants, and cracked boots. As far as Dr. Ward could surmise, his cousin also appeared to be unarmed, outside of the wooden-handled Bowie knife he had strapped to his left hip. Owen looked haggard from what Taig presumed to be many long miles of riding out in the open elements of an eclectic natural world.

"Hello, Owen." Taig finally responded, without offering anything to his new guest, as he was curious to know what the stranger wanted.

"Aunt Sally, back home in Texas, told me where to find you all the way out here in the territories. I told her how I wanted to check up on you, see how things were with your family. I was always Aunt Sally's favorite nephew," laughed Owen.

Judge Graves eyed the stranger with placid concern, thinking Owen Ward had the look of a man of humor, but with dark regrets; the eyes seemed to see more than what was in front of them, or was that by design?

"My mother always felt sorry for you, Owen. I see that she still does." replied Taig, before returning to smoky silence.

"I deserve that, I know I do, and I don't blame you for having your suspicions of me. Neither my father or myself have ever been much for doing good, but I thought that we still had youthful memories from our childhood together, as well."

"Are you still a shootist?"

"I've given up that trade, cousin. Maybe we can talk about it more some other day, but over the last seven years, I've had a *lot* of time to think about my life. Look, I ain't looking for a hand-out or nothing. Aunt Sally told me you got hundreds and hundreds of acres of land and that you've been having trouble finding enough boys to help you till the property for you, and goddamn, boy, you sure *do* have a lot of land, you do! Took me thirty minute ride to cover half of what you got out here. Woo, Taig! Now, all I'm asking for is an opportunity to help work your land, maybe help with the cattle. I was born a shit-kicker, before I picked up the gun, and you remember that. I vow to work hard, not drink any spirits, and fulfill whatever task your hired fellas charge me with completing, and I swear upon the Good Book that I will not cause you or your family any headaches or heartbreaks. The Lord's truth, sir!"

Taig Ward watched his cousin's explanations as a spider weaving its web, setting the trap for its next victim, for the doctor had not forgotten the drunken brawls, the overwhelming demands of so-called 'owed respect' to the local gunfighters in south Texas, a type of weak deference to violent men who Taig viewed as the ultimate cowards, and not the heroes of pulp fiction like writers from the cities depict in their books about the West, where lies are told about the way of the cowboys.

No, Dr. Ward would allow no such hero worship onto his property.

"I am very sorry, Owen, but you are not welcome here. You're a disgrace to the Ward family, if that was at all possible. Why don't you go back to riding with the Jonson Gang again? I've read that they're real good at murdering harmless children."

The mirth was ripped from out of Owen's soul, Judge Graves could witness. The man's face appeared as though he had been punched in the gut.

"I swear, Taig, I had nothing to do with those deaths. I rode with those boys for a spell, that part is true, but I've only ever killed men who aimed to murder me first, I swear on it. I would never kill a civilian!" Owen did not shout, but his laconic voice did rise up in temperament.

"Owen, listen to me very carefully. I don't want you on my land and I certainly do not want to see you anywhere near my wife or children. Now, Gunther here will give you a few gallons of water and some spare pork we had for dinner tonight, and any blankets you may require, or perhaps a hat, unless you prefer to go native, but this is the best that I can do for you."

"I wish you wouldn't be that way, Taig. I'll be sleeping under the stars again tonight."

"Be that as it may, I am sure Redview, being the 'Scarlet Rose' that it is, will be able to accommodate you with enough pleasurable distractions to occupy your time. A good rider can make it from here to Main Street in one hour's time. You better get riding now, though, before it gets any darker."

"I'll stay in town, then; see if I can't get any work. Goodbye, Taig."

Taig nodded his cousin's dismissal.

Gunther showed Owen to the front door, while the judge looked at his friend for a long moment.

"What about him? I admit he appears to be similar to so many other seedy, crass rowdies in town, but does the man know how to shoot?"

"Excuse me, Judge, but just what are you asking me?"

"Your cousin, do you think he might be able to help us with the Neary Gang? I don't like the looks of him, but -."

In normal times, the younger man would never have interrupted his friend, but he could not stand to hear the judge go any further in his current line of thinking.

"He's also a degenerate drunkard, man!" Dr. Ward exploded. "I haven't seen the man in damn near twenty years and now I'm supposed to depend on him for help in this most delicate of situations?"

"Sometimes, in order to defeat a wolf, you need a monster of your own."

"Well, I'm not Dr. Frankenstein, and I don't ask thugs for their assistance. No, sir, you're dead wrong about the man, *dead* wrong!"

"I just thought I'd ask you, Taig. I'm sorry to have upset you so. Consider the idea forgotten."

But the idea was not forgotten; for even as a man comes to the conclusion that he must take on a terrible burden in the distant future, and while he can put this matter out of his mind or attempt to think the problem away, he still remains subconsciously aware of what needs to be done. In all of human history, this has never made the choice or the eventual actions taken any easier. No, not by a longshot.

The men drank and smoked deep into the night.

Chapter 4- Owen Ward Leaves Behind the Way of the Gun

Owen Ward was born a year before his cousin Taig, in Olive Spring, Texas, the first grandson of a petty businessman from New England. Owen's father, Martin Ward, was the younger brother of Ronald, Jr., and he was the first man to teach Owen how to shoot; first, with the purpose of hunting, and then, just for the thrill.

The objective of shooting would become for Owen an end in itself, pulling off shots whenever the inclination warranted him to do so, and thus in the starting portion of life he had been encouraged by his father to become a shootist.

In the days when buffalo roamed throughout the western plains, Owen had spent several summers earning honest wages during his mid-teens working as a buffalo hunter for railroad work crews who operated throughout the West. The workers, broken men of Chinese, Irish, and freed extractions, grew to appreciate Owen's sublime ability to bring in fresh meat every day after his hunts, and not to have to consume any meals riddled throughout with buckshot, causing the eater to have to spit out bits of bullet to be able to chew on the buffalo fat, like the hunters who were poor shots brought in to the work kitchen during lean days.

No, Owen Ward was an excellent shot, aiming small, and limiting the pulling of his trigger until when the wind and timing was near-perfect. Outside of the thousands of hours of monotonous target shooting, the solitary secret to Owen's success as a shootist could be attributed to his grace in allowing his mind to be clear in the moment of peril. His breathing would become shorter, all thoughts and hopes for tomorrow expunged from memory, and Owen was the shark in open waters, eyes sealed and his smiling razor-sharp teeth displayed to the combatants; the smile is what unnerved more than a few of his opponents. Honest and of so good cheer, you'd think that Owen was about to toast your health, instead of trying to be the first man to fire a shot at you.

'But no,' Owen now thought, as he guided his horse along the moonlit, red-soaked path back towards the direction of Redview, which he had avoided on his way over to visit his cousin. 'I am not a gunfighter anymore.'

Owen's first entrance into the central Arizona region had met with his approving eyes, and he delighted in the harsh redness, the same as every man and woman before him. Not having seen so delectable hills and mountains throughout all of his time spent riding and whoring and drinking across the Southwestern regions, Texas and northern Mexico, Owen thought the town of 'Scarlet Rose' may not be such a bad place to lay down his hat, although the man did not possess a hat of which to speak of, as the ex-shootist rode hatless, following the style of old Apache and Yavapai associates of his. The lack of sunshade lended to the bleached gold and tanned look of Owen's face. His brown eyes sharpened to the red stinging wind, as he urged his horse to move quicker into the night.

Owen rode nearer to the as-of-yet unmet love of his mortal life. In all of the years he had wasted plying his professional trade as a gunsman and dealing with the ramifications that ensues when practicing said profession, the free man had never had much of an opportunity to develop more than a passing notion of passion for the opposite sex; although he was very fond of their company in the saloons, dance halls, and brothels throughout his time of being a 'cowboy.' Thus, given the previous work experience of Owen's aforementioned future love interest, Miss Emma Rabelais, the mother to nine-year-old Tom Rabelais, a person might expect to think theirs was a love at first sight, but alas, their love was not. However no, that first meeting between the two, and their discovery of true love, lay still a little further ahead.

But first, Mr. Owen Ward, ex-gunslinger, found himself outside the more respectable saloons built up in less hazardous fashion along Main Street and 1st Avenue, where orange sandstone and faded yellow limestone were cut into smooth rectangular boxes, the pieces fitting together like the parts of a puzzle form a greater jigsaw. The redness in the nearby mountains were obscured at this hour of night, as were most of the faces of the denizens of Redview who were enjoying themselves while interloping along the seven blocks-long main-thoroughfare road; but the color was never absent in the spirit of the people, as it lay always just around the corner. A quick burst of bloodlust; the solitary ideal certain men of Redview could respect whilst interacting with other men in town, and those vague specters of threats from the mere passing-by of uncouth strangers could keep a fellow's aggression in check, if not his jaded jests or half-hearted attempts to mug at his fellow man. Unless, of course, the onlooker happened to be a woman or a shootist, the ruthless gunman who asked no questions and answered to no lawman; then in that case, all other men would fear the way of the gun, or otherwise prioritize their desire to catch the woman's attention.

Although Owen was lost inside of himself as he strolled the dry streets in town, he thought how human he felt not owning a gun anymore, allowing him the opportunity to ease his disquieted conscience, if not protect his mortal person. For what is it to save one's life, just to be lost into the wastelands and received into the devil's desperate, seeking hands? How many years of freedom is a man willing to sacrifice in order to *preserve* his life?

Owen was reminded of his seven years being locked-up and breaking rocks for 15-hour work days, six out of seven sunrises per week. Hearing the sounds emanating from the blood-colored and freshly painted wooden den of vice, he let himself enter into the Old World.

Content in being gun-less, it was inside of Mac's Golden Nugget Gambling Hall that Owen bumped into the vaquero Flores, (self-styled as the 'King of Flowers' owing to the printed petals on the sides of his black boots), a previous associate of the former shootist when Owen was running illegal moonshine, rum, and mescal over the Rio Grande in his late teenage years. The direction of the movement of the contraband alcohol depended upon whether the white government officials were angry about current import prices, the brown government officials were angry about alcohol exports, or if *both* corrupt American and Mexican border agents were upset about their dictated cuts of the profits. Bandits and other rowdies such as Owen Ward and Flores found themselves to be amongst those taking the most amount of risk for the least earned money. Times change and men find better deals elsewhere.

"Flores, boy, how the hell are you doing? What flowers have you painted in Redview to celebrate your latest conquests?" asked Owen of the man with fresh-painted petals on the tops of his boots.

"Aw, 'Mad' Owen Ward, how goes the gun trade?" the Mexican cowboy loudly responded, standing with one foot propped up on a stool at his table near the bar, with no regard to the passed-out white man sprawled out next to him at the neighboring chair. "But yes, the red, orange, and purple flowers that now grace my boots are local renditions of the 'Indian Paint-brush' varieties. I thought these flowers to be of a rather delicate touch, and they match the ways of the Navajo muchachitas who call this land home. Ha!"

The black-leather boots had green shoots that reached towards the tops of Flores's knees, the flower heads bursting into magnetic fireworks across the red-dust encrusted shoes of the cowboy trade. Owen was unsure whether to be more jealous of the man's elaborate boots or his presumed sexual adventures with the local native women.

'Yes,' thought Owen Ward. "Indian Paint-brushes.'

These were the same flowers that grew like weeds on his grandmother's land back home in southern Texas, as he could recall from his long past boyhood. The paint brushes were as clear in the former shootist's mind as if the 'King of Flowers' had plucked the stems from out of Owen's head and placed them onto the middling gunfighter's boots. For although Flores was indeed a shootist, he was also a vain man, who would sometimes forget his proper footing during a gunfight. But besides these issues, Owen had had no major quarrels with Flores, even during their respective years of riding with rival cowboy outfits that were technically at war with each other; Owen and Flores were not the kind of men to let a shoot-out or two come between their brotherhood of camaraderie.

"Now, Mr. 'Mad' man, I know you have merely smelled and looked at only half of all of the flowers and lilies that I have been able to pluck away from the earth in the heart of spring and summertime, but perhaps you can observe me to see what you need to do to be so lucky with the ladies." smiled Flores, as he toasted a glass of water at Owen, as the Mexican national never drank alcohol, a rarity in his line of work.

"It may very well be true, Flores, that I have only slept with about half of the number of women that you have been with, but let the record show, furthermore, that all of my women have been twice as beautiful as the prairie dogs you have found yourself curled up around, boy. Can I buy you another water?"

"Ah ha, cowboy! Very good. As you can see by the look of my companion's face–" Flores gestured to the man still firmly planted into his crumpled hat on the table, "–there is a reason as to why I do not drink. Of course, the man has his own motives to be so foregone."

"Oh, yeah? Just who is this drunken gringo beside you? And how the hell did you find yourself in Redview?" asked Owen, as he ordered a glass of water and licked the end of a cigarette purchased by him from a passing serving girl.

"His name is Bob Channing and why he drank himself into a stupor is because his step-brother was murdered by the Neary Gang, over at the Eye of the Needle saloon, their hang-out. Diced is a more liable term to use to describe what happened to Ted Channing and his friend. Them boys went complaining to Neary, and I guess he didn't appreciate their words all that much. So, now my friend, Bob here, drinks. A lot. As for me, hombre, I am like you. Gunfighters don't have a home."

"I'm not carrying a gun anymore. See?" said Owen, as he proceeded to pat down his own sides and lift up the bottom end of his pants, revealing the inside of his boots to be empty.

At this, the 'King of Flowers' roared out a loud belt of laughter, as one who knows the hope of trying to stop a horse from going further, and realizing that the bumpy trail ahead is far from being over.

"May your enemies only ever be armed with pea shooters!" Flores again toasted with his water glass held up into the air.

"Yes, and the same for all of the angry husbands and fathers who awaken to find you inside of their homes, de-petaling the ladies of the house, you crazy Oaxacan." Owen added, clinking his own water against Flores's cup.

"You have probably already spotted him, but I have also been tracking him for part of the past few days. See the man in the far right corner, his back facing against the wall?" asked Flores, who had lowered his head and voice, and his entire demeanor changed whenever he was discussing business.

"Is that the half-breed cowboy…Sams, I think his name is? What the hell did they call him back in Tucson?"

"The 'Apache Kid,' although his daddy was half-white. Sams has never been caught by any authorities on either side of the border."

"What's the going rate for bringing him in?"

"Around $150 to 200."

"That's it? A kind of dangerous man like that is of better use to you being free and on your side."

"That is one way of looking at it, if you were so inclined. But you are right. I don't have the cojones nor the desire to take in a man such as Sams for such a small payout."

"Then maybe you should let him go. Who knows, we might need him, some day." winked Owen.

"Ha, that's right, 'Mad' man! Now, do you still gamble?"

"Only with money that I do not have."

At that, Owen and Flores started to wager several bets at the faro tables, avoiding further tempting discussion about their possible business ventures together, but never fully leaving behind the friendship by fire owed to a fellow traveler walking down the bricked pathway paved through the actions of the gun.

After the gambling losses of a small amount of money and the telling of many coarse jokes, Owen asked Flores for his advice on where to find 'regular' ladies in town, not those of the 'painted' quality.

"Well, my friend, there are several dancing halls just off of Main Street that the maids, sewing ladies, and serving girls love to frequent. Perhaps there you will find what you are looking for." smiled Flores.

Smiling back at the 'King of Flowers', Owen went through the open door of the Golden Nugget, and he went back out into the night.

Before too long, the ex-gunfighter started to hear a pulsating piano beat, a rapid ragtime melody the younger women went wild for the previous couple of musical seasons. Even respectable girls from high society were known to lose themselves in the current dancing manias. Owen Ward had no particularly strong appeal towards this style of music, but he recognized and appreciated the enthrallment found in the rhythm the younger ladies desired to hear, so he went where they went.

Going into the first dance hall he came across, Owen did not see the name of the establishment he entered, only knowing that the place hummed as a beehive.

The ladies inside wore red, pink, and green, while the men wore sunburnt hats they could barely keep clung to the tops of their heads, as the women danced in circular patterns, the style of the dance demanded by the music being both simplistic but animalistic.

Owen did not recognize the song, but he understood the notes to be quite popular with the ladies that night in Redview. As he sat down at the bar to better scan the hall for a full view of what was on offer, that is when the former shootist saw her.

Emma Rabelais, 25 years old, and an ex-prostitute the past two years, after being painted off and on for seven years of her short, cruel life. Owen Ward, of course, knew none of this, and his feelings for the young woman were born upon first seeing her, and they would have been unaffected anyways, as Owen had relinquished certain judgments upon others after he had entered into the penitentiary. Being a former gunsman allowed him to understand that not everyone in life is given a choice in the world of circumstance.

'Besides,' thought Owen. 'She's a lovely dancer!'

Emma Rabelais wore a red dress to match her auburn hair, the color of autumn born renewed. Owen noticed that she was alone except for a fellow female companion, although both ladies were getting lots of masculine countenances cast their way. Owen moved closer to where his new lady love was dancing.

Not able to get her to meet his eyes, Owen counted himself content to watch the animated pixie dance to her heart's content, as the painted lady-tuned-servant woman worked 14 hour shifts, five days a week. The young lady danced her frustrations away, the sweat starting to pour down her face, before she appeared to realize how thirsty she had become.

Emma and her young friend sat down, taking a break from dancing for a while. Before Owen could make his way over through the masses to the hard-breathing women, another fellow beat him to the women's table, with drinks in tow, just as the ex-gunfighter could overhear their conversation from a couple of feet away.

"Hello, girls, I thought two young dames such as yourselves could wet your whistles with some of this!" the dark-featured man said and then sat down between the women, before they could even acknowledge or welcome his presence.

"Go on, take a sip, gals," said the grinning stranger.

Owen did not have to be a medium to know what Emma Rabelais and her friend thought of this interloper, who had also placed a rough hand upon the nape of Emma's neck, to read the look of distaste on the women's faces.

"We are not interested in any male company this evening, fella. We only came to dance," said Emma's friend.

"Okay, but not even one drink?" the brute hissed through tobacco juice-brown teeth.

"No! Now, shew away, you! Like my friend said, we're not looking for any men tonight." Emma said, full throated.

"Oh, I see how it is, girls," the man made a dramatic show of unbuttoning his jacket's side-pocket, taking out his wrinkled-leather wallet and placing a $10 greenback directly onto the table. "I forgot for a moment that I am dealing with whores. Does that suit you, you bitches?"

Emma then slapped the man across his face, but when he went to strike back at her, Owen Ward had grabbed the man's winded-up and closed left fist.

"Listen here, pimp; be gone from here or I'll be forced to harm you, boy." Owen said in a calm voice.

"Damn you, you bastard! Mind your own business!" the man shouted, as he attempted to hit Owen with his right fist, but the ex-gunfighter proved himself to *not* be an ex-boxer, as he broke the harasser's nose with a single landing punch, resulting in the man reeling towards the ground, before righting himself upwards by the knees.

"Hey, rogue. I see you around Redview again, I'll make sure you taste the dust of this town in your grave long before your natural time on Earth is set to expire." said Owen.

Aiming for Owen's stomach, the man attempted to stab him with a heretofore hidden, short-edged blade, but Owen kneed the man in the mouth, busting out multiple teeth and breaking the capillaries that supply blood to the man's face. Wailing, the man was dragged by the former shootist to the exit doorway in the dance hall, and then the former shootist booted him out of the establishment.

"Thanks for nothing, Romeo!" shouted Emma Rabelais, as she and her friend ran out through the other exit, escaping from the hands of a raging bartender who was angry for all the ruckus. "Now we can never come back to dance here again!"

Owen took chase after the women, because he was not willing to let her flee out of his life, so soon after entering into it. Keeping a safe distance, he watched as the two ladies stopped to talk for a moment at the cross-section of Main and 4th Streets, and then Emma and her friend hugged and parted ways. Owen continued to follow the red-haired beauty.

A few minutes later, Emma Rabelais arrived at the McManus Boarding Home for Christian Women. Watching her enter the building into relative safety, Owen decided that one last night under the open sky, in such a glorious environment, was suitable to his current love-struck mood.

However, as he walked through the lonely streets of Redview in the early dark morning, the ex-gunfighter swore to himself to secure honest employment and a warm bed by the end of the new day.

Chapter 5- A 'Colonel' with No Army

The 67-year-old 'Colonel' William Ridge, addressed behind his back by employees as the accurate title of 'Mister', put down the mid-morning edition of the *Redview Daily* newspaper that he'd been skimming through to look up and take notice of the time.

The tanned, wooden grandfather clock inside of the 'colonel's' office read 11:37 am.

"The bastard's over a half-hour late!" 'Colonel' Ridge groused to himself, while he threw the crumpled newspaper onto his desk.

The non-military man's mood had been exasperated by a lack of sleep he'd been experiencing over the past several weeks. Prone to closing business deals and securing any and all land properties that tickled his fancy in a quick manner, Mr. Ridge found his mind addled by forces beyond his full control. Problems started to stack on top of each other, and the combined weight of his worries became akin to stumbling blocks blowing in a harsh wind.

In prior difficult commercial dealings, the 'colonel' had displayed no issues concerning using rough and tough negotiation tactics, but now the semi-legitimate businessman found himself in a war he was impotent in trying to end. The situation took the man back to when he was in preparatory school, as a very young man, compelled to learn Latin and read the ancient Greek and Roman orators in their original texts, as if they had been released yesterday. Although many years had passed since he had read and spoken in Latin, and he failed to recall most of the words now, while he sat waiting with annoyed expectation, he was reminded of a quote by Plato that 'only the dead have seen the end of the war'. As a civilian with no military combat experience, this saying seemed to be as accurate as any other observations concerning the dead seemed to be.

Glancing upwards again and reading the time as 11:42 am resulted in Ridge standing up and shouting at his office's front door.

"Samuel! Get a boy to run over to the Needle, and have 'em bring me over that damn Boze Neary. Now! I've been waiting nearly all morning!" said the 'colonel' before adding. "And my coffee is cold! Bring me another!"

"Yes, sir," came back a low, pip-squeak voice from the other side of the office's wall. "I'll send Lyndon over, on the double!"

Ridge folded and re-folded the ruined newspaper into a compact small square and then placed it on his desk, while he waited.

"Wait, wait! I see Lyndon and another fellow approaching the office, 'Colonel'," yelled Samuel through the office's wall. "I'll meet them as they enter!"

"Give me a minute before allowing them to enter my office." Ridge yelled back at his closed door.

"Yes, sir!"

The 'colonel' felt for the revolver that he had holstered above his right hip, underneath his suit jacket. The well-polished, unscratched gun had never been fired, but Ridge was prone to thinking that the firearm's mere presence on his person had somehow saved him from a live shoot-out, without giving a full consideration to his habit of posting hired guns throughout his entourage and wide-spread properties and other business ventures that he had founded throughout the Arizona territories. While some men forget the way of the gun, other fellows never learned the method in the first place.

The redness did not bother the civilian 'colonel', as he began to unstrap his gun's holster, ready to draw, if need be, because he truly believed his blood could never succumb to the crimson's claims against mankind.

"Mr. Cotton, sir, the 'Colonel' has made it *quite* clear to you and Mr. Neary that he strongly desires to speak only with your boss. No offense, Mr. Cotton, but–" Samuel said before he was interrupted.

"Call me Jimmy. Or J.C.," said a harmless-sounding young man in his mid-twenties. "And go ahead, now, and tell Ridge that Neary is, uh, feeling under the weather today. I can speak for him, though, so that shouldn't make any difference. And if it is a problem, I can boot on out of here."

"Jimmy, I don't think that is a good idea," said Samuel.

"Shut up, Sam! Send the man in. I'll conduct my own affairs myself, if you do not mind, sir!" rambled the wall.

Jimmy Cotton opened and closed the office door like a thief in the night, but he was a robber who arrived in the bright daylight, all the better to see what he took as he practiced his trade. The gunfighter walked towards 'Colonel' Ridge, not waiting to be granted permission to sit down, but before Jimmy made as if he were to take a seat in a nearby chair next to Ridge's desk, he pivoted into standing at his complete height right next to the much older man, ensuring that the businessman could see both of the loaded guns hung along his hips.

As the right-hand man who helped to cajole the other Neary gang members into a cohesive shooting outfit, Cotton had been recruited as a mere eager-to-learn teenager who'd been given a formative outlet for destruction through the mentoring of Boze Neary at just the opportune time. And so began the relationship forged between Boze Neary, the man from Galway, and his young, enterprising shootist pupil, Jimmy Cotton, a product of the Southwestern lands. Their relationship was reminiscent of that of the late Caesar Tiberius and the rogue Caligula; when the embittered Tiberius decreed that he'd vindictively redress the persistently hateful senators and rude regular Roman-folk by appointing the infamous Caligula as the rightful successor to his throne. Although the ruthless Caligula was brought up and kept alive with the notion of being the future king, he was never taught *how to* rule fairly by design, and Caligula, by default, learned to use the ways of a despot. Neither Neary nor Tiberius had any vested interest in seeing their successors be trained in diplomacy or practice at developing an even-temperament. Both rulers, however, were effective in filing their youthful arrow proteges into sharp, gilded points, ready to strike at the heart of all that a nation holds dear and true. The revolver cares not a bullet for understanding the prevocation for its use.

"Where is Mr. Neary?" asked Mr. Ridge, a planned lack of concern could be detected in his face, and he appeared the worse the wear for his deceit.

"Where do you think? He's back at the saloon, livin' high off the hog, while I'm out here workin'," said Jimmy Cotton, his pointed brow dismissing any perceived deference he may have been supposed to grant his financial backer. "But like I told your rube outside, *I* can do the talking for the Neary Gang, and if *I* feel like it's important enough, I'll go tell it to the old man. Got that, kid?"

"Yes, that's fine." said Ridge, as he looked downwards at his desk, like a beaten dog.

"Good, now that you've been trained, speak, '*Colonel*'." said Cotton with a gruff smirk.

"While I truly do respect what you fellas have done for me recently, that is breaking up all the labor disputes that those damn lazy workers have been fixing to muck up my bottom line, I would hope that I'd need not remind you or Mr. Neary that my strongest desire is to avoid any interference from law enforcement and the government folks. Frank Jones and Ted Channing were trouble, but I *did not* want them to be murdered!" Ridge's voice became louder at this last word, before his tone settled down again. "All that I'm saying is, you boys need to let the blood cool down a spell and avoid open conflict with all parties in Redview."

"The blood's already soakin' in the ground, old timer. We do what we want. And if you're going to pull the trigger of that revolver you've secretly aimed on me, I suggest you do so in the next three seconds, or it will be your last gasp of air."

The 'colonel' re-strapped the gun's holster.

"I guess we can play it that way. I can pay you more money, if that's what will motivate you. Here, look. Samuel! Bring in the gray suitcase, at once!"

Ridge could not bear to look at Jimmy Cotton, although he felt the gunfighter's eyes watching his every movement, waiting for an itchy finger to reach for the revolver, the young gunsman needing just a second to take the shot in his defense. But Cotton's vigilance was unwarranted against a non-fighting colonel.

Samuel barged through the office's door with a tattered, fading suitcase, which the assistant then placed onto the 'colonel's' desk, leaving Ridge to open the travel bag to Jimmy Cotton's noticeable delight.

"Here's double the normal monthly payments, all right? And let us just say that maybe we can keep the increased amount between the two of us? You do what you want with the extra money, but please, for God's sake, please and *please* do not bring any more noise to my operations out here in the West. Son, it's just not good business practice to go around and kill a man indiscriminately. Now, for young men from *my* generation, we were forced to grow up fast, to fight and die in the Civil War, so what do you young ruffians know about what it takes to be a man?" puffed Ridge, forgetting his safety under the guise of disrespected manhood.

Jimmy Cotton took out the .45 caliber revolver from his left hip, and then aimed the gun behind Ridge's ear. Uncocked, Cotton used the barrel of the .45 to smack Ridge's hat from off the top of his head, causing the older man's face to grow as crimson as the dust upon his boots.

"You wanna know the one thing that pisses off a real shootist more than anything else?" asked Jimmy Cotton, as he looked down at the 'colonel' with doll eyes. Ridge shook his head in hurried misunderstanding, as his mind raced to change the subject. "It's seeing an amateur loudmouth showing off with his expensive toy pistol. The mere sight of a gun can incite to violence, can it not, Pop?"

Before Ridge could nod his head in a just-convinced understanding of the man's argument, Cotton put the .45 caliber revolver away, closed the top of the suitcase containing $1,000 greenbacks within it, and carried the 'protection' payment back towards the Eye of the Needle, without uttering another word to the corrupt businessman.

Too furious for words, Ridge picked up his glass inkwell and threw the wet vessel at his assistant, Samuel. The blackness spilled down the young man's fresh-pressed linens as a snaking river.

"I'm sorry, Sam, but I needed to hit *somebody*! We need a back-up plan, and we need one on the double. I think I have bought us some time, but we may need other, more professional assistance in this battle. Are there any gunfighters, *good* gunfighters, around who could take out Boze Neary and Jimmy Cotton?"

"Not any local fellows. Lyndon and I can look into the matter further, however, sir."

"Do that right away, would you, Samuel? And one final thing; where is that *other* idiot I was expecting today, Sheriff Daggs?"

Chapter 6- The Unmaking of a Lawman

Sheriff Tyrus Daggs was born neither a lawman nor a criminal, but instead he started out as a simple man who had developed his own peculiar interests in life. To ask when a man has crossed over to one side of a demarcated line, or the other, is to question the specific time when he first understood his own consciousness. Although a true assessment of the exact moment the bend towards self-debasement and unrighteousness occurs is unknowable to the outside observer, Sheriff Daggs developed a pattern of deceit and corruption that had increased further after 'Colonel' Ridge's arrival into the redness of central Arizona. At the time, deputy Tyrus Daggs, native to the southeastern regions but an adopted son of Redview for the past 25 years, was considered to be the best man for the county job of sheriff, and for a spell of time, this may even had been correct but now, while the citizens recognized that no other more forthright and honest man had wandered into the 'Scarlet Rose' wanting to be sheriff, and so the utter corruptness grew worse with each passing year that Daggs remained in power, making the people's hope for change more severe in the hearts of those he had sworn an oath to protect.

But what of Sheriff Daggs's character and general disposition? Was the man out-and-out evil?

Imagine yourself walking along a straight line; no obstacles in your way, no inclement weather or snapping dogs or nosy fellow travelers to interfere with your journey. Now, picture this: Back in reality, walking up life's inclined road, as the elevation of your steps *are indeed* affected by the nuances of the bumps in the ragged steps still before you, and each passing with a changing new year bringing you closer to your destination, to points not perfectly unknown, but to the end of the line that can never be known to you, either. A journey, sometimes, is only known to have been started by the traveler after he has already set off a ways along the road, and he may not be ready to contemplate what he has accomplished or failed at until *after* the conclusion of the journey.

Not that Sheriff Daggs spent much time justifying his existence; the people had duly elected him every election, so what ultimate right did they have to complain?

What the sheriff had never given thought to, though he would have agreed with the sentiment if spoken out loud by another party, was the idea that *no one* is totally good or evil; Daggs would have nodded, jerking his large, balding head in agreement that an individual's good or evil intentions start insidiously with each and every next step that he makes or word that is spoken by him, for every man lives his life by making one choice, one step, and one breathe at a time for better or for worse. Nobody starts out wanting to be the devil, as even Lucifer himself did not begin his life with rebellion, but rather in service.

Tyrus Daggs was born far from the shade of the devil's shadow. The blessing *and* curse, true for all gunfighters, that the future Sheriff Daggs possessed was the demonic gift of marksmanship. Steady hands are the mark of a steady mind. Tyrus could drink an entire pot of coffee, and his hands could still track, aim, and hit ten out of ten buffaloes for the rich Eastern businessmen who enjoyed hunting in the wild western plains of America but were themselves poor shots, and they did not mind claiming credit for the kills.

The last day Tyrus served as a buffalo hunter was for a man from New York; his employer, not understanding the trade, except the potential for profits, allowed his hunters to be misabused and unpaid. On this particular afternoon, he stood up to the vicious work crew boss who had grown tyrannical in the amount of work hours he was demanding of his employees. Tyrus and a few other fellows formed a worker's council, deciding to elect Tyrus to discuss remediation of grievances with the foreman. As the boss was a quick-tempered man, prone to apoplectic outbursts at any challenge posed by a subordinate, Tyrus was the unfortunate lot drawn to be the speaker of the hunter's council, a job the young Daggs did not want, but would find that he had a knack for public speaking.

'And, hell,' Sheriff Daggs had often thought to himself over the years since people first looked to him for direction in public service. 'Being six feet, four inches doesn't hurt to remedy most folk's feelings of doubt concerning my leadership qualities.'

A tall man, standing with a gun he never has to shoot, works half of the time in preventing crime in most cowpoke towns, and this was true of Redview as well, for a while. But when new men, who are not intimidated by the artificial trappings an appearance of a man provides a viewer with, come to roost in the henhouse, a skill in shooting replaces the cheap flash of threats and words, as the bursting of a gun allows any quiet, determined man to say his piece in confidence.

All those years ago when he was a much younger man, Tyrus the Buffalo Hunter, had been threatened by his boss multiple times, and he was offered a final warning to not unionize. On that day, the teenage Tyrus Daggs had to confront an angry alcoholic who carried an ivory-handled pistol in his left workboot, which all the fellows on the crew knew to carry no bullets inside of the gun's chamber.

Tyrus stood up to his fully erect height, feeling as tall as a redwood tree, and took out an old, LeMat revolver he'd borrowed from a Civil War veteran on the work crew, and then he shot the bowler cap from off the top of the crew chief's head, and the cursing man went galloping back to the nearest town, afraid for his life and telling company officials at business headquarters that he was quitting, as he was through dealing with rowdies and ruffians on the worksites. Tyrus and the rest of his co-conspirators were fired and banned from hunting in the region, but the legend of the 'Righteous and Democratic' Daggs was born, a modern-day victor in the Biblical 'David vs. Goliath' story. So started the drunken saloon stories told by old men growing older with each passing work season, embellishing or fabricating new details of the Daggs confrontation to better amuse a younger generation who'd heard the myths and fairy tales too many times from their parents to believe in Sheriff Daggs as a hero. The younger folks, not able to remember a time before the current iteration of the lawman, had already *seen* his style of justice, and thus understood the man from legend seldom steps into reality, as power can corrupt when given without constraints.

Sheriff Daggs had spent a decade keeping Redview civil and safe from major harm by 1880s Southwestern standards, and he had never been forced into any gunfights over the intervening years, so his battle instincts went greatly unchallenged, and any amateur marksmanship he had was left to languish in memory, unpracticed and unoiled, not ready to face a wolf.

The Neary Gang rode in to Redview on a burning afternoon, the smell of drying blood on their fingertips, but the redness was thought to be as bits of dust clinging to motionless hands, the rough palms guiding their horses along a trail paved with the many wings of cardinals, all of whom fluttered about in beaked agitation.

The human eye can see as little or as much as the viewer chooses to perceive. The mind is more deceptive than the eye, for the eye cannot control the eyelid; 'tis the thinker who chooses to restrict the details of their own solicitude.

A choice was made, perhaps on *that day*, by Sheriff Daggs that helped to lead him into the predicament he found himself to be in, without any obvious solutions to his plight being available. The town's 'protection' had been bought and paid for by the collective goodwill of both the leading townsfolk and Eastern businessmen and investors who had no strong affinity for being shot at and murdered while just trying to turn a profit out in the Arizona territories. Sheriff Daggs had found the terms reasonable enough for him to live with and go to sleep at night, but the old lawman could not shut his eyes tight or long enough, nor could he cover his ears with a more firm hand to drown out the noise of multiple targeted, cold-blooded killings that had occurred in Greater Redview over the last several years, regardless of Daggs's repeated overt and proud exclamations that 'no shootings have happened in the town limits of Redview in over 8 years!' A more honest man knew the true death score, if the truth-teller also happened to be a drinking man in the midst of telling no lies, for the saloon was *the* public forum, a place where both the lawmen and the lawless men gathered pertinent information while playing the other side.

Today, Sheriff Daggs sauntered down chalky Main Street, nodding at random matrons and families as they eyed him walk by. Taking a passing side-view of nearby 4th Avenue, the sheriff decided to continue walking down Main, wanting to avoid the Eye of the Needle, at least for another peaceful hour of the day. Ticking off the names of the faces in the crowd he passed started to tire the aging lawman, but then a new visage met his eye, a stranger to the town of Redview.

Besides the initial shocking sight of a capable newcomer in his town, Sheriff Daggs had found as good a distraction as any to keep him occupied and away from having to visit the Needle.

Owen Ward looked worse for the wear after spending yet another night sleeping on the ground, a habit quick in making a young man old, but the former shootist also wore the look of determined hope in his eyes, as one way or another, he would get a job today and a bed tonight, 'so help the son of a gunsman', Owen had thought as he came into the view of Sheriff Daggs's undivided obsession. The lawman was standing on the short, wooden walkway lining the opposite side of Main, in front of Murray's Butcher & Blacksmith, an odd combination, but a prosperous local business, nonetheless.

The lawman placed a hand on the gun holstered onto his left hip. Owen Ward made a show of brushing off the red dust from his work shirt, and in the process showed that he was not carrying a firearm, just a Bowie knife, same as most harrowed men in Redview. Owen took a few steps forward toward Redview's man of the star badge, who at first only nodded at the stranger, before realizing the man was coming his way. The sheriff sought to meet the man in the middle of the street.

"Good afternoon, young fella."

"Hello to you, too, Sheriff. My name is Owen Ward."

"Daggs. Ward, you say? Any relation to the good Dr. Ward, who lives in the wilds of this county?"

"Yes, sir, Taig is my cousin."

Noticing the lawman's incredulous face, Owen affected an artificial laugh.

"My cousin is a doctor, while I'm a desperado, so to speak."

"Am I to take it, then, that you are an outlaw, Mr. Ward?"

"I figured you'd hear it a-fore too long from some other fellows, so here goes, Sheriff. I just got out of doing seven years in a penitentiary in Amarillo, and I have no particular inclination on going back inside of *any* jail cell ever again," said Owen Ward in an earnest voice. "I want it square between us, as I'm simply looking for ranch hand work, or perhaps trying my hand at the cattle trade, some day, after I make a little money."

"Hmm, you're the only other Ward, besides your cousin, that I've seen around these parts."

"Well, most of them are like me, except dead or still in prison. Taig and his old man were the only good ones in a rotten bunch. But listen, sir, my days of riding with bandits, cattle rustling, and gunfighting are over. I don't even have a gun anymore, nor any reason to use one."

"That's all you'd need, boy, is a reason, isn't it?" the sheriff said, as he stood to his full height, trying to stare the younger man down. "A tough britches such as you, ain't I right?"

"I'm afraid I don't get your meaning, Sheriff."

"Ah, huh, I'm sure you wouldn't. Well, look, what did they all call you back there in Texas? All of you cowboys have those silly schoolhouse nicknames, so what was yours, back when you *used to* carry a gun?" snickered Daggs the callousness of his tone leaving Owen no doubt as to the lawman's intentions.

"'Mad' Owen Ward." the ex-gunfighter stated softly.

"What's so mad about you, boy, ya got rabies? You look like a young man who'll listen to reason, no? So, consider this, you Texas shit-kicker. Any man with a record for gunfighting can only work outside of the town's limits, which shouldn't be a problem, seeing as you wanna find work ranching anyways. Now, I suppose if Taig wants to take you on, that's fine by me, but otherwise your final option is to work for Mr. Ridge; he has a use for ex-convicts like you, Ward.

I can promise to be a thorn in your side, and your employer's side, if you try to work for any unapproved rancher. Do you understand me, boy?"

"I am willing to consider my options, but where do I find Ridge at?"

"Follow along, shit-kicker."

"I will only say this once, Daggs. Never insult me again."

Owen Ward's eyes locked into the depths of Daggs's soul, penetrating the eggshell veneer of a pretend lawman, and sawing off the wooden stilts of the older man's fixed commanding heights that were hollowed out by untried confidence, as an amateur is more prepared than others to recognize the dominating emergence of an actual professional in his midst, or else face his certain detriment and demise. No threat of a gun was needed to know that a blood oath would be sworn by the newcomer if Daggs was arrogant enough to enter open, antagonistic behavior, and it was at this moment that the strong instinct bent on self-preservation that had helped to keep the lawman alive for over two decades of semi-corrupt public service and protection of the public made itself known to the sheriff's consciousness.

"Alright, Ward, relax. I'll tell you what. As a token of my appreciation for your cooperation, I'll ride out with you to Mr. Ridge's property; I could use some fresh air. Do you have a horse?"

"Yeah."

"Well, let's get riding then."

The two men rode in silence, as the scarlet wind filled the vacuum of disquietude.

Chapter 7- 'A Lady and a Servant Woman'

The smooth-skinned matron watched the young servant woman shake the feather duster outside of the open patio door, the sand swirling as a dust devil, caught between low, rocky hills, exploding in lifting, vicious rotations. An incoming low grade wind breezed away the red debris. 'Just as the 'sands of time' dwindle in one's own life,' thought the Lady of the House, who had a decade yet to go before she would turn forty years of age. Seeking comfort and hope, she mostly sought after her own youth.

"Oh, that's quite enough sweeping for one afternoon, Miss Rabelais. Hey, you're also from around these red-soaked lands like me, aren't you?" asked Nelcy Ward.

"Yes, ma'am, I am." replied Emma Rabelais, while she re-entered back into the Ward home.

"Then you must know that, no matter how many times you sweep in a day, there is no keeping up with or keeping out all the redness that seeps inside of your hearth and house."

"Yes, Mrs. Ward, that is true."

"Why don't you sit down with me for a moment? You can have a glass of water yourself, if you would like. I'll take one, even if you don't want one. Would you mind, dear?"

Emma Rabelais picked up the snow-white ceramic pitcher and poured two cups of water. Preferring to stand, Emma handed a cup of water to Mrs. Ward, who happened to be just one of her many employers, as she also worked for several other ranching families outside of Redview. That is to say limited to the families that either did not know or did not care about the young woman's past profession of prostitution. Nelcy Ward had convinced her husband, Taig, that if Jesus could accept Mary Magdalene for her tainted past, then who would *we be* to turn away a young mother in need such as Emma? The reasoning of a wife was successful, once again.

"It has been awhile since you and I have talked." said Nelcy, choosing her words with careful deliberation.

"I would never want to seem too forward by talking to my employers, ma'am."

"Yes, yes, but you know that Taig and I keep you and your son in our prayers, and I just wanted to check in on you, darling."

Nelcy Ward took a sip of water from her cup and then she tilted her body rightward, upon the white-felt couch where she was seated, the better to prop herself up and face head onwards Emma Rabelais.

"Now, dear, I've heard tell that you may have found yourself wandering around Main Street, hopping along at a few of the dance halls, and that you might be spinning the heels on Friday nights?"

"With all due respect, Mrs. Ward, I know this is your home, but what of it? If you really must know, then yes, I do enjoy going out dancing with several of my girlfriends to unwind after a long week of working. However, that does not mean that I'm back to playing the role of

'Painted Lady' or town harlot, again. I didn't know that I would be required to inform you every time I go out to have a good time."

Nelcy stared at the young woman for a moment with a blank expression, before her face caved into uncontrolled laughter.

"Oh, Miss Rabelais, I am afraid you have misread my manner, darling. If only I could convince the blessed Dr. Ward to take *me* out to the dance halls to waltz again! We haven't had a real night of dancing since the days of our engagement, and before the children robbed me of my physique. You know, dear, I'm thirty now, and all of my married friends are also mothers who'd sooner rather keep knitting by the fireside or gossiping over baked goods than enjoy a night out two-stepping with their husbands."

"Ha, a ruined physique, that's hardly true of you, ma'am! Thirty is not much older than me, and I have also been a mother for the past ten years, but I am still quite partial to getting on the floor and having a thrill, even if I am dancing all alone. The music can exist just for me in those fleeting, special moments, unlike most things in this life. Wouldn't you agree, Mrs. Ward?"

"Yes, I would," smiled Nelcy. "And that is why I've so missed talking with you."

Both of the women took the free moment to reflect on their words, which concluded with Emma taking a long sip from her own cup, while she savored the lukewarm water on such a hot afternoon of work.

"Your son, Tom, I believe his name is, has a birthday coming up?" inquired Nelcy Ward.

"Yes, that's right. A week from this Thursday. I had meant to ask for the afternoon off, because I wanted to take the little fellow to the bakery, so that he may select any pie that he would like to eat. It's our little tradition."

"Yes, of course, you may have the afternoon off, dear. Oh, Tommy will love that!"

"Yes, ma'am, but he hates to be called that. 'I'm a man now', he'll say whenever I call him that. For now, at least, Tom can be laughed at by others and still maintain a strong disposition with a sense of humor all his own. I hope that he can keep this way of being his entire life."

"As you yourself have already seen and are well aware of, my own Michael and little Stephen, about a year or two younger than *Tom* is, are like night and day when compared to each other. Mike has a bit of a temper, much as his father does at times, and he does not tolerate laughter at his expense. Stephen, on the other hand, is a sensitive soul, who knows how to cheer up his siblings and put a smile on Taig's and my face. You might as well roll the dice to try to find out who the man your son will be, someday. It seems difficult to predict, but I'd wager that a boy's father will be an integral part of who the future man may be."

Emma Rabelais said nothing, and although there was no emotion to read on her visage, Nelcy Ward understood the look of a woman with a touched heart.

"Oh, Emma, I didn't mean to imply anything about Tom! I realize that his father has passed, but I still know and believe that any masculine influence in a boy's formative years is good, no?"

"I have never introduced Tom to a paramour of mine. No man has shown any real, *sustained* interest in me, lately. And I haven't had a chance to marry a half-way decent fella in a long time now, ma'am."

"Well, dear, always remember this: Every good man *also* came forth from a woman. Where a man's trail ends, nobody can know; but where the boy's journey starts, well, every living woman who's given birth has been blessed with that sacred knowledge and duty."

Short, dab-away tears enlarged under Emma's eyelids, before she swiped them off from her cheeks in haste.

"I apologize, Mrs. Ward. I don't mean to burden you."

"No apology necessary, nor shall any memory of the event be remembered by me," Neley said in a graceful manner, before raising her eyebrows in excitement. "So then, what shall Dr. Ward and I give to young master Thomas as a present for his upcoming birthday? What does the boy like? Both of mine can never stop playing baseball."

"No, Tom never cared much for games; he had to grow up rather quickly, as you may know. But, no, ma'am, I couldn't accept a gift from you. It wouldn't be proper."

"What if I fired you then?" smiled Neley, not meaning a word of the proposed threat.

"I'd much prefer to continue serving you and yours, Mrs. Ward."

"Then please accept a small token of my family's gratitude, meant only as, let me assure you, a nice gesture from one mother to another mother concerning a kind thought…a tin soldier or perhaps a volume of Shakespeare for the lad? I believe you have said that your son is old beyond his years, before."

"A book by Mark Twain would shake his world. He's quite partial to tales of Tom Sawyer, naturally." laughed Emma.

"Indeed, darling. All boys *do* like to roam, do they not?"

'But it's where they end up,' the mothers only thought to themselves, without daring to imagine all of the possibilities.

Chapter 8- From Out of the Green, and Into the Red...

Boze Neary's earliest memories were ones of unleavened hunger. Born in 1833, yes, of course, the future gangster cowboy could recall all of the hardship induced by 'The Troubles' to all who asked about the 'Potato Famine' era of his teenage years. Boze's birth had been an ushering of a new soul into what was already common in those days for the entire Irish nation, a mere continuation of the famine that had already transpired years prior in his home of County Galway. And so, Boze was a child with an eked-out existence who struggled from the very beginning, starting through the wetted womb to the first burst of air that breathed into and out of his fresh lungs with no choice in the course of his life of whether he could satisfy his material hunger or not. This early on in his story, the young gadfly Neary learned to take what he wanted, the angels of both Heaven and Hell be damned to their perditions.

'St. Michael and all the other angels have forever terrified me,' Neary used to say to passerby listeners in his younger, harder, drinking years, 'Why would you trust a winged creature such as those? No, really, really consider the taskmasters of death for God's intentions throughout the scriptures. I tell you this, I dare not tempt fate too much, lest I cause an angel to reveal itself in my presence.'

Long before other men had found Neary to be a quite violent fellow, the young man from the wilds of west Ireland stole his first morsel of food, licked crumbs that were not intended for his own unwashed, itchy hands, but for another sick, dying neighbor child; but the boy soon justified his thievery of the younger boy's piece of ginger cracker in his own mind by reminding himself that the child's older sister was the mistress of an armed British guardsmen in his village. Therefore, self-righteous anger can justify any evil cruelty, as long as the person committing the act feels himself to be 'wronged' in some way; 'it is not evil if *I am* the one doing the deed, is it not?'

At the age of six, Boze Neary had begun to form a rudimentary understanding of calculated chance and risk, regardless of the legality of *any* business endeavor or illicit opportunity. Before he could shave, the lad had deciphered that any given gamble, whether it be a shootout, a turn of the loaded dice, or a stolen kiss from a woman had unforeseen consequences, and Neary found himself only willing to take a chance when the odds were above a coin flip's fifty-fifty percent possibility; long shots were anathema to his way of life.

'Fortune favors the mold,' Neary learned to believe as a youth alone in the world. And how green the mold could be.

'All shades of obscene green,' his mother had once said to him when he stood just above her knee, while she combed his tangled, knotted hair, before she had left for Dublin on her own accord, never to return to see her first born son again.

Whatever his mother's point had been by that statement, Boze was at a loss, but ever since a very young age, the future average gunfighter took the words as a creed for himself, as he robbed for everything else he needed to survive, and he gave definitions to what he witnessed amongst the shaded green of his homeland.

'Each man is damned by his own actions. Whatever good use, then, would an angel bring forth the dimensions of a fool's reasons for his daily stealing?' a younger, more confident Neary drunkenly would proclaim at times, before he restricted himself to his solitary drinking day allowance to mourn his mother, and not on the real day of her birth, as this was unknown to him while he pretended otherwise to any who asked, but on the day his mother abandoned him to solitary tribulation.

'Even an old fool is given opportunity for certain indulgences when supping on tears and whiskey, in a burning man's effigy to his missing mother' an older, less arrogant Neary thought, as he was scattered throughout the recesses of how own mind, trusting none of the old faces from his formative years or young manhood. Lost, somewhere way down there, was the exact memory of his mother's eyes; the green was infinite and overbearing, but he believed the odds to be less than 25% true that his mother could have such emerald-shaded eyes, but still the false memory persisted in its insistence upon his brain. The actual color has since gone away, while the obscene green spread out, greening the grounds all the way down to the blades of grass, to mere inches from being close to his fallible soul. All types of green lended to his physical and mental dismay.

Or perhaps it was just the ubiquitous hunger, clouding his young mind and interfering with an undeveloped thought process, but the young boy from Galway had a devastating, precise way of making his own rules in life, discovering what actions would cause a much older boy to confer upon him blacks and blues across his face, or how to avoid being caught by harsh nanas, as they sat outside of their browned hovels, eyeing the world in harsh tones of feminine corrections aimed ever at a young fellow such as Boze.

The actual name the Irishman was christened at birth did not survive beyond his toddler years, much as the eye color of his mother escaped him, and so, too, did her name for him. But his nickname of 'Boze' was an invention by a peculiar old man, a recluse not without rampant idiosyncrasies, one of which was an odd pronunciation of particular words.

'Hey, you boze, stop stealin' frum my hen huse!', the man of around seventy would crow to Boze Neary and the other neighborhood street urchins while they committed petty acts of crime.

None of those lost boys that formed a loose gang of thieves led by Boze lived long enough to reach the age of 21, but the collective shout intended at all of the hoodlums clung to the personality and spirit of the young Neary, following him eternal, as new individuals, who could not recall the chieftain's beginnings, repeated the word 'Boze', as if it were the man's proper nomenclature.

The past continues to recede at rampant pace, but there survives a connecting, tethered line to both the present and future self. The man and child may forget one another, but the singular cannot be extracted from the plural, no matter the bonfire constructed in a mind so as to burn a man's memories from his soul; if a thing exists, it can never unexist.

Boze Neary's youthful acts of thievery and ring-leading of fellow troublemakers led to more severe consequences, starting during the middle years of the 'Great Hunger', in 1849, when the wayward teenager was arrested and brought to Nun's Island, off the coast of Galway City Center proper, in order to be jailed inside of the confines of cold, dreary Galway Gaol, built ten years before the boy was born. Forgotten may be the color of his mother's eyes, but the memory of the unblinking eye of 'Panopticon' would remain with Neary until the time he closed his eyelids forever.

The Galway Gaol's 'Panopticon' was a principle of prison system design which allowed prison guards and officials to be located within a central tower building inside of the larger enclosed prison walls. The guards walked along various sound-proof platforms that connect the five stories of the gaol. The guards were enabled to peep in on those held within the cells while the confined men were unable to see with a clear view, as the arrangement of metallic Venetian blinds and the physical outlay of each individual jail cell and the angling of each locked room had a deliberate, oblique blueprint quality that obscured a prisoner's external view on the outside of his shared cell. The planned Victorian intention of presumed perpetual surveillance by roaming guards, who jaunted atop carpeted floors so as to conceal their footing when they spied on the prisoners in their schemes, or the prison officials that would watch from above the unrestricted convicts who were allowed to gather in the gaol's small, inner courtyard, was to enable a man bent towards criminality to better develop his conscience, as the convict's moral fiber may be restored by the constant vigilance provided by the guardsmen.

'If the teachings from the Good Book need any assistance in raising these corrupted men in uprightness, then perhaps the unverified gaze of the 'Panopticon' will overcome Man's shortcomings. Imagine it this way; when are school children least inclined towards misbehavior? When the teacher is watching their every move! So will it be here, at our modern prison,' wrote an early warden at Galway Gaol in a letter to his brother that instructed the reader on the ethics of constant surveillance in order to prevent prisoners from continuing to practice their unreformed ways of maladaptive existence. But as with all teachings taught through fearful practices, the lesson was for naught on the teenager from Galway.

The soon-to-be 16 year old Boze Neary, who had never heard of the 18th century concept of the 'Panopticon' or its cumbersome surveillance, nor of its claimed successful methods of helping the mischievous to become less so, would soon realize the meaning behind the words which were sculpted above the gaol's main gate and throughout the walls of the prison, which he saw to read 'Morals Reformed, Health Preserved, Industry Invigorated'. The younger Neary came into Galway Gaol after being forgotten to cruel ambivalence his entire life, and he spared no serious interest towards being reformed. The teenager's sense of others and the ultimate meaning of 'rightness' depended on whether he was being observed or not.

'But how do I know if I'm being watched by the 'Panopticon'?' the young man's paranoid mind raced. The schemes of his soul were not meant to be confined through the actions of men, but the eye of the 'Panopticon', much like God, was mysterious and foreboding in its silent observations.

'How to act without being seen?' was the constant refrain of Boze's first weeks inside of gaol.

The future gun-strapped outlaw was able to grasp how to alter his overt actions, so as to appear cooperative and repentant in front of the authorities and his other social betters. Although the prison would one day learn the young man in the ways a man can be productive in his works, the gaol also taught him how to organize desperate men into disciplined numbers, which led to further growth of his commanding leadership qualities in the form of strategy and tactics.

Located on Galway Gaol's 2nd floor, in cell number 25, and under the presumed eyes of the guards as they circulated as the lifeblood of the 'Panopticon', Neary discovered how to hone his skill at taking prudent chances on worthy gambles. The ancient Latin question of 'who watches the watchers' could never be answered by any individual prisoner with 100% certainty, but sight is not the sole sense granted to men, and while a kaleidoscope might make for a poor telescope in terms of what physical realities can be seen, even an obscured view with accurate, open communication provided by the other organs of the collective bodies of prisoners, could predict the approach of a guard, just as there are ways to detect the presence of an angel.

'Practice your mind on it, my dear fellows,' the drunken twenty-plus year old Boze would harp on. 'Even the Angel of Destruction must come forth on great flapping wings, which by force announce their secretive movements as a bugle.'

According to the man from Galway Gaol, if you could hear an angel, then you could see a guard, even with blinded vision. In the absence of knowledge concerning the sight of those holding the powers of authority, Neary was inspired to only speak as if his windows were ever open, which they were; this skill from prison would be retained throughout the criminal's unreformed career. Another ability was based more on an advanced form of intra-prisoner communication through the use and manipulation of each prisoner's prescribed round shaving mirror. Neary had noticed over the course of his first few weeks of confinement how the guards in the tower might be able to watch the various prison cells at all times, but in order to get a close-up look on the inside of a particular room, an individual guard was still compelled to get close enough to the four-man cage so as to peer in for a scrutinized verification of negligent behavior. The teenage criminal further understood another physical law dictated by the gaol's 'Panaopticon': Although the Venetian blinds blocked the initial, direct presence of a guard on lush, carpeted floors, each prisoner *could see* the passing of the light projected by the guard tower, as every time a new guard moved away from an individual cell, the guard's shadow would be cast underneath the doorway and blinds, indicating that he'd been there strictly *after* walking by. Utilizing the mechanical knowledge that the average guardsman took between five to seven seconds to walk past a jail cell, Boze Neary figured how a guard's movement could indeed be monitored, albeit at a specific time delay; but through delays such as this, and the *knowledge of* this time gap, Neary brought to fruition the idea that great acts of violence and overall centralized control of a jail could be directed by the hands of a prisoner himself.

Although the guard's tower was placed in the middle of the gaol, as a dot in the center of a circle, and this masked a prisoner's ability to communicate with another by reflected light off of the saving mirror of a prisoner in a cell that's in a direct, straight line, the concept of a semi-circle helped Neary to develop a relay system that predicted with reliable certainty on approximately where a guard happened to be located. Picturing a semi-circle in his mind, Neary saw the two points forming the ends of the half-circle acting as a way to circumnavigate the guard tower and have each cell throughout the prison ready to be in reflective communication with their cell's respective end of the semi-circle, and even while accounting for the 5-7 seconds of cumulative delays during the passing of the lights, the future outlaw's mirror system was intricate in design, but leaderless by mere circumstance of his young age, at least at the start of his time in Galway Gaol.

When Boze Neary became Prisoner #4008, the most feared prison gang leader was Michael 'Killjoy' McCoy, a ruthless rapist and rumrunner who'd been brought to Galway Gaol for the murder of two men at a public house in Galway City. 'Killjoy' might not have been a saint, but he knew how to categorize a man by his heart and hand, and further making use of him for his own devices.

'And what use would that do me, boy?' asked 'Killjoy' McCoy of an excited Boze one afternoon. They talked in the small, inner courtyard of the gaol, the light from the sun entering the open-air roof and the bright, white candles from within the tower provided a man some further assurance that if any guard chose to watch him, the guardsman could see his actions in its horrid glory by the movement of flames, if one chose to watch with great care. Above each platform of the guards' walking corridors that existed on all five levels, further carved-in-stone signs reminded prisoners of their mission: 'Morals Reformed, Health Preserved, Industry Invigorated'. The young Neary was indeed quick at work in convincing 'Killjoy' McCoy of the necessity of operating a prison through having selective controlling knowledge as to the whereabouts of the guards at any moment.

'A man could act with near immunity from repercussions from all despotic authority.' said the teenage Neary.

'To what end, you young scrap? You talk big, boy, but I don't see much purpose in getting them other rude fellows trained in how to manipulate optics.' responded the long-term prisoner.

'Leave that to me, Mr. McCoy. It'll only require one man per cell to be alert to track a guard's movement, and we can limit ourselves to the 2nd floor, for now.'

Before the first month of the teenager's prison term was complete, 'Killjoy' McCoy and Boze Neary had instilled a great fear into the hearts of the hundred-odd prisoners present in the cells of the 2nd floor of Galway Gaol, as the reflective-light relayed mirror system developed by Boze helped 'Killjoy' to extort other prisoners for their misdeeds and indiscretions, all under the protection of *not* being watched in a tomb where each guard could serve as a potential witness against you. Any prisoner who refused to aid the relay system was soon dispatched to the gaol's hospital ward with a broken limb or two, and from there the injured, now marked inmate would be transferred to another floor or to a new prison, in the hopes of avoiding their certain demise if welcomed back onto 'Killjoy's' floor. The prison gang leader let the other prisoners know not to harm Neary who, over the course of his prison sentence soon began to further cultivate a charismatic talent for getting brutal men to follow him and obey his every command. The younger Neary's, and later yet the older Neary's, talent lay not in being the biggest or strongest man in his cell, but instead by becoming the most brutal and intelligent.

18 months into Boze's three year sentence saw the teenager at a crossroads with 'Killjoy', and the rift built to the point where Neary feared for his life and safety. Upon being passed word one hot afternoon that 'Killjoy' McCoy had ordered a cellmate of Neary's to murder him for the bounty price of a new pair of shoes, the future Irish-American cowboy acted in haste. Waiting for his traitor cellmate to fall asleep, Neary then utilized his own selected renegades in the other jail cells throughout the 2nd floor to monitor the guard patrol. Signaled that he had three minutes before a guard would pass by Cell #25 again, Boze used the fury of both of his hairy hands to suffocate the thirty year old arsonist who'd been bribed to kill him. The next night, Neary had convinced 'Killjoy's' right-hand man and cell mate, Timothy Skelton, to stab the gang leader to death with a knife that was provided and disappeared by Boze. As the end of Neary's sentence approached, the now 19 year old had failed to be reformed, but his industry of vice and careful, developed sense of self-preservation served to allow him to be the prison's sole reigning sovereign, for all that it was worth to be the kingpin of a tiny gaol in western Ireland, and no other prisoner had dared to look at the young man twice again after Killjoy McCoy's bloody murder.

In 1852, Boze Neary was rendered a free man. Seeing the last of the forsaken hut in the deserted village his mother had forsaken him to, the teenager decided to leave the motherland behind him and venture out to the New World by rickety ship. He then moved along the southeastern seaboard, drifting from port town to port town, before he wound up in New Orleans for a spell of time. In this crescent city of the creoles, Boze plied his trade as a low-level pimp, rumrunner, and part-time advisor to several criminal syndicates that operated throughout the wharves and waterfronts of the regions. Tired of cracking heads for cheap bosses and desiring to avoid the threat of constant arrest in his adopted city, the Irishman left New Orleans after twenty years and the practiced loss of his Irish lilt. At a loss for what to do, he roamed the land in many directions, but still he did not settle down. The West was what called to him, and so he went. Riding a horse had not come easy for Neary, but neither had shooting, but after consistent practice the ex-convict was soon effective enough in these tasks to be considered dangerous to the pacific public. His ability with a six-shooter now added to Neary's ruthlessness, but the outlaw recognized that he lacked the quickest draw to be able to defeat all of his armed opponents, so the man sought out all cowboys willing to work and kill for him; they just needed to do what Boze told them to do.

By the time Neary had become the boss of his own freewheeling posse and heard the siren call from Redview, the last of the obscene green had been culled from out of his soul, and the dreaded red filled his old heart with near-hope. This desired hope was one which knew that the eye of the 'Panopticon' had been blinded, and accepting for the first time on the day of his

50th birthday that he would never again mortally fear the face of an angel, as the old man intended to see the winged beasts when he knew he was already dead.

'I kill the Angel of Destruction by creating evil and chaos, by bringing strife into the souls of all peoples. Any creature, be he man, angel, or beast, who dares to look into my soul shall know death. Follow me, brothers in arms, if you thirst for blood.'

The wolves and riders of the red dust knew all trails, and all trails knew tears and pain and strife.

Chapter 9- Owen Ward Meets the 'Kid'

Owen Ward's eyes followed Sheriff Daggs along his horse, as his own mare breathed in slow, trickling breaths, her nostrils flailing in great dilated circles, as her eyes bulged against the trailing wind and dust. The lack of a hat while riding, as in the Indian style, had brought many comments over the years about the former shootist, including that the man was vain in showing off his long dirty blonde hair and that he'd 'turned Injun' in his habits, adopting their style of stirrups and tracking methods, but the former ex-gunfighter had in particular perfected the art of squinting in the bright sun due to his hatless ways, and his trail sight allowed him to scout the horizon faster or ride away from potential danger long before a less adept horseman. Losing time, Owen watched the bottoms of the sheriff's horse's black hooves turn a ruddy brown, as the lawman and his charge splashed their self-made paths through several slow-flowing creeks, the clear stream waters dampening the feet of the horses, and as the small party moved further along the dry red dirt trails, the ground marked the animals in a visceral paste that took on the patterns of splattered lightning strikes of blood tattooed onto the hides of the beasts of burden.

Not wanting to ask Daggs any questions, Owen assumed that the stone-gated fence that they passed through belonged to the self-proclaimed 'Colonel' Ridge, whose property stretched for hundreds of acres in all four corners' directions, the landscape only surpassed by the owner's supreme vanity grasping at the straws of superficial eminence. Handfuls of Mexicans and white ranch hands worked in small crews throughout Ridge's premises. After speaking with a light-skinned Mexican man in jangled Spanish, Sheriff Daggs directed Owen to follow him and the ranch hand to a nearby riparian area, where the cottonwood trees were long and thin and pale, spindly white creatures freckled with black spots etched into their bark as if by fingerprints of embers, and they grew next to a small river that rolled along the southern line of Ridge's property. A watchful eye could detect the presence of ladybugs, the red-orange insects rummaging for food amidst the green wetness of veined-leaves grown downtrodden by the weight of the winged bugs, and Owen's sensitive ears could hear the soft trickling of the ebbing river floating through the red lands before he could see the translucent waters.

The relief at the sound of water was short-lived, as Owen witnessed a group of about twenty-odd men and boys that were trying to build a precarious bridge across a steep section of the river. Spotting a particular fellow, Sheriff Daggs waved and shouted out, 'Alonso!', at the large, balding man, who was directing two young boys to carry a small log down to the river.

"Hey, Alonso! Up here! I've got another guy who I think could help Mr. Ridge out on the ranch."

Daggs and Owen commanded their horses to halt and both men got back down onto the rocky earth, waiting for the rotund Alonso to approach them. The Mexican approached at a slow pace bearing a sweaty, scarred face, as Alonso was the survivor of multiple knife fights, a storied victor who was fortunate to only be slashed along his ears and neck, instead of being blinded by the knife or silenced into the great undead. None of them men nodded to acknowledge the other.

"Alonso, this here is Ward, he's a gunfighter turned honest citizen. My money says Ridge could convince Mr. Ward here of the necessity that a man who's skilled in the use of firearms is far more critical then having another swearing grunt to lift heavy things for the boss, but we'll see."

"Senor Ridge is not here today, but this Ward fellow can toil for tonight's supper and cot if he starts working right now," puffed out Alonso, still catching his breath. "The fighter can talk to Ridge about any specific arrangements later on."

"I'm not a gunfighter anymore, Alonso. I'm just here to ranch and brand cattle." Owen said.

"That's *jefe* Alonso to *you*, Ward, and today you're here to help build this goddamn bridge that Senor Ridge has been insisting for weeks that we rig across the river." fumed Alonso.

"What in hell does he need a bridge for?" asked Daggs, more out of boredom than curiosity.

"Loco gringo boss says to work this maldito puente, then we must work this maldito puente. I ask no questions, sheriff."

"Well, you fellas oughta know that the bridge should be moved to a more shallow section of the river, no?" said Owen, pointing to about thirty yards down the river from where the skeleton foundations of the bridge were being set-up. "See where the bridge is now, how far the bottom of the structure will need to be underwater, at such a deep section in the water? Tell your men and boys to-."

"Hey, gunfighter, what difference does it make to you?" Alonso was quick to interrupt the newcomer. "Just kiss Ridge's ass and he'll see that you're fed, have a bed, and a whore by your head. You fight for him, and he'll pay you *whatever* you want. However, as I have already said and will only repeat a final time now; I'm jefe of this work crew. I got 22 men and ninos that are getting paid to hustle and rustle the land, which includes carrying out the personal, self-drawn blueprints of Coronel Ridge. We are only following the specific orders of el 'coronel', tu pendejo!"

Alonso paused to wipe a large accumulation of sweat that poured over his face during the humid, hottest part of the day, and watching as Sheriff Daggs hopped back onto his horse and took his hat off of his head, the Mexican smiled up at the lawman.

"Did Ridge ever actually specialize in engineering at any school, civilian or otherwise?" Daggs imposed his question upon the incredulous Mexican.

"Of course not, Sheriff! The man has no training or aptitude for anything, excepting his pride!"

Both men roared in laughter, and the sheriff grasped at his hat to prevent it from falling to the ground, before he turned to ride back into Redview.

"Alright, then, Alonso, just let Ridge know that I stopped by to pass on this new worker. And, Ward, now you listen and listen good. Alonso and his men here have my permission to deal with you in any way they see fit if you get out of line, or if you're uncooperative towards Ridge's requests." Daggs nodded back to the standing perspiring men.

"Things will be dealt with in proper time, one way or another, Daggs, and you can bet on it, Sheriff." winked Owen Ward, as he tied up his horse to a tree, and prepared to put on a clean work shirt and new boots.

Not watching the lawman leave from out of their viewpoint, Owen then trotted after Alonso, who'd returned back down closer to the river, by the soon-to-be constructed bridge. Wanting to avoid further issues with his current employer, the former shootist became determined to remain silent.

"Niños, niños! Aquí! Over here!" Alonso thundered over to three boys, whose ages looked to range between ten to twelve years old. "Hurry, tu changuitos!"

All three of the pre-teens, two Anglos and one Mexican youth, breathed out in harsh coughs, as they were unused to running uphill at such high elevations. Alonso told them to catch Owen up along with the rest of the work crew, and walk him through where the first timbers will be laid for the bridge. The boys spoke English, Spanish, and a mixture of the two, and they were, down to the last lad, happy to escape the more arduous and dangerous work of assisting the lumberjacks or leveling the earth for the bridge's initial foundation ramparts on either side of the bridge, the back-breaking work which caused the pre-teens to lull away hiding for a couple of hours break, and they were not quick to give up escorting the newcomer around just to return back to the toiling drudgery.

"And over here is where they are whittling the overhanging beams," said the Mexican boy, nicknamed 'El Cid', who sometimes nodded his head when the other boys used the name, 'Jose', in recognition, but only to his great consternation.

"Yeah, we had to help carry the containers that were shipped and waggoned in, and my wrists are still swollen," said 'Stone Wall', the boy who liked to talk at length about the Civil War at all hours of the day.

"Well, mine don't hurt, and I lifted twice as much weight as what you did!" yelled 'Tom Sawyer', the smallest of the three but also the liveliest.

"Okay now, fellas. That'll do it," said Owen Ward, as he stopped to watch the free flowing river. "Let's cut out the noise and go down this side of the river again, just one more time. I know they're building the foundation into too deep of waters. You boys take down the measurements I ask you to make, and I'll record what we get."

"What if they need our help building the bridge?" 'Tom Sawyer'asked, looking to be disruptive but helpful.

"Let's avoid it unless they absolutely need us. It won't be safe to be one of those first timbers out there on the water. Come, now, let's see how deep the river is a little over yonder." Owen cajoled the boys to follow him.

After recording specific measurements for a half-hour, Alonso and two other ranch hands then approached Owen Ward and the boys.

"El Cid, Stone Wall, let's go!" shouted one of the men.

"We need help laying down the timber, Sawyer!" added the other man.

"Wait, I'll help you out, Alonso. The work of one man is more than a match for any expenditure provided by three boys, no?" said Owen.

"Sure, now let's go, let's go, all of you who desire to be paid today, let's get to it!" yelled Alonso, as the men and boys raced along the river bank back to the location of the would-be bridge.

'Okay, we're ready on this side of the river! You men on the ends head out into the shallow parts of the streams, and we'll then pass the beams on to you!" exclaimed Alonso to his entire work crew that was gathered near him on the sandbanks.

Exhausted men were heaving the 12 foot long timber logs into the shallow water, with a few men standing at each designated spot in the river where elevated cement platforms would serve as the position where the new wooden beams were to be emplaced into. The delicate task of guiding the timber into their placements required care from smaller hands like those of a boy, as a child's hands were more adapted to not over-forcing the severe weight of the uplifted logs. Although Owen Ward could see that the work crew would be able to secure a few of the beams into their cement-based platforms, the two in the middle of the river, where the water was at its deepest and rushed the quickest, would be impossible to safely secure the timber into. 'El Cid' and 'Stone Wall' joined in to help two of the platforms closer to the river's edge, while 'Tom Sawyer' was ordered to swim out to the farthest section of the water. 'Sawyer' looked back to Owen, who shook his head to indicate to the boy that he should not dive into the river, but the yelling threats and severe consternation from Alonso harangued the boy into pacing his way over to the middle platforms, swimming through several swift currents before grabbing onto the physical safety provided by the scaffold. Owen was quick behind 'Sawyer', as there were only two men at either platform, when there should have been four present on each one.

Swimming out past the two men, Owen could better see the struggling, dehydrated ranch hands fighting against the current, as some of them gasped through the water for air.

'This foundation won't be able to hold,' thought Owen Ward, as he clung onto the cement platform that sheltered 'Tom Sawyer' from the waves.

'Sawyer' stood on top of the platform, near the hole in its center, where the 12 foot long timber log was designated to be planted. The two ranch hands who'd swam over to that particular cement platform had failed to lift the heavy timber, as they struggled against the roaring current of the river and they were forced to balance their combined weight all the while being bombarded by the white waves; breathing in the wet air in quick gasps, the men held onto the log now out of fear, not letting the timber go, as the wood would drift down river with the tumbling currents.

"Wait a second there, fellars," throttled out Owen Ward, huffing in rushed oxygen into his lungs, and finding small footing in the shifting sands on the bed of the river lined with smooth, white stones. "Be careful, 'Sawyer', and watch your fingers!"

The small group of now three adult men were able to uplift the timber log sideways onto the cement platform, and the beam lay secured in a horizontal position near 'Tom Sawyer'. Sweating out beads while maintaining the log's weight atop the platform and starting to lose the traction present in both his hands and feet, Owen was just able to provide a major final push upwards to put the beam into an upright, vertical bearing, as the two other men moved to hold either side of the timber up from their angles. 'Sawyer' waded in from the river and continued to watch, the small boy waiting to play his part and guide the wooden beam into place, as he grabbed onto the platform.

Looking back down into the moving water, Owen observed the initial crumbling of the cement platform the four of them stood upon, as the combined weight from the timber log and the surging charges of the river's currents proved to be too strong of a force, and the platform's disintegration was seen by those close-up to be inevitable.

"Okay, now look. All four of us are gonna drop the log, and then we'll leap out into the water, away from where the currents are strongest." shouted Owen over the deafening din of the river.

While preparing to jump, one of the men lost his bearings, and he fell splashing into the water, where his head struck a rock. As the beam of wood started to fall in the direction of the remaining three fellows still on the platform, the other ranch hand stared at Owen with cold eyes, before he leaped into the safety of the river, swimming towards the sandy shoreline without sparing a look back. Having a single moment before the giant log could fall onto and crush the diminutive boy, Owen grabbed 'Tom Sawyer' by the scruff of his soggy shirt around the back of his neck, and then the man yanked the boy into the currents with him.

The fallen log cannonballed, making its presence felt in the bursting ripples launched upwards and outwards, causing Owen and 'Sawyer' to attempt to just only avoid the timber log, while the boy was wrapped tight around the man in a death's grip. Owen held the bottom of his chin secured against his neck, in order to hold onto the youth, where the child's hands were now squeezed into, and the ex-gunslinger swam hard for dry land. Approaching where he could touch the riverbed easier, a few of the other men swam out to meet Owen and take 'Sawyer' back onto the shore, and another man shouldered Owen's body weight underneath that of his own, as he helped Owen to struggle to walk along the slippery rocks.

Panting for several moments, Owen turned to face the boy, before speaking.

"Are you okay, kid?"

"I think so," 'Tom Sawyer' responded softly.

"And tell me something. Why aren't you boys in school? Does your Ma and Pa know that you're working out here, instead of learning how to read and write in the schoolhouse?"

"My mama works real hard to get all of the things we need for the two of us," 'Sawyer' looked down in shame, while coughing to catch his breathing. "I tell her I'm going to school most mornings, and that I only work for Mr. Ridge on the weekends, but I know mama's too smart for all that. She lets me get away with it, and allows me an opportunity to earn a little bit of money to help us survive."

The river water dripped off in droplets from 'Sawyer', and his hair and clothes were soaked to their minutest fibers. Catching his own breath in the sun, Owen eyed the approach of the obese Alonso.

"Alright, we were able to catch Garrity floating down the river. He's a little shaken up, but the man'll live." the rotund man stated, as he looked down at the wet Owen Ward.

"That's all you have to say to me?' glared Owen at Alonso.

Alonso held out an empty hand, reaching down to Owen, who accepted the open-handed grasp. The large man lifted up the newcomer with relative ease, as Alonso weighed 250 pounds, not counting his work clothes and boots.

"Now, perhaps you were right, gringo, and I'm glad no one died, but Senor Ridge is the one who set the specifications for the construction of this bridge, as I have already explained to you earlier today."

"Then let's move the bridgehead! Because next time, somebody will die out there. To hell with Ridge, we're the ones doing the dirty work." said Owen, while searching Alonso's face for any reasonable understanding of their collective predicament.

"Well, for a gunfighter, you seem to know alot about carpentry, don't you?"

"No, but by living off the land, and traipsing across the Rio Grande, you learn a few things," said Owen, as he rubbed his face dry. "Now, let us get five fellows together to start double-checking my measurements for the river's depth a little ways down river from here."

Losing himself in the work, Owen Ward struck a look towards 'Sawyer's' direction, who by now was surrounded by 'El Cid', 'Stone Wall', and several other excited, chatty boys.

"Hey, 'Sawyer'? Why don't you wait until I'm done later this afternoon, and then I can walk you home, and perhaps we can see if I can talk to your Ma?" asked Owen, in a polite tone.

"Sure, I'd like that." grinned the lying 'Tom Sawyer'.

Winking at the boy, Owen soon returned back to his work.

Several hours later, Owen was unable to locate 'Sawyer', and most of the other boys claimed to have not seen him leave. Searching around Ridge's property for a little while, a clanging sound projected off from the ringing supper bell brought Owen's attention to his unfed stomach, and his mind much desired to find a cot with dry sheets to crawl into that night, the first soft bed he would have known in several months.

Chapter 10- Dr. Ward and Judge Graves Share a Drink and an Opinion

Dozens of sitting denizens were riddled throughout the entire claustrophobic environment of Baker's Bets, a gambling hall that specialized in poker; the smoke so opaque, even the cheating card dealers could never be certain that the half-drunk prospectors and coachmen and men of derelict creeds were able to catch the quick flashes of tricks or not. Murders had never occurred within the structure, but nary a night would pass without the beating of a fellow by a man who had felt his luck to be foiled by a dealer's designed intemperance.

Near the den of vice's bar area, far from the main gambling floor, there sat less than ten men, most of whom had either lost most of their money or were bartering with their conscious under the influence of ignorant liquid confidence, that misplaced notion of a man seeking his own path to be void of all humanity, and damned to live within his head. The gamblers bought themselves another drink, to help them decide on whether to sell their boots and hats for spare coins, or perhaps see if a fellow ruffian would make trade for a gold tooth or two.

Two refined and dignified gentlemen sat at one of the few bar tables present in the room, and they were left undisturbed by the obliviated degenerates near to the entrance of Bakers' Bets. Dr. Taig Ward and Judge Graves drank their beige whiskies with the slowness of thinking men who had through misfortune not of their own making become unsure of themselves. The judge was delighted to be out of the house and away from his wife, and he did not mind the initial direction of his younger friend's conversation, but over the course of their distilled spirits, the old legal scholar wondered at what the doctor thought of him, and if their long friendship would be affected by new developments.

"I don't know, Eugene,' said Dr. Ward, as he shook the strong liquid contents around inside of his cup. "I still find it suspicious that Sheriff Daggs hasn't thoroughly investigated the Jones and Channing murders at the Needle more than he has. It seems he hasn't bothered to leave the bars for weeks at a time, when he isn't palling around with members of the Neary Gang."

"Well, maybe the rumors about what happened to those boys, heck, *boys*, more like drifters, are true but I digress," gruffled Judge Graves, as his burning throat derived further pain from the man's exposure to air as he continued to speak. "You know how drunkards and cowpokes love to tell tall tales. Daggs might be on the take, but he couldn't possibly ignore murder charges, no matter who committed them."

"Yes, I suppose so, but I'll tell you what's been bothering me more than our corrupt sheriff. That damn Ridge keeps making these infernal demands against claiming my property and land deed. I mean, how much can one man possibly want and need to call his own? He already *has* damn near half of the available public land in this bloody county, but he still desires my small part of this here earth. "

Judge Graves spoke to the bartender to order another drink, but was silent about the concerns of Taig, so the doctor continued to ask the question which had been needling him for weeks.

"Have you looked further into being able to issue any of those injunctions, like I asked you a stretch of days back when?"

"Of course I have, Taig, but his lawyer keeps drawing things out with continuations and trial misdirection, which unfortunately is legal. You just need to wait it out, young man."

"I guess I have no other choice but to do just that, then, wouldn't I?"

Taig Ward finished the rest of his only whiskey glass of the evening, shaking his head at the approaching barman as to the unwanted second nightcap. Judge Graves took another of his frequent bird sips from his own whiskey, and then placed his hand over the top of his cup, also declining one for the road, which would make for his fifth in the last hour.

"What's to say we get back to a poker table? We can play a few more hands; I mean, we've only been out a little over an hour, and I'm sure our wives would appreciate their free evening even further to have more time towards quiet domesticity in their homes."

"Is it granite or is it sandstone, because I forget which it is?" asked Taig, willing to risk injuring the feelings of his aged friend.

"What do you mean, sir?" laughed the judge, and then the 63-year-old man placed his large, venous hands onto the table in a show of contrition.

"The new courthouse being built up there on Grand Avenue; the building a handful of the local robber barons are paying to construct, all in the name of being good business for the common folk, I'm sure, no?" the doctor eyed the judge without blinking.

"I hope that you are not implying that Mr. Ridge is bribing me to take your land. Don't think that just because you're a quarter-century younger than me that I won't give you a severe pommeling, Doc," the older man spoke in half-drunken fury, but was tempered by his embarrassment at the entire situation. "You think I could survive out here in the Arizona territories for this long if I did not know how to fight and survive?"

"Just answer the question. Will the outside walls of the new courthouse be made of granite or sandstone?"

Recognizing the man's determination, the judge gave up.

"Red sandstone."

"I don't know the law around here anymore, Judge," Taig said, more out of resignation than disgust. "Men are being murdered in broad daylight, our sheriff is a drunken coward, and small ranchers like me don't have the coin to compete with rich fools of the colonel's breed. You think an honest man can win in this life, Eugene?"

"Come on, let me buy us another whiskey, ones that are not as strong."

"Yeah, you owe me that much, don't you?"

After the bartender had supplied another drink, Taig Ward was quick to empty the last of his glass, his head becoming less clear with each sip. Finished with drinking for good on this night, Dr. Ward stood back up from the barroom table, looking to make his way back home to his family. Grabbing his hat and overcoat, the doctor was about to exit the gambling establishment.

"Hey, don't you want to play for a little longer?"

"No, but while you gamble some more, please at least take a moment of your time to ponder what I have said to you tonight. We've known each other for many years and have been friends for quite some time now, but you aren't being on the level with me."

"That's not true, Taig, it's really not like that. It's only Ridge's bastard lawyers who're the ones steering this ship of depravity towards our town. They have been driving the hard bargain on all of those land deals. If only Daggs would-."

"Yes, indeed, it is always 'if only' in this life, is it not? Every man knows how that goes."

At that statement, Dr. Ward exited Baker's Bets and rode off home in a fugue, and he was near to forgetting the correct trail to guide his horse over, as if he'd never before been on his way to domestic sanctuary.

Judge Eugene Graves sat back down and drank alone, until a little red rooster crowed thrice the next morning.

Chapter 11- What If Your Love Had Never Been Born?

Owen Ward awoke to the loud sound of tired men farting, their cots groaning underneath the deadweight of ragged ranch hands, while still others rewarded themselves through the breaks of self-abuse. The eyes of unseen dreams were quick to hope to re-enter ignorant good-humor and the quietude afforded to a man while he slept, but the former shootist saw the futility in trying to go backwards in time; instead, he put his work clothes and tattered boots on, and started to venture outside, seeking hot coffee for his head by the burning campfire outdoors. Witnessing the warming yellow light of new morning through the cabin's sole dirty window, Owen could almost forget the lower back pain and cawing right knee problems that had been inflamed by yesterday's burdens, his old injuries from breaking rocks inside the yards of the South Texas penitentiary not lacking in making their awareness known to the ex-gunfighter.

But still the man sought no gun, even while foolish young men left their unpolished revolvers, unguarded and unsecured, propped upwards inside of their boots, the sweat and grime of the footwear rendering the guns near useless to a future firefight. His forgotten ways of the gun could not yet unsee the practiced disciplined tenants of his previous vocation.

After the prior day's work along the rushing river waters, Owen had received a cooked meal of burnt carnitas and cowboy beans, unsalted to the taste, but the food allowed him the comfort to relax in his drying clothes, as he savored any source of fat and protein. Before the sun had set, the stout Alonso had shown him to the ranch hand camp quarters that the men were expected to share, six fellows each to his own cot inside of a small, wooden cabin. The Mexican informed him that all hands were expected to be ready at 6 am tomorrow morning, and the former shootist nodded back his acknowledgement of the working terms expected of him by the civilian 'colonel'.

Easing his way through the first few hours of work, Owen tried his best to nurse away the soreness of his aging tendons and muscles, while also helping to prepare the laying down of new wooden foundations for another bridge approved strictly by him, as he continued to draft and redraft crude blueprints based upon the bridge's measurements from yesterday. He watched as Alonso joked around with the work crew before starting on his approach.

"Do the new blueprints look good?" asked Owen Ward.

"Yes, they do. Go ahead and roundup the boys that're fishing down there by the river, and tell them we have much work to do. Oh, and Senor Ridge says you can have the morning off and that he will see you in his office in Redview tomorrow at 11 am." replied Alonso.

"Why can't I just meet with him right here on his property?"

"Ridge does not like to meet with the help in this way, gringo," laughed the jiggling mass, as several other of the more brash ranch hands joined in the obese Mexican's mirth. "You think you're gonna join him for dinner tonight in his dining hall, perhaps even share a drink?"

"Alright, I'll go gather the kids and get them started on mixing the cement."

A half-dozen boys, including 'El Cid', 'Stone Wall', and 'Tom Sawyer', were using weak, brittle tree branches and cotton yarn to cast after fish, much to the chagrin of all when Owen discovered them at work for their lunch.

"Good morning, fellas," smiled Owen, who motioned the children to come closer and listen to him. "Now, this being Saturday, I can use all of you. But from here on out, I only wanna see you younger boys on the weekends, after church on Sundays, and when school lets out during the rest of the week. We'll see if we can get you paid the same for working less."

Most of the boys' initial rage at Owen's direct forwardness in dictating the order of their lives was salved by the promise of an increase in pay while reducing the hours of back-breaking work they were expected to endure. Bursting at the seams with ebullient cheer and tired of their failed efforts to catch any wiggling trout, the young would-be ranch hands braced themselves to ask the newcomer a most pertinent question, one that no boy was quite brave enough to salvage the courage to query Owen if he really was a cowboy, supposedly even a noted gunfighter, to hear Alonso and the other men talking around the campfires the previous night. 'El Cid' and 'Stonewall' had decided to gang up on 'Tom Sawyer', and a few of the other taller lads pushed the younger 'Sawyer' towards Owen, telling him to ask about the man's past.

"Come on, 'Sawyer', the fellow saved your life yesterday! You should be the one to ask him," said 'Stonewall' to his friend.

Taking notice of his charges' overeager discomfiture, Owen Ward affected a wide grin, loving the idea of playing the role of an unwitting fool.

"Ask me what?" the sly Owen Ward said, as he sharpened his focus directly onto 'Sawyer'.

"Nothing." replied the young boy, while staring at the ground, wishing to avoid eye contact.

"Come on, ask him!" exhorted the rest of the boys in unison.

"Fine, then, you jerks," said 'Sawyer', his freckled face starting to redden with anger, and his awkwardness becoming insurmountable while everyone looked at him. "What *they* want to know is, are you a gunslinger or not?"

"A gunslinger?"

"Yeah, a cowboy. Word is, you've been hiding on the lamb, maybe a cutthroat cattle rustler, or even a bank robber." surmised 'Tom Sawyer'.

"Well," began Owen, as he spoke in a soft tenor voice. "I'm out of that line of work, fellas. Now, as of yesterday, I'm in the same trade of business as the rest of you, so what say we get started working?"

"Wow!" exclaimed a tall and lanky pre-teen boy.

"Then it's true, you *are* a gunslinger!" said another boy.

"I knew it, I told you guys!" said 'El Cid', as he jumped up and down, losing his hat in the process.

"Now, settle down, fellas, settle down. I'll tell you all what's what, if you're all so interested in that kind of life, and I can tell you stories about what it was like, riding on the outlaw trail, but all of you first need to promise me that you'll report to the schoolhouse every morning and learn the day's lessons well, the best you can. Is that a deal, gentlemen?"

"Deal!" the boys thundered back.

"Okay. Toss the fishing rods, and let's get to work on this new bridge."

The work of mixing rocky cement platforms, felling obstructive and hazardous trees, and leveling more ground went on through to the torrid late afternoon, and then carried over into the clear evening. By that hour, Alonso finally called for the work crews to take a break from their job duties and head home for the night. As the other boys drifted away into the dying light after hearing a particularly raucous story about the former shootist's time in Dodge City, Owen stopped 'Sawyer' to have a personal conversation with him.

"You left early yesterday. I had wanted to talk to your mother and father about what happened, but then you disappeared."

"My father's *dead*, but I am sorry about shirking off like that, Mr. Ward."

"Call me Owen."

"Alright then, Owen," the boy smiled. "It was just that I didn't want anyone to tell my mother about you helping me out on the river. Not only will she be liable to whip my hide for almost drowning, but she'll be even more furious to know that I have been ditching school, even though she kinda already knows that I do that. Besides, I had never met a gunfighter, before now, that is!"

Owen Ward looked back at the smiling nine year old's face with neither humor nor malice, but with a genuine regret for the sorrow the boy would have to confront over the course of however many years God has seen fit to grant to the poor youth. The man wanted to explain to the child that while indiscretion was natural, as a boy is liable to skip the schoolhouse some days for a lark, but the time for games concerning cowboys had reached an end. The roughened would-be ranch hand did not know how to whisper these words into the ear of a boy, let alone make the wisdom stick in his mind, without also inflecting the gruff tones of dissatisfied age into applicable temperate advice.

'How do you teach a boy to be a man when you don't quite know how you got to be there yourself?' Owen Ward thought in his mind.

Either way, Owen recognized in 'Sawyer' a spark of life that the man had failed to elicit within his own most recent years of existence. So instead, lacking any better alternative arguments, the former shootist aimed for bribery.

"I won't tell your mother about the accident along the river, as long as you don't keep being truant from school, 'Sawyer'."

"Yeah, but," the small boy paused for a moment, running his tongue along the bottom of his incisors, as he thought about the grave injustices that erupted from the schoolhouse in the past. "What's the point in school, anyways? Mama told me that my father owned his own ranch of many acres, and how he never spent a day in the classroom in his entire life. Of course, he *left* mama, but still he did something under the sweat of his own brow and industry."

"There are certain things you can only learn in life while you are still very young. I know that nine years is a long time, but when you're an old man, one day, and your ears are taller and your nose is bigger and full of tiny, growing hairs, there will be lessons that come back to you in those tired years that you'll remember learning from, way back when. Now is that 'when', sonny, boy. So, what say we go on into town, and take you back home to your mother, eh, 'Sawyer'?"

"Okay, Owen," said the boy, before he took another step closer to the ex-gunslinger. "But you must promise me that I can still work here after school is out."

"Yes, sir, I promise."

The man held his hand outwards to 'Tom Sawyer', and the boy shook it. Owen was proud of the child's strong, firm grip.

"Okay, Owen." Sawyer repeated, as the two fellows made their way to Owen's horse, determined to ride into Redview, the dusty town also known as the 'Scarlet Rose'.

The washed and brushed horse trotted for an hour, past the saloons and bordellos of Main Street, and then the travelers entered 4th Street. The boy was pointing at the McManus Boarding Home for Christian Women, and several young women and children sat and stood around outside the two-storied building meant for charity, watching in particular the movements of the man.

"You live here with your mother?" broached Owen in a nonchalant tone.

"Yes, since I was eight."

"Does she have red hair?"

"So what's it to *you*, Owen? How did you know that mama has auburn hair?"

"Lucky guess, I suppose," Owen smiled at the petulant youth. "Do you wanna go in and talk to her first?"

"Yeah, that'd probably be better. I'll be right back."

The petite boy ran up the short steps and in through the front entrance way, not waiting on a response from Owen.

'What should I say to her?' thought Owen Ward.

The ex-gunslinger could not remember if he'd ever been in love before. In lust, yes, he was most certain of this, but not in love, as the man could not recall a memory of that peculiar feeling ever being singed into his heart and soul, not even as a youth or so much as puppylove.

'The woman and her son are sheltering in a boarding house because either her husband died or he left them,' thought Owen. 'How awful, but what could I say?'

Running along the steps formed in the image of his words which he built inside of his mind, the former shootist happened upon a question to ask, just as the most physically striking red-haired woman he'd ever seen in his life walked back into his life, as she followed little 'Sawyer' to the front entrance door of the boarding house.

"Owen, this is my mama, Miss Rabelais."

"Tom, you know that I *do not* tolerate young people referring to their elders by their first names. You are not an adult quite yet, young man." said Emma Rabelais, whose eyes struck a jolt of shock into the depths of Owen's being, and the proof of this was his rising heart rate.

The man thought the mother smelled of dewey lilacs in the summertime. Smiling at her, he nodded a heavy head, and then he extended his hand outwards.

"My name is Owen Ward, Miss Rabelais, and I'd hoped to talk to you about your son; alone, if possible."

"Certainly, Mr. Ward. Tom, go into our room and pick out your clothes for church tomorrow."

"But we *never* go to church!" 'Sawyer's' voice was raised to a higher pitch than normal.

"Well, we're gonna try to tomorrow, boy. Now, get inside, mister!" the mother's eyebrows arched into a sharpened triangle, and her son stood at attention, listening to her command.

"Goodnight." waved Owen to the boy, who nodded back in silent farewell as he entered the boarding house for the night.

Emma Rabelais saw a squint in Owen's eye and a wry smile upon his mouth, a similar look that he had adopted when he used to ride the hidden back trails of the country, escaping from the searching marshals, and the same expression he wore upon his face the other night when he had beaten the rude fellow who had been harassing Emma and her girlfriend at the dancing hall. The woman was immediate in her feminine recognition and she was determined to make a direct response to the scruffy stranger.

"It's you! Because of *you*, I can never go back to the Dancing Prize again, as they already thought I was still a pros-. Well, never your mind," the red-haired woman caught herself before she remembered her heart's priorities. "What are you doing with my son?"

"I help to work on Mr. Ridge's property, ma'am. Your son has been assigned to my work crew, so I just wanted to say hello to you."

"Is that so, Mr. Ward?" Emma herself squinted into Owen's visage. "Do you pay visits to *all* of the mothers of the boys working for you?"

"No, just you," smiled Owen Ward, before he leaned in to ask the mother in a low tone. "Is it okay for me to pose a question your way?"

"I suppose you can." Emma raised an eyebrow.

"Assuming a man is not already in your life, and that you are not the right hand in a doomed lover's tale, do you want to live to be a great old age, look back over the years of your life, and ask yourself without knowing the answer, 'What if your love had never been born?'."

Chapter 12- Then I Suppose I Never Would Have Known Love, but Only Imposters

The blue-eyed woman, Emma Rabelais, pierced arrows into Owen Ward's soul, and then responded back to the man's question.

"If I were to consider the truthfulness of the question, then I suppose I never would have known love, but only imposters. No?"

At a fast clip, an old, severe matron approached Emma from behind, exiting the boarding house like a missionary intent on spreading the Good Word to the ignoble savage.

"Miss Rabelais, shouldn't we all be heading in soon?" asked the wrinkled woman, noting Owen with a vague notion of detestable toleration.

"No, I always go out to dance on Saturday," murmured Emma. "I promise to be back by 11 pm, Mrs. Garfield."

"But you only ever go out with your *female* companions." Mrs. Garfield exclaimed in harsh tones, as her eyes shot daggers in Owen's general direction, not appreciating the developing conversation.

"Betsy had to cancel tonight, but Mr. Ward here has volunteered to be my chaperone, and as he is the employer of my son, who in turn works for the 'colonel' on his ranch outside of Redview," noted the mother, taking on the tone of a respectful daughter. "I wouldn't think you'd mind if we wanted to go out dancing for a spell, ma'am, if that's alright by you?"

Looking concerned but born prone to excessive forgiveness meant for all of womankind, the wearied matron nodded her head in slow approval.

"But you simply *must* be home by 11!" responded Mrs. Garfield harshly.

"Okay, ma'am, and dinner will still be served to Tom?" asked the mother, as she took notice of the older woman's further nodding acknowledgement. "Mr. Ward, let me just go inside to kiss him goodnight."

The former shootist watched the woman in her mid-twenties bounce along the steps of the boarding house, her feet seeming to not even touch the ground, as she caused a fluttering of tangled nerves throughout his body while she did so.

The man was now most certain that he had never been in love before, and he could not tell for sure right now if he was or not; but he wondered. Or *prayed* that he was, with great hope.

Emma came back outside to the top of the steps, her red hair pinned-up with yellow bow ribbons in a style meant for dancing; she had also put on a simple white dress that did not show off the curves of her youthful form. She smiled and laughed at Owen, as she watched his eyes follow her every forward progression towards him. Catching himself grinning far too wide, he held out his hand, hoping to take hers.

"Where should we go dancing tonight?" Owen asked.

"Certainly not to the Dancing Prize, after your own rather unique performance there the other evening," Emma shook her head in false chastisement, which was given away in quick feminine chuckles.

"Isn't there any other place to dance within all of Redview?"

"Of course, dear; come on," the woman said, as she tightened a light coat around her small shoulders. "I'll ride with you, on your horse. We can go a little across the way, to the other side of town. Maybe they won't know you over there. Just don't beat anyone up this time."

Owen felt content enough to simply wear his tight-lipped smile, once Emma was at his back while they both sat atop his horse, and the world's red dust was just another feature of this life that attempted to distract him from the most beautiful woman in existence. The pressing of her body weight, and the grasping of her delicate white hands along his middle, reminded the man of the woman's realness, in his secret moments, and the exhaled breath she breathed onto the nape of his neck tempted his lips beyond redemption. Yet still he waited for the right time.

The ex-gunslinger rode in silence, while Emma continued to talk, but Owen did not mind listening to a woman, because even as he had never been in love over the 37 years of his life, neither had he been given the opportunity to be so near to an unpaid woman for so long a stretch of time, at least not since he was a growing boy; the man rejoiced to the sound of her voice.

The one item Emma Rabelais refrained from disclosing to Owen on the ride through Redview was that she had once been a paid lady herself. She looked for a secured moment to expose this part of her to him, but the clock never struck the proper delicate time. For the entire ride, Emma was surprised to discover anyone, be they man or otherwise, who'd listen to her continuous prattle about any old matter that came into mind. Most of her employers looked down at her from the dizzying heights of respectability, on account of her former profession, and her son, Tom, had grown more despondent over his beliefs about his mother during the preceding few months, and he was less talkative around her then the boy had ever been before in his short existence. Emma thought the ride was nice, as she was heard by a man who seemed to want to listen to her, and she was excited to dance with him.

"Here, take a left off Main," said Emma, as they entered a new section of Redview. "There's a place kitty corner to 7th Street that the girls and I like to go to on Saturday nights, because the pianist there plays at a fast, ragtime clip. You might even say he plays like the devil."

Going at a slow trot in the commanding direction, Owen Ward guided his horse to a hitching post near The Black Rose, a single-story dancing hall of redstone bricks, and both of them could hear the music from outside, the notes of pulsating vibrations meeting them in the sandy street. Inside of the hall, a crowd consisting of a couple dozen men and women danced and twirled around the wooden floor, their drinking at a lull, as the majority were there to go trotting along to the sounds of the small brass band plus the accompaniment of the upright Tack piano, and the ensuing, thralling energy released by the instruments was contagious to all who had ears to hear and senses to feel. The ranch hand and servant woman drew near to each other, the sides of their upper thighs and hips grazing one another while they walked past the rollicking couples.

The brass band was deafening, but Owen could just hear Emma ask if he knew the melody of this tune. He shook his head to the negative, and he had to lean in even closer to the woman in order to hear her shout her second question, a query pertaining to whether he'd like to dance to the current song, regardless if he knew how to step to it or not. Owen nodded yes, and the mother clasped both of his hands into hers, leading him out onto the dance floor. The man had not danced since before he was incarcerated for the previous seven years, but the natural grace and the alluring hair and smile of the woman enticed him to ignore all of his internal doubts, and resort back to his carefree grammar school days. After an hour of non-stop dancing together, they both plopped down in small chairs to drink a glass of water, as the salty sweat dripped down their bodies, the woman's white dress becoming soaked, and the material clung to her body, hugging the curves underneath.

Owen turned to look at Emma straight in the eye, and they both burst into laughter, as they recognized the exhaustion on each other's faces. Neither one of them had said a word to the other since they had started to dance, owing to the loudness of the brass band, and both the ranch hand and the servant woman felt as excited to talk again as they had been when first looking into each other's eyes, earlier in the evening at the boarding house.

"Tell me something," said Emma, her guile revealing nothing on her mind.

"I think that you're the prettiest girl to ever walk upon God's green earth," replied Owen, as he brushed a few stray hairs from off of his forehead.

"No, tell me something I haven't heard before from a man, if you can." the woman jabbed him softly on the shoulder.

"I obviously don't know you very well, Miss Rabelais, but I suppose I can inform you of two matters at the same time. Now, the first issue concerns something I've been waiting to tell you all night, but I have lacked the moral courage, and been further distracted by…well, let's just say I've had a lot on my mind. The second matter, however, can only be of use by starting with the first."

"Okay, out with it, then, Owen!" Emma exclaimed in feign exasperation.

"I used to be a gunsman, an outlaw, so to speak," Owen began in a slow, unashamed voice. "I was in a county jail in south Texas for many years, but I am a changed man now."

"Oh, God, you are a criminal?" Emma moved her head away several inches from Owen, not wanting to believe this revelation.

"A *former* shootist, Emma. Please, you must understand. This is not easy for me, but I always want to be forthright with you. How can a man ever pretend to care about a woman if he starts off by lying to her?"

Emma appeared to be about ready to scoff at the new ranch hand, but Owen continued to speak the hopeful words that sprung into his mind.

"Now, you may have heard compliments paid to your beauty before me, but I say this as a man who knows," Owen risked taking her left hand into his own, and the woman did not pull away from his soft grasp. "Yours is the kind that keeps a caged man dreaming of soft nights, the delicately etched looks that even a damned man can come alive to at the mere thought of a caring world made for sweet touches and whispers of caressed promises. I've never met you before, Miss Emma Rabelais, but I went to sleep every night for seven years inside of a cell praying for an angel like you to bless me. And I'll keep waiting, as a free man, for as long as I have to."

"An angel? Is that what you think I am?" laughed Emma, in spite of herself, as she stood up and moved back closer to the dance floor.

"To some folks, angels are like statues, pieces of marble that you sculpt and place in front of churches," said Owen, approaching a foot closer to her, not wanting her to fly away again. "The problem with that is, an angel formed of stone is made to get shit upon, and corrode and fade to dust over the passage of time. But my thoughts concerning you are different. Yours is the angel that I can soar to the highest reaches of heaven with, as you are the winged creature to let me roam the solid, firm depths of my heart and soul, helping me to discover myself, if not to find the Lord's good graces. Remember, Emma, when I say angel, I do not mean to imply a divine being without knowledge of humanity's wicked sins."

"I used to ply my trade as a painted lady," Emma blurted out, wanting to see if the man's angel would have her wings cut off with this new unholy knowledge about her past. "I started when I was fourteen, as my daddy departed this world young and mama was left with many children to support, so I lived on my own. I had Tom when I was fifteen, and I don't know who his father is. Some women weren't meant for wings, you know."

"Then maybe those women weren't meant to dance with a fellow like me," said Owen, as he stood right in front of her, close enough to breathe in her scents. "Shall we go back out there, then?"

"I'd love to." said Emma, grabbing his hands hard enough to leave red imprints.

Dancing until the hour grew closer to 11 pm and the yellow ribbons loosened to the point of falling out of her hair due to vigorous gyrations, the mother informed her suitor that they'd need to head back over to the boarding house before Mrs. Grant could go into conniptions, and while Owen did not like the idea, the man listened to her request.

The ride home in the dark night cooled off the sweat from all of the earlier physical movements, even if the air could not quite stay the passionate feelings they felt growing between them, and the light projected from the stars above allowed each other to catch glances into reflective eyes, which broadcast what the beginnings of creation may have looked like, to any vulnerable man and woman daring to imagine the cosmos together.

After reaching the McManus Boarding Home for Christian Women, Owen Ward helped Emma Rabelais down from his horse. The time was just past 11 pm, and both of them could feel the elderly eyes of several matrons cast in their direction, and this prevented the former shootist from being too forward with the mother. The woman, however, desired to be kissed.

"I had such a lovely time tonight," Emma cooed.

"As did I. We'll have to go out dancing again, maybe next Saturday night?"

"Indeed," Emma approached ever closer to Owen. "And perhaps we can end the evening with a soft goodbye?"

Owen leaned in to gently touch the white dress shoulders of his date, and Emma placed her arms around his back. After a moment's kissing embrace, but right before Mrs. Garfield started to yell from the second floor window about the lateness of the hour, Owen brought his head backwards, to look again into the woman's soul.

"Will you keep dreaming about me, Owen?"

"Until the stars burn out."

After a second kiss, and the further frantic rantings from Mrs. Garfield, the two separated and made their ways into different beds; but they dreamt the same tempting dream.

Chapter 13- Nelcy Ward Makes the Case

Nelcy Ward and her two daughters, Rachel and little Elmira, exited Zeke's Fixtures and Wares clothing shop, on 9th Street and Main Street. The Ward ladies had depleted their sewing supplies at home, so the mother decided to pick up new materials and fabrics while in the tiny shopping center of Redview. While they were already out about town browsing, Nelcy and the girls had decided to buy a book for Tom Rabelais, the young son of Emma, the thrice a week servant woman at the ranch home of the Wards, as the boy's birthday was fast approaching.

Walking along the shaded wooden pathway that ran parallel to the street in order to avoid the crimson dirt from staining their dress shoes, the family next entered into one of the town's few bookstores, where Nelcy spotted several of Redview's leading ladies, who were the authority concerning all matters related to high society in the 'Scarlet Rose', and a person's worth and ability and proper station in this life could be decreed by these ladies at an instance's glance by them. The women's hats were made of bright colors and contained white and black feathers; Nelcy's own hat was gray and plain, and she hated all types of feathers.

"Mrs. Ward and the girls, please come and join us!" said the exuberated Mrs. Hamel, head matron of Redview's edict on how a modern, and thereby sophisticated, woman was supposed to act, appear, learn, and condescend to other, like-minded civilized creatures.

Nelcy Ward had been born inside of her grandfather's cabin in what was, during the time of the American Civil War, the capital of the Arizona Territory, Prescott, long before the seat of local governmental power was moved to geographic points further down south. The thirty-year-old woman adored Redview's skies during the summer evenings, on any clear day, right when the sun has just about surrendered to the night, and the fireworks burst of red, orange, pink, and yellow is almost too gorgeous for human eyes to behold, and a mortal mind starts to wonder as to how God could make the domain of heaven even more beautiful than this broken land, where red ground flows beneath the toes of all who dare to walk so near, and so close to perfection. But the mother was not blinded by the ingloriousness of freedom, and the endless choices that life often forces a poor soul to make. For whether a cause is righteous or not, like the wicked Neary Gang and the havoc they create, where clearly the men's direction was lost, the woman understood that violence was a facet of existence, a feature built into this world, and a person could either accept this reality, or instead run off to fret their time and humanity away, pretending that man is not what he is *at times*, an irrational beast who *chooses* not to think.

'Good men should be made of proper judgment, prudence, and be prepared to use violence only in the most extreme of life's circumstances,' Nelcy had once remarked to her quarreling sons, who yelled at one another that *he* was a 'man', while the other was just a 'boy'. 'And I can say the same thing for a good woman, Rachel and little Elmira, as I'm talking to you, too, girls.'

Although the red lands attracted the bad seeds of destruction, the area had also been sown with the tree of love, and the tree's roots had long ago spread underneath the ground, pushing back against the eternal darkness. By reaching for the light, mankind can find their place in this blackened universe.

Nelcy Ward begrudged no lady her right to her own opinion, but she herself was a woman in possession of passionate and strong convictions, ones which went against the tides of crashing against others with salted words, the damaging comments meant to cut deep, and those horrible eye rolls concerning another lady's ruined reputation serving to only further marinate the martyred woman's wounds in vindictive vinegar.

Nelcy nodded her hello to all three ladies inside of the bookstore, and she did not need to encourage her young daughters to return the politeness of the moment, as they were both well-behaved and correctly trained. All three of the matrons nodded and laughed their approval at the girls wanting to purchase a book before they could properly read.

"Well, that's splendid, girls," said Mrs. Hamel, as she finished talking about the two novels she had just now purchased from the shop. "What were you looking for in particular today?"

"We are actually here for several different items," interjected Nelcy Ward, who felt that her ten and six year old daughters had tasted enough from the richness of high society's golden cup for one afternoon. "For the girls, I think the collected works of Jane Austen will make for stimulating reading, while for my boys and young Tom Rabelais, Miss Emma Rabelais's soon-to-be ten-year-old son with his birthday coming up, I was hoping to acquire the works of Mr. Mark Twain, with a focus on any of his books that have 'Tom Sawyer', as I believe Emma's boy is quite fascinated by the character, apparently."

The two ladies with Mrs. Hamel guffawed in a quiet, feigned disgust. Mrs. Hamel only turned her eyes upon her companions, without altering the position of her head, which continued to face Nelcy and her daughters. The smirk that ran across the lead woman's visage caused a sharp pain to occur within Nelcy's heart. The mother within her allowed her to stay her tongue, but that same maternal forbearance was further connected to an instinct ready to deal with harm in no uncertain terms.

"That's rather a little curious, is it not, Mrs. Ward?' asked Mrs. Hamel in a practiced nonchalance, long cultivated over a lifetime of having others *to do*, while she herself spent much of her time doing *not*.

Bracing her words, Nelcy kept her voice in proper check.

"And what is it, exactly, that you find to be so interesting, ladies?"

"I know that you were not born in Redview, darling, but I had assumed that it was not a common occurrence for a lady from a decent home and background to treat her help like they are her *friends*." said Mrs. Hamel, allowing the trueness of her words to sink into Nelcy.

"Yeah," said another of the laughing ladies. "They're paid to wash your clothes, honey, not to pretend like they care about you."

Nelcy only needed to make two steps toward the intrusive woman for her to stop laughing, by which time the mother of four had come to her senses, and she elected to avoid physical violence, at all costs. Taking another deep breath, Nelcy sought to make Emma's case against the ignorance of the polite, controlling world.

"I could suppose that you would hold no other value for people besides what they can do for you. You are indeed very rich, Mrs. Hamel, rich in the ways you hurt those around you."

Mrs. Hamel and the other women's faces darkened, with the head matron exhibiting a further mixture of surprise and genuine distress upon her elderly features, her feathered red and green hat shaking as a weather vane on top of the old woman's head; the tempted tempest now looked to inflict a punishing pain upon Nelcy.

"Is it my correct understanding that Miss Rabelais has not *always* been a servant woman, Mrs. Ward?" began Mrs. Hamel, her voice turning into concentrated humorous hatred. "Mrs. Stevens, Mrs. Weir, and myself wouldn't know for sure, as we have never employed the dreadful woman, not even for a single day, but *you have* for quite some time now, haven't you?"

"I think we're done talking, ladies. My daughters and I have better matters to attend to than nonsense such as this. Come on, girls, let us carry onward."

"Hmm, that's interesting, isn't it, ladies? While the rest of us women of finer upbringing and civilized behavior would sooner die than see one of our daughter's become painted, other women would see fit to allow a first-class whore, a master jezebel of Main Street to come into her own home and gallivant about around her little girls, and God only knows what else her *husband* may get himself into."

The heckling laughter came to an abrupt end when Nelcy Ward slapped Mrs. Hamel on the cheek with an open palm of her hand, before she made a quick apology.

"I'm very sorry, girls," Nelcy said as she looked down at her daughters. "Rachel, my love, and my baby, Elmira, please understand that what mommy did was not a *good* thing, but sometimes *good* people must defend themselves from *bad* situations. Now let's leave here, girls, and find another bookstore to patronize. The air inside of here is all stuffy, and filled with no breathable or worthy substance."

The Ward women left the store in unabashed silence, and they were able to purchase their novels from another shop in relative peace, ignoring the cost of the books, as the only offered choices were all first editions. Nelcy Ward paid the money for her purchases and then laughed deep within herself

'Either way, you pay,' the wife and mother thought, as she corralled her girls in the vain hope of returning back home before the hour grew too late into the afternoon.

Chapter 14- Dr. Taig Ward Rides the Land

A man rides into the desert not knowing if he shall ever return home again. He accepts this agreement with nature through an incomplete understanding of free will and the unpredictable determination of providence, not granting the intemperate tendencies of the wilderness a respectful nod of acknowledgement at his own risk, which shall then manifest into the man's pathway, as he thought he was to be gone on the trail for an hour, when the trail instead may become the way towards death. Of course, no experienced traveler ever thinks of himself being faced with actual peril, living only to be kissed by dying lips, and this was never more true then when the itinerant man in question is also a trained medical doctor.

Dr. Taig Ward rode on the back of his gray mare, who was long in her tooth but quick in assured dusty step, and the father of four was far from contemplating dying as he navigated the land of infinite, clenching redness, alert to the fact that this was the second time this week that Ida Tollinger had failed to produce the baby that had been growing inside of her for near on nine months now. The doctor was not angry at his daily tasks but appreciative, as the journey over dozens of riding miles allowed him to move through dry, sandy washes out in the high desert country, where he could see jagged crimson hills and snow-crested mountains far to his north and all of the shapes that the human mind could construct them into being, much in the same way people provide names and finishing touches to the clouds in the air, or the stars in the night sky.

Quail ran back and forth across the permanent riding trail, the animals seeming to have a design on death, or at the very least an arrangement towards preparing for a trampling that thundered down heavy hooves upon them, before the black-faced and crowned birds managed to dredge out of Taig's way, the gray mare's clopping not close to grazing the quail, whose tiny chicks followed their mothers in straight lines, much as ducklings accompany their mistress towards the cool waters of a forgiving pond. A new grouping of the soundless birds made their way in front of Taig once again further down the road, and the doctor looked upwards to venture a guess at the day's approximate time, without consulting his watch, by looking at the position of the sun.

"Noon, by my sight," said Taig Ward, who was at easement with the events of his day thus far. "A baby may not have been born out in the desert this afternoon, but it's still a glorious day to be alive."

Not untrained in the ways and means of the high desert, nor easily distracted by the illusions of personal safety or his own inner thoughts as to God's Grace for all mortal sinners, Dr. Ward heard the soft feint noise of a small, dry twig breaking just behind him, and Taig jumped down from his horse, right as his hat was shot off from atop of his head, the hollow tip of his hat bursting into many streaming fabric seams, as the debris tumbled into the dirt and cactus on the ground.

Taig reached out for the gray mare's reins more out of protection than for affection, and the doctor cursed himself for not taking an extra moment earlier that morning to grab and secure his hated revolver. Instead, he had kissed his wife, Nelcy, goodbye and said he may go for a short ride after Mrs. Ida Tollinger had given birth to her baby, if the day permitted him enough time to do so. His wife laughed and kissed him on the forehead, comparing him to a tickled schoolboy who just wanted to 'go on a lark'. In retrospect, Taig realized he would not have had his departure from Nelcy end any other way then how he'd last seen his wife. Except for that damn gun, as much as he detested wearing one.

'At least she knows how I feel about her, even now,' thought Taig Ward, as a second bullet ricocheted off the flinty rocks near him on the ground, the shrapnel piercing the sand all around him.

Fearing annihilation, he stood up in sheer desperation to yell out to his hunter.

"I surrender, sir, as I have no firearm," shouted Taig to the empty desert, holding his hands skyward as he continued to beg for mercy. "Please, this is not a fair fight, and I am a married man with four young children at home. Please, sir, if you want money, I can give it to you, of my own volition. I swear on it!"

Silence met the doctor for the longest moment of his entire life up until that point of its 36 year duration. The dryness of his mouth had caused Taig's throat to become itchy and his voice had started to crack. But into a hope, a good man places all of his doubts, regardless of the unknown future outcomes.

A noise came a short distance to Taig's left; from out of a collective of green and high juniper bushes, there came forth a native rider on a black stallion with ruddy brown splotches along the rump and hindlegs of the beast. Based on petty rumor, half-drunken innuendo, and how he had been described at various lunch functions and suppers with the good citizens of Redview, Taig was certain that the armed Indian riding towards him with aimed long-rifle was the notorious bandit, Sams, the wanted half-breed known to law enforcement and the newspaper-reading general public as the 'Apache Kid'; the native was wanted by several government agencies that offered a reward for his capture that the doctor could not, at this moment, recall just how much the outlaw was worth. Neither did he care about such superfluous notions as money.

The native rode closer to Taig, keeping his rifle pointed at the chest of his prey, daring him to run off into the white-pebbled wash, where the sinking silk-sand would soon exhaust Taig and allow Sams to take target at ease, outpacing the doctor as he would soon run out of breath.

"Is that you, 'Mad' Owen Ward?" said the 23-year-old 'Apache Kid', as the Indian eyeballed an image seen only within his mind, while physically staring into the face of Taig.

"No, sir, Owen is my cousin," said the doctor, as he cursed his cousin's name, wondering how the man had got him into this predicament. "My name is Dr. Taig Ward, and whatever your business with my kinfolk may be, let me assure you that it is of no concern to me. I hardly know the man, since leaving our childhood days long behind us."

"But it *is* of concern to you, pale medicine man," said the man of dark, unresting eyes, whose grip made noise as he tightened his brown fingers around his gun. "Owen was eyeing me the other night at Mac's Golden Nugget; most of the damned fools in Redview wouldn't dare to try to capture me, but your blood is of a special kind of dunce."

"On this we are in agreement. Now, sir, as it seems that you can recognize that *I am not* my cousin, perhaps we can allow the matter to be laid to rest, and you may afford us both an opportunity to simply ride out of here, going our separate ways out of this wash?"

Sams cocked back the hammer of his Springfield Model 1880 trapdoor long-rifle, which was surely stolen, as they were only issued to service members in the United States Federal Army; Taig further noticed that the firearm's bayonet was missing, but that did not mean that the outlaw did not have the steel weapon hidden elsewhere, ready to be used for the coup de grace. The native allowed the hammer action of his long-rifle to serve as an answer to the doctor's question.

Acknowledging the Indian's pointed silence, Taig Ward was determined to change tact, not neglecting that his life depended on his next carefully chosen words.

"What can I offer you to spare my life? Money? Jewelry? Laudanum? It's stronger than the finest of whiskies, and I got plenty of it back in my home office."

"Your cousin," began Sams, who had not blinked over the course of their entire conversation. "He says through the grapevine that he has given up the way of the gun. Is that true?"

"What is it to me? The man claims to no longer be an outlaw, but how would I know the veracity of that claim, sir?" the white man's voice started to increase in speed, and he could just hear himself start to ramble for his life. "I've only seen him one time in the past 15 plus years, when he recently arrived at my home unannounced and unbeckoned by me, and he soon found out that he was *not* welcome inside of my family's humble abode. I don't know what else I could offer you, Mr. Sams, besides the money in my pocket and this chained-watch that my father-in-law gave to me on my wedding day. You can also have my mare, if you must, but I will not allow you to have my wedding band, as my wife would sooner kill me if I gave it to you, then before you could kill me for not handing it over to you. Just for the record, and all."

Sams almost appeared to smile, but just in his watery brown eyes.

"Men like 'Mad' Owen Ward are born with a troubled soul, and he will soon become untethered to the waking day. He knows the cost of being a shootist, as I know the price of every man's soul. Your cousin is the type of man to either have on your side in war, or to fight to the very death against, to the last spit of one's teeth. I'm born to lose, medicine man, but still I keep shootin'. You tell your cousin that I'm not worth the price for what it costs to hunt me down."

The 'Apache Kid' uncocked his long-rifle, and then he placed the gun into the black felt holster on the side of his black stallion. Neighing at the animal, the native hopped up, and turned to leave Taig behind in the open dust.

"I promise to tell him that if I ever see him again," said Taig.

The young outlaw looked back to face his former capture.

"No man can outrun his past or bleed out all the blood of his family which flows through his veins, Taig Ward. Don't ever forget that."

Sams started to ride away, down the pebbled wash, avoiding a bundle of tumbleweeds to either side of him and his horse, as he moved back into the desert just as quick as he had emerged from the red lands.

Riding back home along the other side of the wash, Taig had concluded to himself that he'd never again be out in the windswept land without his revolver, no matter his hatred of firearms, but he was not committed by the millstone inside of his heart, the hardened notion that somehow his kin was *bound* to him, much as the noxious wet scent that clings to a sick, dying dog soils the air around him.

'No,' the doctor thought, as the golden ranch home appeared within his eyesight after the setting of the sun, the rays of light blinding him, as his hat had been destroyed by the bullet of the 'Apache Kid'. 'I don't owe a thing to any Ward. I have my own family to protect and attend to.'

Watching as his two youngest children, Stephen and Elmira, stopped playing in the front yard after they saw his approach, running out to see him in gales of laughter, Dr. Taig Ward swore a blood oath to himself to never let anyone bring harm to his family.

The affirmation he'd taken prevented him from falling asleep later that evening in bed, and the doubt followed him very deep into the night.

Chapter 15- The 'Colonel' Experiences a Set-back at the Eye of the Needle

Mr. William Ridge, civilian, walked around the outside premises of the Eye of the Needle saloon on Massie Lane in the town known as the 'Scarlet Rose', smoking another endless self-rolled cigarette after he had already smoked an entire pouch of tobacco he had bought earlier in the afternoon. His nerves had refused to become steady through the increased nicotine, which was another reason for him to avoid active shooting exchanges due to his jittery hands, so long as he could pay enough to other men to fight his battles for him. However, after one of his assistants, Lyndon, had quit from Ridge's employment because of the constant hounding threats and tauntings voiced by the loose affiliates and female associates of the Neary Gang, the harassment had not only ended Lyndon's termination of employment, but the young man was further compelled to flee from town, exclaiming to all those with ears to never work for the non-military man.

Attempting to prevent his last remaining personal secretary, Samuel, from skipping out of Redview, as the youth had sworn to his boss that he would if need be, the 'colonel' vowed to handle this current trifle himself, as he could not afford to lose another assistant; the town of Redview lacked a surplus of learned men willing to be treated as an indentured servant at a minimal salary.

'Besides,' Ridge had thought. 'Neither Samuel nor Lyndon possess the mental fortitude or corporeal gall to carry out what needs to be done.'

Stamping out the last ashes of his cigarette into the red dirt with the toes of his boot, Ridge used the bottom of his cane to open the front door of the Needle further ajar tp pass through, and then the gray-haired man entered into the smoke-filled front room, inside the den of ambivalent knaves. A few men sat around a short grubby table playing a game of cards, while a handful of painted ladies mingled with a sporadic crowd of cowboys and ranch hands present near the bar, hoping to earn silver and gold coins.

Not recognizing any man by their appearance, Ridge made his way to the bar, grabbing the bartender's attention by holding up a crisp ten-dollar greenback in a delicate, manicured white hand.

"Hey, fella, suppose I can trouble you to tell me where I can find Jimmy Cotton? If he's not around, perhaps you could even pass the good word along to Mr. Neary, and let him know that 'Colonel' Ridge is here to speak with him? There's more money where that came from."

The 'colonel' handed over the money to Jake the bartender, who was quick to palm the bill and disappear the paper into his upper jacket pocket, nodding his head in an openly sardonic manner.

"He should be back any minute, sir," Jake zeroed his eyes into Ridge, providing a false veneer of friendliness behind unkind orbs. "Why don't you take a seat, '*Colonel*' Ridge, and wait for ol' Jimmy to get on back from all the business he's out attending to? Got any drink you want."

"Any scotch?" Ridge looked over Jake's head to scan the bottles near the back of the bar. "A *decent* brand, that is?"

"Right away, best in the house. You got the bottle, boss," said the barman, as he left the bottle after pouring out a three-fingered glass for his only customer standing at the bar.

Having his first sip from his drink, the 'colonel' was enjoying the burn of the alcohol spreading down his throat, as the scotch *did* calm his nerves somewhat, mellowing the overflow of nicotine in his flighty bloodstream. Finishing the one, Ridge was even more liberal with his second pouring into the glass, but he was careful not to spill a drop of the liquid gold onto the bartop. Relishing the taste of the smoother second scotch, the civilian turned to face the rest of the saloon, investigating the scene through the hazy, dim lights with aged, tired eyes which never failed to ache at any irritation. Ridge found the environment to be odd, as first one man, then another man, and still yet another fellow kept coming through the entrance way of the Needle, until the whole saloon was packed to the rafters with degenerates and drifters, ready for some kind of pent-up explosion to be released; without realizing that he was aware of the thought, he could not see where any of the women had gone off to, almost as if they had vanished into the smoky air.

Looking at an opening near the back of the rowdy crowd numbering around a few dozen uncouth men, Ridge saw Jimmy Cotton emerge from the void to shake hands with a few of the fellows, grinning and hemming and hawing at the appropriate times in the course of their exchanges. A muffled voice standing somewhere between Cotton and Ridge mumbled something that sounded like the word 'lynch', but the 'colonel' failed to hear the rest of what the man had said. Considering what to do next, Ridge bided his time by emptying the contents from his glass, and then poured a third, smaller scotch, and he was still sipping the toasted and thrice-blended drink when Jimmy Cotton stood next to him.

"What in hell do you want?" said Cotton in a cold voice, as he used his right thumb to push the brim of his brown hat upwards and out of his visual field of sight.

Ridge wanted to have another drink, but Cotton grabbed the bottle from out of the civilian's hands, as the much older man was trying to pour a fourth glass with a shaky hand.

"More," said Jimmy Cotton, as he poured himself a four-fingered cup, taking his time in an open challenge against the 'colonel'.

"What?" replied Ridge, uncertain as to the point the young gunslinger was driving at.

"You'll need to pay up more money if you want to be drinking in here." hissed the young man, after he had guzzled all the liquid from his own cup.

"I've already paid up with the barkeep, but if it's a matter of pride for you, sir, I will not drink at this establishment again after today. I was only operating out of sheer desperation to get a hold of either you or Mr. Neary-."

Jimmy Cotton slammed the scotch bottle upon the bartop, and then he proceeded to move within breathing distance of the 'colonel'.

"You need to pay *more*, from here on out, and you need to get it through your thick skull that you only deal with *me* now, ya got that, Ridgey?"

"Well, I just thought that-."

"Nope, I figured you for the type that wouldn't know when to listen; guess I was right, eh, Jackie?" asked Cotton of a man near him, unseen by Ridge.

"Damn right, boy, light him up, Jimmy!" came the gargled response.

"That what I should do, *colonel*?" growled the gunfighter, as he poked Ridge in the chest. "Should I take out my .45 caliber revolver and then lay *you* out for good, eh, boy?"

"Sir, I just wanted to tell you fellows that there's a rumor, from good sources, that federal agents and maybe even Pinkerton detectives could soon become involved in the personal affairs concerning the town of Redview," Ridge aimed for wise advice given to a man unwilling to listen. "The killings and the violence, it needs to stop, Jimmy. This cannot keep going on. It's bad for business and *no one* will make any more money."

"Then I want more cash, right now. And we double your monthly payments again. That makes it around another $500, to leave you paid in full to the Neary syndicate's good graces."

"I don't have that much greenbacks on me right now!"

Wasting no moment to respond, Jimmy Cotton punched Ridge square in the head with a closed fist, rupturing the capillaries along the bridge of his nose. Taking the fighting initiative further, the cowboy grabbed the scotch bottle and then he smashed the half-filled container into the knee of the older man, crippling the 'colonel's' balance, and Ridge fell to the saloon's floor in screaming pain. Cotton started to kick Ridge in his ribs, the tip of his boot landing again and again, to the loud enjoyment of the roaring crowd's approval.

In a whisper, those who first saw him standing on the second floor balcony became silent as the gravedigger's tomb. When friends pointed to the man floating above them, each successive fellow closed his mouth to all utterances. The vaunted man took a step closer to the edge of the balcony's bannister to present a fuller eye's view of his presence, until Jimmy Cotton himself became aware of his boss's sudden appearance from out of the gang leader's personal room at the Needle, where his harem tended to his considerable needs.

"Enough, Jimmy," said Boze Neary in a clear and concise tone, for all men present to hear him. "That will be it for today. Cut Ridge loose."

Hesitant for a mere moment, and with a begrudged glint showing on his visage, Jimmy Cotton released the 'colonel' from his clutches, and then Ridge hobbled along from out of the Needle and through the seething crowd of men, the blood from his face dripping onto the floor in red rivulets of paint, while some of the cowboys spat on his head and backside.

After the beaten man had dragged himself through the Needle's exit, Boze Neary remained in the exact position that he had been standing in on the balcony. Watching Cotton for another second, the gang leader removed the elongated Bowie knife from his side, and then he stabbed downwards into the wooden hand-banister that was emplaced into the second floor up to the knife's hilt, the knife remaining turned upside down after the gray-templed Irishman had succeeded in his thrusting aim.

"And, Jimmy? No more making deals behind my back. Your time will come, young man, but I'm not through pissing and fucking and bossing just yet. Don't cross me again."

Not wanting a response, Boze Neary ventured out from viewpoint, as he walked back into his den, and slammed the door shut behind him. The Bowie knife remained plunged into the banister.

Jimmy Cotton nursed his pride by imbibing long and hard from a new bottle of scotch throughout the rest of the day, and on into the dim night.

Making his painful final steps into his personal office on the other side of Redview, the awaiting Samuel, Ridge's personal secretary, saw to the aid of his employer, as the younger man washed away the crusted and browned blood from the older man's face, and he sought to find fresh linens to put on the wheezing and coughing fellow.

Appreciating the new glass of scotch the most, the 'colonel' soon yelled his frustrations into the direction of his assistant, unafraid of the weakling's response.

"Damnit, Samuel, now what the hell developments have been made towards finding someone to take out the bastard Neary clan? They're out of my control at this juncture in time, and the only consistent theme I can ever get out of them is the demand for more, more, and *more money*!"

"There are a few hired hands that are located right here in Redview, sir, and I have taken the liberty to secretly discuss possible arrangements with each of these men, including minor shootists such as Flores, the so-called 'King of Flowers', and the unreliable Bob Channing, a known boozer, but they all say that a couple more expert gunsmen will be needed to take on such a ruthless and sophisticated outfit as to what Neary has riding behind him."

"*Sophisticated*? Bah, Samuel, damn your hide and eyes to hell!"

"By that, 'Colonel' Ridge, I just mean that Boze Neary and Jimmy Cotton have loose control over approximately twenty to thirty men at any given time, and they have *a lot* of firepower, sir, I'm very sorry to say. We need as many skilled shooters as we can find, according to all the fellows who are in the know of such concerns, if we truly intend to rid this town of Neary and his ilk."

"Then keep looking, you skinny little bastard! Find me some killers! The only way to defeat a merciless man is by utilizing one of your own. Do you understand what I am telling you?"

"Yes, sir, I will keep looking and talking around with any worthy man I can get."

Leaving the bloodied and bruised old man alone to his own drunken devices, the personal secretary closed the office door behind him with delicate care as he left, not wanting to cause a sound that would disturb his employer's drifting focus, as a parent does when shutting a sleeping child's bedroom door.

Chapter 16- The Ranch Hand and the Servant Woman Enjoy a Picnic

The gruff, callused hands of the man carried the white wooden basket up a small, rocky hill. The young, auburn-haired woman followed near behind him, and she made to unpack the meal that she herself had prepared earlier in the morning soon after reaching the top of the red knoll. However, before Emma Rabelais could grab the basket from his hands, Owen Ward insisted on first laying down the blue blanket he had borrowed from a fellow ranch hand who was in possession of a little more pocket money then was available to the former shootist. Emma had bought a loaf of sourdough bread from the bakery on a whim, and she had ordered her son, Tom, to round up and collect all of the fruits and vegetables and cheeses he could find by rummaging around the cupboards inside of the McManus Boarding Home for Christian Women, where the mother and son had been residing the past couple of years. The mother had smiled upon the success of her son's completed mission.

The man and woman glanced into each other's opposite colored eyes, the different shades of brown and blue, and then they sat down to catch their breath, collapsing onto the careworn quilt. Following a moment's time to steady his heart rate, Owen was patient to wait for Emma to take a first bite, but then the remembrance of long past youthful manners returned to the ranch hand, and he held out a small slice of bread after cutting the white loaf into jagged pieces. Emma ate a tiny bite from near his fingertips, and then she grabbed the rest to feed her greedy mouth. Owen adapted her example, but taking a larger piece of the sourdough for himself, as hungry as a lion.

"Have you picnicked on this hill before?" asked Owen, as he held up his hand to block the sun, so his hatless head could continue to enjoy an unobscured view of the woman he was slowly becoming infatuated with, like a schoolboy falling for his first sweetheart, his shoulder-length blonde hair blowing with the hill's breeze.

The ex-gunslinger desired to avoid coming across as a lovesick fool, but the more he saw of her and learned of her mind, the more he could not prevent himself from being victimized by her charming enchantments of his tired, guilty soul, which had long since been wearied by the absence of hope and love for anyone or anything. The mother's wit and determined will assured the man of her raw committal to live a glorious life on her own terms, but he could still perhaps dare to try to win her heart.

The couple's conversation evolved into stories of their childhoods, as the picnic environment had caused both Owen and Emma to relive both the common and unique experiences from damaged youth gone by. Neither of them could quite recall the early years of the Civil War, but the ranch hand and the servant woman could recount family picnics in the backwoods, where fathers and uncles and other gallant men, some missing limbs or toes and fingers, played the instruments and sang the songs about the war between the states, which were constant and unrelenting when they were children. The violin's tone may have changed chords in more recent years to suit current musical tastes, but Owen and Emma could just hear the music from those days now, as they sat alone on the red hill, under the eyes of God.

Lost in old memories, Owen and Emma failed to see the rumbling monsoon clouds move into the nearby mountains near the red hill where they were picnicking; the lightning was restrained, as most summer downpours tended to be, but the waters came fast, and soon after the magnetic burning smell of the stormy sky alerted the man and woman to the rain with large, pregnant droplets pelting their bodies, the heavy liquid which hurt when they struck the pale eyelids and uncovered forearms of Emma Rabelais. Gathering up the picnic items, Owen shouted for Emma to grab his horse and follow him to higher and flatter ground, as the edge of the hill where they were located was surrounded by washes, and the ranch hand could hear the distant roar of moving water coming from multiple directions below them, which until this day had not seen any rainfall since the monsoon season of two summers prior. The flash flood was a horseman's living nightmare in the desert.

"Up this way," yelled Owen, as he carried their belongings further up the redness.

Emma followed at a quick pace with Owen's horse, who needed just the slightest of nudgings from the woman to escape the deluge sound emitted by the instant river that came with the rains flowing downwards into the washes. The rapturous thunder echoed across the great rockfalls of the red mountains, the echoed vibrations a consistent, low dirge, ready to remind any listener of Nature's true intent aimed towards mankind, if they dared to ignore the epic wonders of the world.

"It's okay, Owen," Emma said, as she stood next to him in a small clearing that was enclosed by skinny ponderosa pine trees and juniper bushes, with their green berries ripened to the point of explosion. "The storms around here can be fierce, but they tend to be infrequent and short-lived. This should pass us soon."

They watched the ebbing waters destroy the ruddy dirt side-walls of the overlooked washes, as clumps of soil and rocks and pebbles tumbled into the just birthed muddy river, the brown flowing waters pushing tree branches and debris further down the wash at destructive speeds, and soon passing the man and woman by, much as the days of one's life gone past, never to be seen by mortal eyes again.

Lost in beautiful despair, Owen Ward felt a soft touch needling at his unoccupied, dangling right hand, and he looked over to Emma Rabelais, but her eyes were facing the now thoroughly wetted washes. Looking back at the created tributary for himself, Owen gathered her small hand into his with a gentle grip, the warmth from her palm eliciting a faith for something he had never realized could exist. He wanted to fly with her, above the dark clouds, and into the bluest of heavens.

"And when was the last time you saw a storm this bad?" asked Emma, as she moved her thumb over Owen's own scarred one, rubbing the digit with tender emotion.

"Hmm," mumbled the ranch hand, as he dug into the dented past of his lost youth. "Well, I suppose it was not nearly as bad as it seems in my mind now, but for my money I'd say the storm that set off one night when I was about 14 or 15, that twas a real barn breaker, and it ripped apart my grandmother's grain silo to bits, and after which I refused to help rebuild it, I had to run away from home and I did not have much else to do with my father; the man lived his own hard lifestyle, you see?"

"But why would you run off from your family for these reasons? Didn't anybody else, your mother, miss you or look to see where you went off to?"

"My father blamed me for shoddy work done to protect the grain silo from the winds and rains of the storm. My mother died in childbirth with my younger sister when I was two. After the storm, I was very angry, and my father was deep into his cups when he was alive, always drinking grain alcohol, especially in the end. I told him I would never live in my grandmother's house again, which is where he kept my sister and I until I grew up to be too much of a burden for the old woman to bear."

"Did you never see your father again?"

"A couple of times or so, as I approached the age of 21 and before the old man had been institutionalized. I bumped into him at the saloons, near some of the towns my gang and I liked to stir up trouble in, especially as I developed my own shooting instinct. My father, you know, he was a shootist, too, before the alcohol got to him, but I was no longer afraid of his ability to reach his gun first, and I saw a man much reduced by age and drink. After making my way towards him, my father took much rousting and convincing for him to see that it was I, Owen, and not a debt collector or lawman seeking to jail him. The last thing my father said to me was 'don't lose your soul, son'. My old man was a gunsman like me, but he was meaner and more cruel in his criminal pursuit of life. I've tried to become a better man, ever since I left that drunken fool behind in that dank saloon all alone to die by himself, but I often feel that I have failed. Although I have lost years of my life to hard time and given up strong alcohol, loose women, and too many other un-Christian-like vices than I care to number, at least not in front of a woman with eyes as kind as yours are, Miss Rabelais, but still I do not seem to be redeemed. That's not to say I blame my father, because I know what he had to deal with growing up, surviving his own harsh father. I just never understood the man."

Emma kept her left hand holding onto Owen, while she brought her right hand to touch the cheek of her man, and then she turned to face him, looking into his dark eyes.

"A child does not grow along a straight line; he diverges from the path and develops in ways that you cannot dare to imagine. Perhaps the same is true for you, Owen, because as a boy becomes a man, is that man then forever set in stone? No, he continues to change and takes on a form mixed with all that he has within him."

"Including the bad?"

"Including all that which he is capable of doing."

"I think a man could grow tired of preventing himself from pulling you into his arms; from trying to stop from kissing you, eternally."

"Then stop fighting it, Owen," whispered Emma, as the mother brought her body upon his, and the man's guiding hands helped to temper the writhing weight of the woman against his person.

The rainwaters of the wet wash would long since start to become dry again, and after the monsoon had moved away, leaving behind a clear blue sky, before Owen and Emma rode back into Redview.

Chapter 17- The Agreement Between a Husband and a Wife

Dr. Taig Ward tried to wash his hands free of the dead young woman's blood; her mother stood crying soundless tears, as the old matron cradled the wailing newborn babe in the elbows of her arms, the clear visceral hanging over the boy's face and body before being wiped clean. The doctor continued to stare down at his hands, scrubbing the drying, browned blood and fecal matter away from underneath his fingernails and palms and between the white creases of his knuckles.

"You should bury Ida before too long," said Taig, not without empathy but detecting a powerful stench of death, as he started to rinse his hands off with fresh, boiled white linen.

"I know, sir, but my mind is scattered at this moment," said the old woman and new grandmother. "I am cursed in this blessing, a beautiful boy given to me while the Lord has taken my Ida. I am lost, doctor."

"Well, Norma, let's have some of the other ladies look after the child, and I'll go fetch your husband, to tell him that you will need to rest for a while, dear."

The doctor looked back down at the woman, and he closed her hazel eyes to the living day and night forevermore. He checked to see the time, but was unable to; forgetting like a fool that he had removed his timepiece before the operation, Taig noticed there were no clocks in the room. He suddenly realized he didn't care if he never knew the hour of the day ever again throughout the rest of his existence.

'I have lost patients before,' though Taig. 'Children, babies, and good folks, but why does this one hurt so much?'

Nodding his head to several women standing near the bed where Ida Tollinger's corpse lay motionless, two of the young women gathered on either side of the matriarch, starting to guide her towards the bedroom's door, as still a third youthful female took possession of the baby. Taig stood by the aged Mrs. Smith, but he refrained from placing a hand on her.

"Please do watch over that boy," bellowed the grandmother, and Taig now comforted the woman with a small squeeze upon her shoulder, not wanting her to chase after the newborn child.

"Yes, I will, Mrs. Smith. I promise to be *most* careful." declared the caretaker, hugging the baby tight in clean cloth wrappings.

Not saying goodbye, Taig exited the death room and set off outside of the house in search of Mr. Smith, but the old rancher found Dr. Ward in the front yard first.

"Doc, I got the sheriff over here, say's he lookin' for ya!" hollered Mr. Smith, with the dour Sheriff Daggs huffing up a small hill behind the farmer.

"We need to talk, Ward," puffed the red-faced lawman, tired after exerting himself while walking the increased, rocky elevation to reach the medicine man.

"In a moment," said Taig, ignoring Sheriff Daggs, as he looked at the grandfather. "Mr. Smith, I am terribly sorry to have to inform you of this; I am afraid that Ida has passed from this world, but your grandson is alive and well and screaming for life. You need to see to your wife."

"Oh, dear," the old rancher cried out, his white whiskers dancing across his face. "Where is Norma?"

"Enough of that prattle, now, Smith! I have important business to discuss with the doctor here." sneered the sheriff, as he pushed forward to make his heavy, official weight closer to Taig Ward.

Not wasting a moment, the doctor released his own boiling emotions against the intruder of sorrows.

"You need to remember *your place*, Sheriff," said Taig, with the voice of fire. "This man has just lost his daughter. You *will wait* your goddamn turn."

Seething in his own look back at the doctor, the towering Sheriff Daggs made neither a sound nor a movement towards creating harm upon Taig.

Ignoring the eyes of daggers, Taig looked back into his charge's face, recalling his proper duty to the aggrieved, and the medical advice soon gave him an escape hatch to hide from his feelings of worthlessness, of unending blame for *his failure* to save a young mother's life.

"Now, Mr. Smith, your wife will need to lay down and rest for a few days, as she has experienced quite a shock; she exhausted herself over these past twelve hours, and I fear that she is too old to make a quick recovery without forced rest. You should be there to comfort her, and when she wakes up, give her a sip of this, every six hours. Here. This will help her with the melancholy."

Dr. Ward reached into his satchel bag, rummaged for a few seconds, and then handed over a small brown bottle containing the cheap laudanum to Mr. Smith, as the tincture of opium that Taig had had supplied to his office was of low quality, but he figured a small relief for the matron might have a large, beneficial effect for the grieving grandmother, 'at least while she can still dream of her daughter', thought Taig. 'If dreams ever return again for her.'

"Yes, I will do this, doc," said Mr. Smith, before he shook Taig's hand and ran into his ranch home, calling after his wife.

Taig felt like running away home and holding his family close to his bosom, but combatant reality intruded upon his misery.

"Okay, Taig, now let's chat. That is, if you're done mouthing off to me, boy." said Sheriff Daggs, as he gripped the handle of the hanging and holstered gun upon his left hip, shifting his body's position to appear even bigger than he already was.

"Just get to your point, Daggs, if you have one. Ida Tollinger was in labor for many hours, and now I just desire to go home to be with my wife and children."

"Well, bonesaw, you *do* get mighty mouthy and then some, but I'm here on urgent business for Mr. Ridge."

"Playing delivery boy again?"

Sheriff Daggs spit out the entire brown wad of juicy chewing tobacco he had been sucking on, clenching his teeth in a harsh grinding noise and then he unclipped his gun holster.

"I ain't no delivery boy, bones, you understand me?"

"And I'm an unarmed doctor, lest *you* forget that. Now, get to it!" hissed Taig Ward.

"Ridge wanted me to try to talk some sense into you, see if you wouldn't change your mind about his offer. He said he'd be willing to consider giving you a higher amount of money than he'd previously offered to you, if you would only just listen to what he has to say."

"The answer remains the same; not that Ridge will accept that. Now with that, Daggs, I'll be on my way back home. I grow tired of your face."

"What did you really know when you received that first offer? You won't even consider taking a good deal from the rich old bastard, even when he's offering you decent cash to just vacate your little plot of land? Well, I ask you this, then, what would you know?"

"I understand what my own business is, sir. What I *don't know* is why hasn't Neary and his band of thugs been arrested and brought to trial for the murders of Theodore Channing and Frank Jones? Perhaps *you* might be able to shed more light upon this question for me, no?"

"You watch yourself now, Ward, or you'll end up needing to stitch your own person up, lest your innards fall out from your bowels. And as far as Channing and Jones goes, there are no bodies! A matter of fact, and just this morning, a couple of young ranch hand fellows have attested to seeing them boys out drinking the other night or so ago, along the saloons of 5th Street."

"Either that's a lie you just told or those men who sold you that nonsense are liars, but it makes no difference to me. I'm going home." said the doctor, as he jaunted past the corrupt lawman.

"You may live just long enough to regret that, Ward."

"Never forget why you don't have a deputy, Daggs," said Taig over his shoulder, as he got on top of his old gray mare. "Nobody would be that suicidal as to sacrifice his life away walking by the side of such a dirty scoundrel as you."

Sheriff Daggs looked akin to the demon confronted by the all-seeing light, watching as Taig rode away from the Smith property with black eyes. The red dust that Dr. Ward's horse launched into the air melded together with the mists of the law man's mind, the rage gathering as the calm before the self-righteous judgment of fury.

Taig Ward arrived at his ranch home in a state of walking sleep, and he required both of his male servants to assist him in getting down from his mare.

"Send Loretta to get new shirts and pants for Dr. Ward," said the older houseman, Gunther, a German immigrant "And quick!"

"No, sir, just take away these bloody undershirts," said Taig in a daze. "I wish to speak with my wife at once. Where is she?"

"In the garden, sir, reading the newspaper." Gunther replied.

The roses were yet still in bloom, the whites, yellows, and reds casting vibrant welcomes to all viewers even in the fading dusk of light, but the green remained ever at the ready to combat any reaching creature, the thorns piercing all those too greedy to not simply enjoy the mere sight of passing beauty, as opposed to wanting to possess their fading, youthful grace into haughty human hands.

The doctor's wife and four children sat together on beige rattan chairs, the mother reading to the boys, while the girls read their own books. Not wanting to interrupt their tranquility, Taig started to walk back into the house, and away from the fleeting peace of the garden, but then his youngest child, Elmira, spotted his retreat while looking up from her reading.

"Father!" the child exclaimed in a cheery tone, forgetting all about her book.

After this utterance, every one of his children stood up from their chairs to greet him, and his wife smiled at his visage, before she recognized the distraught look her husband wore.

"Children, let your poor old dad rest, as he's been working all day long. Go inside to your rooms, now!" commanded Nelcy Ward, as she started to have the nearby servant woman direct her children to go inside of their home. "Sara, please have Michael and Stephen start their baths before supper, and girls, please change into proper dining attire for tonight."

"Yes, mother." responded the downtrodden but disciplined children, as they left their parents outside in the rose garden alone to themselves, not daring to linger on the private words of the adult's conversation.

Not knowing where he should begin, Taig accepted Nelcy's open, outstretched arms, and he let his wife hug deep into him with a close embrace, as he looked around at the different colored petals of the roses.

"Was it so awful for poor Ida Tollinger in the end?" Nelcy asked after a moment, while she listened to her husband's quickening heartbeat.

For a time, Taig did not answer, as if his silence could somehow prevent the young woman's death from becoming confirmed truth. If there is no confession, can there be any absolution?

"She lost a lot of blood, Nell, and there was no way to save her," stuttered Taig, through hushed tones and harsh tears. "I sewed her up as best as I was able to, and it was all that I could do just to keep the babe alive."

"I know, darling." Nelcy said through her own tears.

Looking into his wife's eyes, Taig found himself to be more hesitant than he'd been on the ride back home, thinking over selfish future problems, but he started to tell her.

"Sheriff Daggs ran into me, right after I delivered the child. He's a rotten man."

"What did he say to you?" Nelcy asked, wiping away both streams of their tears.

"Oh, the usual nonsense concerning Ridge and why can't we just pick up and leave our land, but you know what? This time he made a true threat. He made no specific remark, but Daggs may not be bluffing this time."

"Do you know what it is that you need to do?"

"I haven't a clue, Nell. I've gone to the law, written pleading letters; I've sought sanctuary through all legal avenues, and even my old friend Judge Graves cares not enough to assist me, as long as he receives excess funding to build his precious new courthouse."

"This is Redview, Taig, and like I've told you since the day you proposed to me and you told me that you wanted to live and raise a family in this town, forever and ever, with the girl of your dreams. But in this town, if not in life itself, you cannot stand for something while living your days kneeling down, husband. Always remember that."

The eyes of his wife penetrated through his anger at Sheriff Daggs and the civilian 'colonel', and her sentiment salved the sting in his belly.

"What would you have me do, wife?"

"We need more guns. I know you have your old hunting rifles and revolver, but maybe we also need to arm the servants and hire a few more ranch hands to live on the property," pausing for effect, Nelcy then made her most important proposal. "I think we should also reach out to Owen for help."

"Owen!" shouted Taig, not wanting anything to do with his cousin. "That man is also a rotten bastard, like all the rest of the Wards I choose not to remember. That old bank robber isn't fit to help himself, let alone our family. Besides, I just don't trust the man."

"But people seem to think that he has changed. There's talk around town about how he saved the life of Tom Rabelais, and that he has an honest job ranching, and according to Miss Rabelais, he appears to have gone straight."

"His kind *never can* go straight, Nelcy! Fine, we can get pistols for newly hired men, but we *will not* be seeking help from that bloody charlatan, Owen Ward."

"Then are you prepared to stand up for what is *ours*? The soils of this land have known much spilled blood. Can we dare try to stay living here?"

"I suppose I no longer have a choice."

"But you always have a choice, Taig. We just need to be ready to choose the most difficult choice, to remain alert to what the wicked world throws at us."

"Like we always have, Nell," said Taig, leaning in to kiss his wife.

"Like we always will." said Nelcy, before she kissed her husband back hard.

Chapter 18- A Birthday for Tom Sawyer

Emma Rabelais, Tom 'Sawyer' Rabelais, Owen Ward, and the boys known only to the adults as 'El Cid' and 'Stonewall' sat down on ragged blankets set upon the ground by the mother, and the small birthday party began in earnest in the front yard of the McManus Boarding Home for Christian Women.

"Tom, honey," began Emma Rabelais, before she was interrupted.

"'Sawyer', mama!" demanded Tom, annoyed by the snickering of his friends.

"Right," said the mother, as she herself was just able to contain a hidden chuckle. "'*Sawyer*', we all wanted to wish you a special tenth birthday, baby. I brought you your favorite, blueberry pie. And Dr. and Mrs. Ward were kind enough to buy you this book, written by one Mr. Mark Twain, whom I'm sure you'll be excited to read about, Tom, eh, I mean 'Sawyer'."

Emma smiled as her boy grabbed the book from her hands.

Tom exhaled his excitement and promised his mother that he indeed would make sure to thank the Wards for their gift. He flipped through the first several pages, growing rapt in his absorption into the written, fictional world, soon taking no further notice of his birthday party. When finished after several minutes, Tom closed the hardcover, and the five of them shared in consuming the blueberry pie, and the boys were quick in becoming antsy, as they basted in underutilized energy.

"If it's alright with you, Emma, I did bring along a surprise present for 'Sawyer'," said Owen, who watched as the ten year old boy's eyes lighted to the color of full pale moons.

The ranch hand dug his palm into a saddlebag on the side of his horse, which was tied to a nearby hitching post, and then he hid the surprise gift behind his back, as he re-approached the birthday boy, jaunting over in casual slowness.

"You fellas often ask me about shootin' when we're working on Mr. Ridge's property, jawwing my ear off and such," began Owen, who absorbed a wry look from a startled Emma, before glancing back to the excited Tom. "And no, 'Sawyer', I *did not* get you a gun, so no getting too crazy now, okay? But any good shootist worth his salt has always started out practicing with one of these bad boys, when he was a younger person."

The man revealed the hand from behind his back, and then he tossed over a crude sling-shot, made of polished oak. The elastic material that was designed to be pulled-back to launch a projectile consisted of black India rubber, and the solid handle had the small-print letterings of 'Property of Tom Sawyer' carved in straight lines onto its surface.

Shouting out a squealing 'thank you', Tom was just as excited and surprised to watch Owen pull out a small cloth bag filled with steel-ball bearings, smooth and solid circles the size of marbles.

"The trick is, son, to practice on quail, jackrabbits, and tiny sparrows. Forget motionless targets; if you can shoot an animal, you can shoot a man," Owen laughed and winked at Tom, while Emma gave her paramour a half closed-lidded look, and her eyebrows arched into a triangle of slight disapproval.

"But before you boys go off shootin', I need to show you all how to use it," Owen said, before looking at Tom's young friends. "This goes for you, too, 'El Cid' and 'Stonewall', as I know you fellas are gonna want to borrow the pea-shooter any chance you get. So let's go."

Emma Rabelais sat and watched as the ex-gunslinger stacked cairns, small flat rocks, on top of the boarding house's deteriorating back yard fence, and the three boys' enthusiasm grew unsustainable as Tom practiced cocking back the elastic India rubber without a steel-ball loaded into the leather holding pad, and his two companions started to shout out unheeded advice on how to handle his weapon, much to 'Sawyer's' chagrin.

"Okay, Sawyer, now before we load it, I want you to pick a spot on the rocks to target and then aim for; concentrate on your *breathing*. Even a focused bad shot is better than a rushed good one. Practice with a small pebble first."

The four of them continued to take turns at targeting the cairns, and the boys enjoyed taunting one another's failures, while admiring the precision of Owen's targeting ability.

"You *can* shoot, Owen!" they all repeated to the ranch hand, while the watching woman laughed in silence.

While continuing to observe the slingshot shooting gallery out of grave motherly courtesy, Emma thought of her father, a man she had neither seen nor heard from since she was five years old, when he was still married to her mother. The much older Frenchman had brought over a teenage girl from the Motherland town of Rouen, and Emma and her siblings knew of very little personal warmth or bracing touches given by the hands of their father, a man who was in constant debt and at frequent odds with the authorities, so he was soon to be out of Emma's life, but not before leaving her with a final memory of his existence; she didn't know why she had lied to Owen about her father being dead, but to her, he had died, so long ago.

The mother did not believe the memory of a bright, sunny morning to be her own birthday, but instead a day her father had decided out of random necessity to reward his youngest daughter with the sole present he ever gave to her. The sewn doll had blue eyes and hay-colored hair, an ugly thing in the judging sights of the world, but Emma loved the rag-doll as soon as her eyes saw her father bring his own hands from behind his back to reveal the gift, much as Owen had done for Tom.

'It's a dolly, *mon cherie*,' said her father, as he spoke to the five-year-old girl in her mind.

Emma could not recall if she had thanked the old man for her present or not, but for years she would refuse to go to sleep without her doll 'baby' crooked in her arms. Somewhere in between the many moves across various towns and cities along the northeastern seaboard of the United States with her mother and siblings, Emma had lost the blonde rag doll, and the repaired torn stitchings that the girl had learned from her mother how to fix and spent many hours over the years to mend were all for naught, and her ten year old self's heart never quite recovered from the loss, until the day her flesh and blood discovered the lost piece of her love, Tom, and the hole in her heart was rejuvenated by an unending fountain of devotion to her son. But the rag-doll remained lost in time and its remembrance.

Wondering at what she wanted her son to have in this life, and hoping to will into existence the kind of man he may become, Emma could see into a future where the boy was successful enough in his endeavors to wed a good woman and have children of his own to spoil, and the mother could just make out the older face of the gray-haired man standing by her side, as he smiled at her as the father both she and Tom had never been fortunate enough to have known, until the arrival of Owen Ward into Redview.

'I want my son to know love, kindness, and strength. Tom deserves to have both a mother and a father in his life,' Emma prayed to the Lord above the clouds.

Not willing to let the changed man fail to see how happy their lives could be together, the ranch hand was watched by the servant woman's hungry eyes, and she was determined to confess to him how she felt. Emma's desire could not be held back and neither did she want it to.

Taking a break from teaching the rowdy boys, Owen Ward approached Emma in tired laughter, as he looked back over his shoulder to ensure that 'Stonewall', who was next up in the shooting order, was still holding the slingshot's handle in the correct fashion. The ranch hand was stirred to the bottom of his soul by the grin she shot at him.

"Where have you got to in your mind, my red-haired siren of the desert?" asked Owen, while he sat down beside her.

The boys were too distracted by their shooting to notice them any further.

"I was only dreaming, mister," said the woman, the sun's light sparkling into existence, a facial curiosity, a most vivacious look in the irises of her eyes.

What words do you choose to speak to a man whom you're in love with before you are sure that he loves you back in return? The question busked around inside the recesses of her mind, but self-doubt gnawed both at the answers she wanted to hear, and those that she could never apprehend.

'If not now, then when?' the mother said to herself, at last.

"Yeah? What were you dreaming of, Miss Rabelais?"

"The past makes no difference to us, right, Owen? I mean, we've both lived lives that are now long behind us, so why would we dwell on old days when bright, future ones lay right in front of us?"

"I'd like to believe that a person's history doesn't matter all that much, but I don't know as to the truthfulness of that declaration, Emma. However, I do agree that tomorrow is an idea any person can stake their hopes onto and build something out of their life towards," Owen hesitated, for just a second, before he leapt from the full heights of passion. "Look, I don't know how else to say this, but no matter what happens tomorrow, I just need you to know that I love you."

Emma was in near-shock and close to tears, but the reciprocation of her feelings stated by the reformed man revived her back into the blessed moment, whatever the future may dictate to mortals.

"You bastard, I was just about to profess my own love for you," the woman said, grabbing his face with both of her soft hands. "But besides stealing my heart, you just had to go and take the initiative, too, *hmm*, Mr. Ward?"

"Yes, ma'am," Owen cooed, as he began to kiss Emma, and the hummingbirds soared above their heads in spurts of glory, lost in their search for succulent honeysuckles, if only for a mere drop of fleeting sweetness.

Chapter 19- The Judgment of Judge Graves

The emptied old courthouse in the town of Redview sat in a silence known only to Pharaoh's tomb, or perhaps another dead rich man's mausoleum, except for the ghastly presence of two aged men, with both parties having achieved a certain amount of respect in the arena of polite society presiding over their collective community within the 'Scarlet Rose'. Neither man desired to be seen in the presence of the other, so the dark Sunday night during the off-construction work hours at the courthouse allowed for Judge Eugene Graves and 'Colonel' William Ridge to avoid any unwanted attention from a distrusting and gossiping general public. The building was made of fading wood, whilst the 'new' courthouse was cut from marble and sandstone, the better to avoid the malignant threat of Arizona wildfires.

Besides the usual discreteness that such matters demanded, the judge came prepared to force a separate legal issue, making an argument meant to be precise and clear for the non-military man to comprehend. Reviewing the gathered legal documents and court injunctions for the third time that evening, and for which he had belabored upon through caffeine-afflicted days and restless nights throughout the past week, Judge Graves handed over to Ridge a single piece of paper for the semi-legitimate businessman to peruse.

"What is this?" Ridge expressed a disdainful puzzlement in his voice.

"A very brief summary of all of *this*," Judge Graves said while he patted a large stack of papers on the table in front of him, the green-glass lamp between the two of them providing the sole luminescence within the building. "You can have any lawyer you want read through my decisions, but the gist of it is this, Mr. Ridge: The offers you have made to Dr. Ward are subpar, sir, and much below the property's prospective market value; that is, if the given real estate market is considered to be *open* and *fair*, you see. And look, I will be further forthright with you, the pulling on the strings of your demented Neary puppets needs to end. I'm sure you've heard the rumbling rumors concerning Federal troopers arriving in the Arizona territories at some point in the near future, no?"

"Is it true?" asked Ridge, in a frantic display of visible fear, forgetting the matter of money, for the moment.

"I have my reasons to suspect that the headwinds may indeed be true, but we *are* discussing the Federal government here, so who the hell really knows if and when they may arrive? Either way, Mr. Ridge, the town of Redview can no longer afford to give home and food and whore to the den of Neary and his small army of cowboys. Now, what do you intend to do about this?"

"As if *I'm* the puppet master in control of Boss Boze and Jimmy Cotton? These animals do not listen to me," the faux 'colonel' looked like a spoiled child not getting his way. "Why don't *you* sick the law onto these savages, eh?"

"Sheriff Daggs works for *you*, dammit, now stop the bullshit!" raged Judge Graves, as the force of his pounding fists hitting the table caused the green lamp to quake in loud vibrations.

Looking away from the judge, the 'colonel' waited a time before he dared to build enough courage to respond back to the accurate accusation.

"And what, then, is to become of your new courthouse? Excuse me, I mean *Redview's* new courthouse?" Ridge leaned back into his wooden chair, smiling and ruminating on the judge's reluctance to answer his own question.

"I'm afraid you have only just served to confirm a sneaking suspicion of mine, and this will backfire on you, as this has also furthered my resolve to completely prosecute any crimes connected to murder throughout this county to the fullest extent allowed to me by territory law. And let us keep it clear, sir, that you have one final week to offer Taig Ward a higher property valuation, a price considerably more fair for the man's land, or you will forfeit all attempts on Lot #492 for the duration of no shorter than sixty months time, after which its conclusion you may make another offer for the land to Dr. Ward, or to whomever may be in possession of the property at that point in time. Are there any questions?'

"I will remove all of the funding that I've delegated to put into the new courthouse, leaving you in this half-deconstructed one." Ridge said, his eyes the size of beads.

"Fine, Ridge, then we may let the new, vacant courthouse to sit empty, as the unfinished monument that you were kind enough to donate to this town, a tomb which represents the content of your empty character, if not of the actual conduct that is written by the cruel whispers of your untempered soul. I find you to be rich in land and gold, but I judge you poor in consciousness, and I refuse to play the fool to your grand show any longer. Dr. Ward is an honorable man; I wish I could say the same about you. Good evening, then, sir."

The judge pushed back from the table, standing in a hunch due to the soreness that echoed and ached throughout the muscles of his back after days upon days of writing.

"You're not leaving me with any options here, Graves! Why can't you propose a fairer counteroffer to Ward for me? I'll even give you a 2% commission for your trouble."

"Money is not the priority here, Bill, but honor. Again, goodnight to you."

Judge Graves made his way to the exit, passing by Samuel, Ridge's personal secretary, who'd been hidden in the dark, listening in on his employer's conversation. The judge paid him no heed, as he entered into the night, guiltless in conscience for the first time in many months.

'I can only pray that it is not too late to assist my dear friend,' thought the judge.

Gauging the mood of his boss from a distance for a moment, Samuel was then quick to accept from the 'colonel' all of the paperwork left behind by Judge Graves. As he stood at attention, the assistant awaited further instruction.

"Everything is going to hell, Samuel! I've got to write a letter to that idiot Daggs, and I need you to deliver this most delicate of requests to him immediately. I don't want there to be anymore killings or death, but perhaps just a little bit of greased pressure will persuade Ward to be bought off. I *want* that bastard's land, and I will get it! But first, is there any bloody good news for me?"

Hearing his cue, Samuel stood more erect, and nodded several times in quick succession before he replied.

"Yes, sir, I will certainly deliver any message you ask me to, and with great promptness, but I shall have you know that I have made contact with the half-breed gunslinger and noted killer, the 'Apache Kid', and the man seems open to negotiations."

"Hmm. Hold off on that for now. Neary and his fellows are trained specialists in terroristic tactics, as you know, young man. We may need them alive, at least for the moment, until after the doctor has been dealt with in no uncertain terms."

"As you wish, 'Colonel' Ridge. I will also refrain from alerting Flores, Bob Channing, and the rest of our designated gunfighters against Boze Neary until after the Ward kerfuffle is properly handled."

"Excellent, Samuel, now let me draft this letter to the sheriff. Damn the bloody bastard if he does not stress the utmost importance to Neary that no major harm should occur, and *no killing* needs to be involved to get the message across to the doctor."

Writing in urgent strokes, Ridge chose his words carefully, while his secretary read the wording over his shoulder, causing Samuel to scrunch downwards, in order to make the short sentences clear in the restrained lighting provided by the small green lamp.

"There we are, my boy. Please express to Sheriff Daggs that *no one* is to be maliciously harmed. I just want Ward to come around to our way of thinking, maybe have him remember that Redview is within *my* purview."

"I will see to it, sir." said Samuel, as he ran outside of the courthouse to find his horse, so that he could ride to the jailhouse to speak to the sheriff, before the lawman set off to satisfy his own vices amongst the petals of the 'Scarlet Rose'.

Chapter 20- Desperate Men, with the Smell of Wolf Upon Them...

Taig Ward had been scheduled to conduct two surgeries on a particular morning in the late summer heat. The doctor would be gone for most of the day, and word had a tendency to circulate the saloons and gambling halls of Redview, the same as anywhere else. The father of four scrambled out from the comfort of his bed before the sun's first scintillating rays of light invaded through the curtain-less master bedroom windows, but he did not leave until he had kissed his sleeping wife, Nelcy, on her forehead. The woman's eyes remained shut, but she wore a small smile upon her face as he exited the bedroom.

Not wanting to wake his children, Taig spoke in hushed tones with his head manservant, the aged Gunther, about the vagaries of the planned events for the day, and then he proceeded onwards towards his destinations, his doctor's bag and sharpened scalpels and jagged-tooth hacksaw at the ready, although his supply of diluted morphine was close to depletion; his hated pistol hung low in the holster across his upper thigh. As red luck would have it, new firearms ordered by the Ward family would not arrive until the end of the month.

Jimmy Cotton and five members of the Neary Gang waited a full half-hour after watching Taig ride out into the far distance of the red lands, ensuring that he disappeared over the boiling orange horizon. Riled to bloodthirst, the wolves roved the Ward ranch house property, seeking and then finding three unarmed ranch hands, who were dispatched with by being knocked unconscious by metal pipes, gagged, tied, and bound by rope, so as not to alert the other sheep present inside of the silent sanctuary.

Jimmy Cotton glanced through a back window and followed the movements of the younger manservant of the Ward family, as he approached the back door of the house. The youth was lost in focus on his chores for the day as he exited through the door, and he did not hear the swooshing sound of the pistol that cracked the back of his skull, leaving the man useless to the world. While he lived, the young manservant would for the rest of his natural life experience blinding headaches whenever his eyes were exposed to bright light for prolonged periods of time. Two of Cotton's henchmen laughed as they pilfered through the comatose man's pockets, not bothering to tie-up his hands, as the blood poured forth from out of his ears. Cotton had passed on the word to his skeleton crew concerning Ridge's warning to not murder anyone, as blue soldiers had been spotted heading points just due west of Albuquerque in the past week, but other than that, the future kingpin and heir to Boze Neary's criminal syndicate had explained to his pack how they needed to visit a wrathful reminder to the good citizens of Redview concerning who was in true control of the county, regardless of what the Federal troopers, Judge Graves, or the corrupt Sheriff Daggs might attempt to proclaim in their safe, far removes from the violence. Dr. Taig Ward had either forgotten or never learned the lesson that a wolf will track his prey for miles around him, once he has obtained a scent of weakness, and the taste of blood must always be sated.

The wolves in men's clothing drew closer to the windows, and then they enjoyed the waiting calm, salivating at the freshness of new flesh to bite into. Watching through the opened back windows, the cowboys saw two housemaids, Sara and Tabitha, working throughout the kitchen, trying to prepare breakfast while being bothered by the fresh-eyed Elmira, who sought to help to prepare the day's meals, but instead she made herself more of a distraction to the servants than a source of aid.

The head wolf noted only a single man remaining on the premises, the 61-year-old Gunther, a Bavarian immigrant and Dr. Ward's longest tenured manservant. The old German instructed Elmira, in accented English, to vacate the kitchen, and he enlisted the servant girl, Tabitha, to assist him in his herculean task of convincing the child of the wisdom of his command to find another task to engage herself in.

After Gunther, Tabitha, and Elmira continued their engaging conversation outside of the kitchen and into the dining room, that left just the diminutive housemaid, Sara, all alone on her own to continue cooking over the open flames of the stove. Cotton motioned to three of his fellows to go around to the front entrance of the home, while the co-leader of the Neary Gang and two others would burst through the back door, next to the kitchen.

"Wait for my signal to kick in through the front," whispered a grinning Jimmy Cotton.

"And what signal will that be?" asked the tall man, a sharp-toothed rapist feared even amongst the other beasts in the wolfpack.

"The cry of the servant bitch. You boys leave the Ward womenfolk alone. I'll deal with them."

The three men forming a separate grouping disappeared around the corner, gaining their way towards the front of the house.

Waiting thirty seconds to provide his cronies enough time to get to the other entryway, Jimmy Cotton took a deep breath and then he kicked in the back door, waiting for the other two men to enter before he did, lest the servant girl had access to a hidden firearm, but all the young girl could do was yell out in impotent fear, unsure what else to do.

"Mrs. Ward, there are intruders inside of the kitchen!" the servant girl screamed.

The words were her last before the cowboys punched her in the face multiple times and covered up her mouth with heavy, hairy hands. Cotton looked down at his two underlings, as they rolled around on the floor with the struggling housemaid, not yet inflicting further physical pain upon the girl, but Sara's eyes were terrorized by the sight of their blood-covered, callused hands, as they grasped and pinched and reached all over her body.

The two wolves looked to Cotton for his desired direction.

"Aren't you boys gonna taste what this young lady cooked up for you fellars, or not?"

The men turned their visage away from Cotton, and the allowed screams from Sara did indeed project out towards the home's front door, where the wooden frame was soon broken apart by the other Neary men, who were then able to quickly capture the confused Tabitha, before she could escape into the Wards' master bedroom, where Gunther had managed to forcefully throw Elmira and then push the sleepy Rachel towards their mother, and while Neley

Ward hugged at her daughters in shock, the German slammed the bedroom door shut behind him and then locked the entryway, leaving the poor Tabitha to her doom.

'Gott sei Dank, at least the young boys are far away fishing with their friends for the next three days,' was all Gunther could think to himself at that moment.

While the tall serial rapist banged at the master bedroom's door and bellowed out dire threats, the wolf was quick to remember his already captured prize, as he heard Tabitha's screaming. Dragging her closer to Taig and Nelcy's room, the man wanted the others to hear what was their future fate.

"Out of my way, you chicken-livered bastards," exhaled the tall man to his two weaker companions. "I'm first. Now, hold her there, and hold her down!"

Inside the locked bedroom, Nelcy attempted to console her daughters' crying, as she coldly observed Gunther pressing his full weight against the entryway. Centering his bifocals, the Bavarian spoke to the head mistress of the house in a hallowed voice, as if he were the officiant at a funeral mass.

"Madam, I believe you have a gun, don't you? A family heirloom from your papa?" the elder gentleman looked desperate, as he waited for Nelcy to answer him, his glazed eyes racing around the room for any reachable protection.

Nelcy looked out of the small, closed window in the bedroom; while too small even for a child to slip through, a gun could pass through the opening and be fired with relative ease.

"Yes, Gunther, I do," said Nelcy, as she unlocked a large treasure chest made of iron at the foot of her bed.

After placing five bullets into the revolver's empty chamber, the lady of the house explained her plan to the frightened manservant.

"No, Mrs. Ward, we may need every bullet against these thugs!" shouted Gunther.

"But a few shots fired out of the window will be a good call for help to our neighbors. Someone may hear and come to our aid." retorted the lady of the house.

"Never, madam! These Neary dire wolves are vicious beasts, as I'm sure that you've heard the rumors-."

"We have no other choice," Nelcy interrupted the older man. "This is my home and these are my daughters. I'm going to fire three consecutive, spaced-out shots, in the direction of Ridge's property. Ridge may be a louse, but his men are sure to hear us."

Gunther shouted in unintelligible German but he did not try to prevent his employer from opening the window, yelling 'help' once, and firing off her father's gun three times, before yelling one final time for assistance.

The solitary sound Nelcy heard back in response to her anguished pleas was the laconic sound of Jimmy Cotton's mocking voice.

"Oh, Mrs. Ward, I've been waiting all week for you, saving myself from those wicked girls on Massie Lane for *right now*," cooed Cotton, as the other unoccupied gang member standing next to him by the doorway laughed like a hyena. "Servant wenches, paid whores, loose women, you name it, and I've been avoiding them. Now, all that is stopping me is this small door, isn't that right, darling? Do me a favor and just open up for me. If you do things my way, I'll see to it that your daughters won't have to watch while I give you what's coming."

Nelcy Ward cocked back her gun, knowing she had two bullets remaining. Whispering soothing sounds to her girls, the mother was distracted when Gunther stole the revolver from her soft grip.

"I am sorry, Mrs. Ward, but horrible actions may need to take place, and your husband would never forgive me if anything happened to the three of you." said the German.

Before Nelcy could speak, a Neary cowboy penetrated through the master bedroom's doorway, and Jimmy Cotton had his dead-eye focused upon the armed Gunther.

"Hey, now, daddy, slow down!" said Cotton, as he assessed the situation in the master bedroom.

"What you do to the servant girls is one thing, but you will not be allowed to harm the Wards in my presence!" shouted the old man.

The manservant aimed at Cotton's chest, but the shot went left and wide, missing the gunslinger and hitting the far side of the wall. Side-stepping into the bedroom, Cotton fired a shot of his own near Gunther, to entice the man to drop his gun. Out of fear for his life, the gun shook out of the German's jittery hand.

"Grab the gun, you fool!" yelled Cotton to the lone henchman available for him to direct.

The scrawny, unkempt wolf grabbed the firearm and checked the chamber.

"Only one bullet left, Jimmy, goddamn!" laughed the outlaw.

"He ain't much of a shot, is he, boy?" asked Cotton out loud, although the comment was directed towards no one in particular.

"Let me have my gun back, and all I'll need is that last bullet. I know how to put down a rabid dog." said Nelcy Ward, whose daughters still clung to her hips and nightdress.

Cotton cast his granite countenance at the Ward matron. The ice encased within his stare caused Nelcy to gasp outwards in fear, but her fury had not yet abandoned her.

"Well, Hans," said Cotton, as he turned to look directly at Gunther. "You can't shoot for shit, but let's see if you can box, eh?

Before the Bavarian could brace himself for crushing impact, Cotton had punched Gunther across his left eye, breaking his bifocals and causing the orb's blood vessels to burst open, and the eye was quick to be sealed closed by a puffy, purple eyelid. In brazen confidence, Cotton then slapped the older, defenseless man around with his open palms, causing Rachel and Elmira Ward to shout in terror each time the strikes forced the blood to drip down their 'uncle' Gunther's face; the girls could also hear the guttural screams in pain from both Sara and Tabitha, with brief sightings of Tabitha's exposed breasts through the damaged doorway, into the adjoining room where a man lay on top of her, which caused the prepubescents to become even more scared for the fate of the rest of their family.

Jimmy Cotton's excitement grew with each roaring, crescendoed cheer from his skinny fellow outlaw, who delighted in Cotton's practiced destruction of the old man.

Upon growing bored with the crumbling German in a prone position at his feet, Jimmy Cotton left Gunther bloodied and injured, as the man struggled out through nostrils and lungs clogged with dark red mucus.

"Alright, enough of that, boy," grinned Cotton, as he walked closer to Nelcy and her girls.

"Get behind me, Rachel and Elle," said Nelcy, eyeing the two intruders while hovering her arms behind her backside in a semi-circle of protection against pure evil.

"Mmm, I know *I will*," snarled Cotton through clenched, clattering teeth, as the sound unnerved the mother more than she would have thought possible.

"I'll murder you where you stand, you bastard!" screamed Nelcy, as she edged her daughters further backward, until they were touching a corner of the master bedroom's walls.

Jimmy Cotton kept approaching the Wards, chattering his teeth together in loud, quick succession, as a coatless man stuck outside in a winter storm would in response to the cold weather's serious deprivations. The noise was endless, and grew louder with each passing step the gunslinger took.

Disheartened, Nelcy watched his dark eyes, which showed no signs of repentance for the ill deeds of his past, and no hint of contemplation on changing his path of vengeance against the world for simply being denied the throat of his prey; the redness in the gray prince of wolves overwhelmed the mother.

"I don't stick the help, woman, but I do fuck royalty. Not that either one of us is liable to enjoy it much, ol' Nelcy gal, as I do like 'em a little *younger* than you," chattered Cotton, as he looked from Nelcy to Rachel, closing the ground between them. "Perhaps not *that* young, but I am willing to-."

A few feet short of Nelcy and the girls, Jimmy Cotton felt the faint grasp of a hand grabbing onto his left ankle. Peering down to investigate the source, the wolf noticed the aged German bleeding onto his boot, while Gunther breathed out in harsh, gasping sounds.

"Gunther, no!" yelled Nelcy.

Cotton lifted up and then brought down his left boot onto the hand of Gunther, breaking the man's thumb and forefinger, and inducing the beginning stages of a heart attack in the old immigrant, as he clutched at his chest and emitted erratic, wet noises which sounded like calls for help.

"Enough crying, bitch," said Cotton, while he began to unbuckle his belt and unzip his pants.

The final moment was interrupted by the distant sounds of gunfire, which was soon followed on the heels of the tall man running into the master bedroom to alert Cotton of the enclosing danger.

"There must be twenty or thirty of them damn fellars out there, boss," said the tall serial rapist, as he struggled to keep his unbuttoned pants up, having lost his belt during the attack on Tabitha.

"Federal or local?" asked Cotton, while still continuing to stare at his intended victims, not wanting to throw his caught fish back into the saving waters.

"Just some yahoos, probably some dumb boys from over there on the damn Ridge place, the old cuss! Can't even be trusted to keep his own peasant ranch hands at bay while we do the deed."

"Shut up! Go tell the others to get riding at the double, but be ready to start blazing if necessary," began Cotton, as he daggered Nelcy Ward with the vented hatred of his eyes. "This isn't over, woman. The fear only makes me want you more. Take care, for now, precious."

At that, the Neary Gang became gray ghosts in the mist, gone as quickly as they had appeared.

In the moments right after the fleeing of the wolves, the feet of many men sounded throughout the ranch house, and the Ward women ran to find their saviors.

"Taig! Nelcy! Are you there?" shouted Owen Ward, who held a wooden club between his fingers, ready to swing at the drop of a hat.

Rushing down the hallway and holding both of her daughters in either hand, Nelcy almost did not recognize her husband's cousin at first, thinking that he might have been Jimmy Cotton, returned to finish the devil's deed, but the appearance of several other of Ridge's workers, who also worked the Ward's land at different times of the summer and fall seasons, assured the mother of her family's safety. An instant relief washed over her trembling body, and she rested easy as she realized that a long lost family member such as this was in charge of the rag-tag army who, excepting a few men with ancient revolvers inherited from their fathers and grandfathers, were armed solely with shovels, knives, and baseball bats. The sight of the advancing crowd of men brought out a shout of joy from the woman, and Rachel and Elmira were soon able to control their non-stop sobbing, as they hugged their mother close to themselves.

"Nelcy! Are you alright? How are your girls?" asked a frenetic Owen, who then directed several men to continue scouting throughout the house and to assist the injured servants laying on the floor.

"I'm fine, Owen, but oh, Gunther is hurt very badly!" said Nelcy, ashamed that she had forgotten about the man in her great haste to escape from the torments of her damaged bedroom.

"Marquez, get on that horse of yours and see if you cannot find my cousin. Where did he go today, Nelcy?" said Owen, as he picked up and then held little Elmira in his arms, even though the frightened girl was a stranger to him.

Struggling to recall where her husband ventured off to this morning, she tugged upon the strings of her hazy memory.

"He's over at the Cooper home; he's operating on old man Cooper's foot, I believe."

"This is more important. Ride fast, Marquez, and be sure to tell him that his womenfolk are unharmed."

Walking up nearer to the teary-eyed Nelcy, Owen Ward forced a small smile at the woman, and with a gentle delicateness, he started to pat a hand onto her shoulder.

"You *are* okay, right, my dear lady?" asked Owen.

"I'm fine, I promise you, but how are Sara and Tabitha?"

Owen Ward removed his hand from her shoulder and then winced back at his cousin-in-law.

"They'll survive, but those Neary bastards are living demons; some of the boys are fixing them up the best they can, at least until Taig can get back here."

"Please send for Loretta Smith, Ridge's old cook. She's also a midwife, and perhaps a more delicate source of comfort for the poor girls than a ranch hand could possibly be. Both she and I can see to the wounds of the women."

"Yes, ma'am, will do," said Owen, as he turned to a few men standing near him. "You heard her, men, let's bring the wounded women into the parlor so they can be properly attended to."

As he turned to leave with his fellow ranch hands, Owen heard Nelcy Ward squeak out a few mumbled sounds.

"And thank you, Owen, oh so very much," said the mother, before she ran over to the former shootist and kissed him on the forehead, not giving a damn about matters of impropriety. "I'll always have a tender place in my heart for you for saving my family. That's the Lord's truth, good sir."

Owen Ward winked once at Nelcy, and then he walked away down the hall, and into the furnace of war.

Chapter 21- A Response to Violence

In the enclosed and claustrophobic space of a dilapidated workshed, a single shred of light shone in the midnight's penetrating darkness; the slight warm breeze blowing in the Indian summer during a red dog night through the splintered holes of the shed caused the candle's brightness to flicker the shadows of five figures across the shed's perforated wooden walls, while the men studied several quickly drawn crude maps of the county and surrounding desert countryside placed on top of a short-legged, wobbly table. Each man, in proper turn, was expected to say out loud the time and place he was relied upon to be at if their grand scheme were to be successful. Except for an individual ranch hand, all of the fellows were armed to the teeth; the single unarmed fellow had his principled reasons for being so, or as some of the other rough riders present believed, his 'unreason' for still not carrying a firearm.

"But why even bother to help your cousin any further?" asked an incredulous Flores, known in the outlaw world as the 'King of Flowers', for the distinct designs colored onto his boots and wild claims concerning the fairer sex.

"Yeah, don't the doc believe that you are somehow responsible for Boze's attack on his family? How in hell ya gonna square that one, boy?" hiccupped the tipsy Bob Channing, who held onto the side of the centered table with both of his hands, the better to steady his balance.

"There's no one else capable of targeting the Neary Gang. Judge Graves' hands are tied, and as we all know, Sheriff Daggs is a traitor to the badge, a sell-out to all dishonest men who pay the right price. We're it, gentlemen; there is no one else," said Owen Ward, speaking in a calm voice. His face was hidden in semi-shadows, but his eyes were clear for every man to see. "Now, look, this doesn't *have to be* a shooting war. All we need to do is follow the plan and we will cripple the gang's business in Redview. If we can strangle their finances, most of their cowboys will vanish as soon as the money dries up. They have no other reason to be loyal to Boze Neary or Jimmy Cotton."

Taking a moment's pause for effect, the ranch hand turned his visage upon the two newcomers, away from the small circle of men that Owen already personally knew and vouch for.

"So, what about you two fellows? Bob Channing speaks for you, and you all seem like you understand the plan." said Owen, in anticipation of watching their faces, more than listening to their verbal responses.

"Well, just a minute, Owen; I know *of* them. They *don't* work for Boze Neary or Ridge," said Bob Channing, as he slapped the back of one of the new men that was nearest to him, much too hard as the alcohol clouded his depth perception. "But I also further *do not* know how good a shot either man is in a live gun-fight. I seen 'em shoot the hell out of still metal cans and jackrabbits, though!"

One of the new men straightened his back and leaned onto the table with the heavy weight of his belly.

"My name is Tex Willis, a feared gunfighter throughout Harris County in Texas. I have also been known to give them Comanche Injuns a dose of their own fire water," baritoned the Texan, with tobacco juice running down the sides of his mouth, and both of his huge hands emplaced upon the top of his holstered revolvers.

"Never heard of you," said Owen in a dispassionate manner, but not out of spite. "Anyways, you'll be riding with Bob here. Are you sure you know the four hide-out cabins to target? By heart and without the use of a map?"

"Damn right. You got it, 'Mad' man," said Tex Willis, in a more subservient manner, after brushing away the brown liquid from the sides of his mouth for a second time. "Me and Bob will hit up the first cabin before the break of day, tomorrow morning."

"At what time *specifically*?" said the suddenly agitated Owen Ward, as he leaned in closer to the large, boastful Texan.

"The stroke of midnight." Tex nodded once.

Satisfied enough to leave his fellow countryman alone, Owen then turned his head towards the other unknown quantity of manhood present inside of the dark workshed.

"And what about you? You're gonna be riding with me. I'm going to be carrying one of Flores's guns, but just for appearances sake; it won't be loaded, but are you sure that yours will be ready to shoot at any interference attempting to disrupt our schemes?" said Owen, looking at the silent man with soft, fair features.

"I'm Otis Staals, sir, and I'll go with you to the gates of hell, 'Mad' man," said the fellow in his early twenties.

Tex Willis snorted out a derisive laugh, blowing out a gob of tobacco spittle onto the floor in the process, but the rest of the men made no outward signs towards the quiet fellow's passionate declaration.

Glancing for a long moment at the fresh-faced, boyish looking man, Owen Ward was unsure if the newcomer could shoot, but the former shootist believed in the ability of their plan to be carried out without a single gunshot needing to be fired. The strength of Owen's convictions allowed him to believe in a type of purer fighting principles, as man is wont to do on the eve of a great destruction, despite the history of humanity's tree bearing no good fruit on that front.

"Alright, then. I guess our final order of business before scattering tonight is to ensure a sawed-off shotgun for Mr. Flores," said Owen, as he pointed to the smiling Mexican.

"I already got one, jefe," laughed Flores. "You think I need a *gringo* like you to get me strapped?"

"Get some rest, then; we first hit them tonight, and then Otis and I will light 'em up bright and early in the morning, just in time for the girls to arrive on site." said Owen.

Caring no more to ponder any concerns about the plan, Owen Ward picked up the rudimentary maps, blew out the candle, and then followed behind his posse out into the night that covered the redness, but which could never prevent the violence from becoming manifested in the souls of all who passed through the land.

"There's nobody in there, hot damn!" Tex Willis yelled out into the silent, hot night.

"Shh, boy, lest we wake the damned dead or snakes, and I don't know which is worse," said Bob Channing, as he took a final swig from the half-full whiskey bottle, before the amateur shootist proceeded to pour the rest of the bottle's liquid contents around the base of the Neary clan's rickety, wooden hide-out base of operations ten miles southeast of Redview.

Bob and Tex Willis had searched the small log cabin long enough to find a cache of hidden greenbacks, which the cowboys were quick to pocket before burning down the first safe house.

"Welp, my watchpiece reads midnight by moonlight, boy, what say you?" asked the drunken Bob Channing, who was still able to stand on his own without leaning against a sturdy object.

"I ain't got no watch, but I don't give a good goddamn *what* time it is, let's get to burning this bitch down and hurry on to the next safe houses, before Neary and the rest of his bad company arrive ready to raise some hell at what all we've done."

Bob Channing poured out the remaining whiskey throughout the one-room structure, and then he struck a match, letting the tip burn for 15 seconds, before dropping the tiny piece of wood and running back outside of the cabin.

"You ride to the south-west hide-out," commanded Bob Channing, as he caught his breath. "Even if you don't got no timepiece, I'd reckon it'd be damn near close to the 2 am burn time that Owen wanted you to stick to the schedule by."

"Yeah, yeah, I got it, Bobby boy," said Tex Willis, as he started out riding alone into the shadows of midnight, yee hawing loud enough to send a small group of quail running to new juniper bushes for coverage.

Bob Channing calmed the whinnying from his horse by laying a gentle, rubbing hand upon the male's muzzle; with his other hand, Bob reached into his side-saddle bag to feel for the half-dozen remaining whiskey bottles.

"One for the road never hurts a man," said Channing, before taking a slug from a fresh bottle, before he guided his horse in the direction of his next target.

There came a rampant, persistent knocking upon the Eye of the Needle's 2nd floor master bedroom's door. Jake the bartender was hesitant to keep pounding on the metallic entryway, but he feared more what Jimmy Cotton would do to him if he did not interrupt the current employer for the sake of his future boss.

"Mr. Neary, I'm real sorry about this, but Jimmy wanted me to break the bad news to ya," said Jake, his voice low but firm.

"Ahh, you bastard!" roared the old Irishman's muffled voice from behind the door. "Get up and go answer the door, girly; then pass me my Pamplin pipe."

A blonde painted lady belonging to Boze Neary opened the bedroom door; her clothes were put on in what appeared to be with great haste, but over her bruised shoulder the bartender had full view of the nude, spread-eagled Boze smoking a Pamplin red clay pipe on his king-sized bed. He held the pipe's long wooden stem betwixt his teeth and a left forefinger and thumb.

The young woman stood still for a moment, not knowing what to do, but fearing the physical repercussions for failing to do what Neary wanted to absolute and unknowable perfection.

"Get out of the way, whore, so that the man can be let in!" shouted Boze, as the smoke left his mouth, much as the vented steams near the lands of Yellowstone turn the local air into hazy smoke right in front of a man's eyes, before the devil can take him.

The blonde did her best to further shield her nakedness, but not before passing a damning look at Jake; while the woman had no chance for any recourse or restitution from her actual employer, the bartender could see from her face that she would have much to say to him later on, while drinking from the available intoxicating liquids down at the bar; free of charge, naturally, and out of the personal expenses of Jake himself.

Jake stepped inside of the bedroom, and he was stunned by the sight of all the snowy white hair that ran down from his boss's burly chest to his groin, and onwards to the man's hirsute feet. The barman almost forgot the reason why he had intruded into the lion's lair in the first place.

"What is it, then?" demanded Neary, in between puffs on his red clayed Pamplin.

"Jimmy's downstairs coordinating a plan of action. He's all riled-up. I guess the hide-out near the Perez Ranch has been burnt to cinders. A few of the boys could make out the fire from here at the saloon, as they telescoped the vicinity of our drop-spots."

"Send a couple of 'em out to poke around the site, but no more. We may need the rest of the fellas at our own disposal."

"Yes, sir, that's what Jimmy said."

A new voice could be heard yelling from down the hallway, through the master bedroom's open doorway.

"There's been another one burned down!" said a man, as he ran along the hallway, pounding closer to Neary and Jake.

Arriving at the door was the tall man, a serial rapist of brutal renown, and he struggled to catch his breath before repeating his earlier screamed statement.

"They got us again!" said the tall man. "This time it was the house by the Bloody Basin Wash."

Sparing no moment's thought, the boss jolted into action, as he sat upwards, while still clutching onto his pipe, the vespers strongly emitted from his nostrils.

"Tell Jimmy to split everybody into groups of two and three men, and have them go to each hide-out to salvage what we can. Take *everybody* with you."

"A lot of the boys are passed out," said the tall rapist. "Are you sure you don't want to have a few of the fellas stay behind here, maybe protect the Needle?"

"I'll stay," seethed Boze Neary. "I ain't finished with that blonde bitch yet, and Jake here knows how to shoot any mouthy customer. Besides, if need be, we can roust awake a few of those dead drunk skunks."

"You got it, boss." said the tall man, as he exited from the bedroom to go back downstairs.

"Keep both eyes on the place, Jake," winked Boze. "And call back that girly for me; I'll be down when I've had my fill."

Jake nodded his head, and then he went out into the hallway. After the woman heard his call, the bartender could see with clearer eyes all of the girl's bruised and battered face in a quick side-glance as he absconded away from his employer's presence, and he understood that his job could always be worse; the succeeding cries of pain emanating soon from Neary's room reassured the bartender of that notion.

The Mexican gunslinger waited with steel determination across the darkened street of Massie Lane, watching the barman push out the last few unruly customers from the Eye of the Needle. The time was near 3 am and Flores, the 'King of Flowers', was happy to see that only Boze Neary, a handful of passed-out cowboys, and a half-dozen painted ladies remained inside of the outlaw establishment, as far as Flores could make out after surveilling the scene for the past 15 successive hours. Checking over the sawed-off shotgun a final time, the native of Oaxaca strutted his way towards the saloon's entrance, and ensured the firearm was hidden underneath the back of his long brown duster jacket; the jacket was speckled with red from the blowing wind, as were the flowers painted onto his new boots.

The bartender had just locked the inner door of the Needle's entrance, when Flores began to knock on the door's upper glass window, softly at first.

"We're closed for the night, so go home!" Jake yelled through the pane glass.

"No está bien!" responded Flores, as he affected the bearing of a drunkard.

"What, you damn Mexican? Either go home or drink somewhere else!"

Flores started to pound harder on the window, and as soon as Jake opened the door to punch the Oaxacan, the 'King of Flowers' revealed the hidden shotgun that was behind his duster jacket.

"Alright, gringo, now take me to the safe." Flores smiled.

"We don't have one *here*," gulped the barman.

Flores then slapped Jake across his face with an open palm, while still keeping the shotgun aimed steady at the man.

"You lie to me again, and you no longer have a face, cabron! Comprendes?"

"Fine, that's fine," said the bartender, as he thought of the revolver stashed behind the bar's iron-hatch safe.

Following Jake into the Eye of the Needle, Flores looked upwards, scanning the 2nd floor balcony for the Irishman.

"Where's Boze at?"

"He's laying a jezebel, boy; what of it, are you afraid of 'em? I would be, too, if I were you!" grinned the bartender.

"Open and empty the safe, or I'll shoot you where you stand."

Taking a second to settle down his breathing rate, Jake steadied his fingers enough to dial open the lock on the safe.

"Hand it all over; put the money into this," demanded Flores, while he handed the captured man a gray satchel bag, as he continued to eye around the upstairs balcony for any sign of movement.

Smiling to himself, the bartender, with a well-practiced nonchalance, attempted to use his right hand to take the greenbacks from out of the safe and into the satchel bag, while at the same time maneuvering his left hand behind the iron safe, as he searched for his hidden revolver.

"And know one thing, gringo. If you pull out that gun you're reaching for there, you'll never have back problems again, *friend*."

"Bastard," fumed Jake before he calmed his nerves. "Well, listen; ya gotta rough me up a little bit, though, or else the boss man is almost sure to do much worse to me than you ever could, for letting you rob us."

"No problema," laughed Flores, as he hit the barkeep with the smoothed butt-end of the shotgun, the force of which knocked out one of Jake's golden teeth from his now bloodied mouth.

While Jake groaned in ruffled pain on the saloon's floor, Flores kicked the man into further pain, only stopping after he had heard a rib crack. Letting the storm pass from out of his consciousness, the Mexican steadied himself.

"Don't forget to let Boze know that his businesses are finished in this town. By death, by gunfight, or by loss of money, the Neary Gang won't be able to run this roost any more. Redview is free again."

After Flores ran out the front door with the stuffed satchel bag, the bartender brushed himself off in great pain, bracing for the lies he'd need to tell his employer in order for him to survive long enough to see another sunrise.

The pale yellow sun rose above the distant corners of the earth to greet Owen Ward and Otis Staals's tired eyes at 5:36 am. Both of their horses chewed at the grassy cud of the land, while they scanned the brown vista with make-shift telescopes. The 21-year-old new gunfighter-to-be hoped in vain that 'Mad' Owen Ward wouldn't take notice of just how nervous the young man was becoming, with each passing moment bringing the break of the action closer to occurring, and the realness of the deed coming to pass from plan into action.

The former shootist became aware of Otis's fears before the boyish fellow himself could begin to fathom the great depths of dreaded despair when contemplating the odds of being shot and dying.

"Can I tell you something?" asked Otis, as his eyes looked downward in shame, but they remained wide open to the world.

"What is it, kid?" responded the ranch hand, choosing to look forward, so as not to add further embarrassment to the youth.

"I ain't ever been in a real skirmish or nothing like this before," said Otis, through a slight, childish stutter. "I didn't want you to take me for a dirty liar, neither, b-but-."

"Remember to breathe, Staals," interrupted Owen as coolly as could be. "Don't think about all of the things that *might* happen in a fight. Instead, you need to be strong enough and be prepared for what actually *does happen*; you can only control yourself, and not much else."

Owen leaned downwards on the back of his horse, looking to fish out the eyes of Otis, so he could stare directly into the younger man's face. Otis was red-cheeked and big-eyed, but he did look back at his idol.

"Listen, I will take the lead and do all of the talking. The solitary thing I require from you is to just keep an eye on the driver and the pimp, and I'll do the rest. Watch their hands for any sudden movements, but don't be too quick on the draw of your long-rifle. And remember to breathe naturally."

"You got it, 'Mad' man."

"Just Owen, from now on, okay? And don't forget that my gun is no longer loaded, either."

"But don't that, in a way, just make you a new breed of crazy?" Otis asked the older man with no humor in his voice.

"Fair point, kid," laughed Owen, in spite of the graveness of the hour; he felt good laughing. "Now, hey, I think I see them driving up near the vista. See the high-rising dust over yonder? That's gotta be them. You ready to ride, Staals?"

"Yaw!" yelled out Otis Staals, as he kicked his horse to race in the direction of the incoming stagecoach.

Owen Ward followed the petulant young man at a slow gallop close behind.

"Slaugh-ta, wut iz takin' us so long, eh?" squawked the Englishman from within the black stagecoach's plush sitting cabin, and through the open window.

"I'm very sorry, Mr. Dalrymple, sir, but there appears to be a heavy log in the middle of the road, just up ahead," said Mr. Slaughter, the driver of the stagecoach. "From here, it's hard to tell if the tree fell over due to the laws of Mother Nature, or if it was caused by bandits. Perhaps it may be wise, sir, to return back south to Yuma-."

"A pox on yer hide, you worthless rotter! Weed lose the betta' part of a week if we did tha'. I can assures you that Mr. Neary, money-grubbing mick that he iz, will not take so well to tha' idea, ya fool!"

The pimp from Portsmouth, England, felt compelled to take out all of his rage on one of the five painted ladies seated adjacent to him throughout the stagecoach's inner cabin. However, when the souteneur went to strike the nearby brunette woman whose cheeks were covered in rouge, Dalrymple remembered that Boze Neary had once broken the Englishman's nose for having beaten a girl who was intended to be the sole possession of the old gang leader; the man from Galway did not punch the pimp out of a deformed act of chivalry, but instead struck him with the understanding that Neary had strict discretion with regards to "teaching" the new painted ladies how to act and behave whilst working at the Eye of the Needle.

Fearing the wrath of Neary, the pimp pulled his hand back from a forceful hitting position. The other women witnessed Dalrymple's display of weakness, and they wondered at what the middle-aged man was capable of doing to them, if anything at all. They snickered in silence.

"Ya jezzies jus' watch yerselves!" hooted Dalrymple, as he felt ten haughty female eyeballs searing hate into every fiber of his being. "Slaugh-ta, are ya gonna git up close to the tree to move it, or are we to die out here in the desert heat?"

Before Slaughter could turn his head back towards the stagecoach's open window to respond, a shot fired from a long-range rifle ricocheted close to the brake lever of the wagon. The powerful sound awakened the sleepy creatures of the wilderness from their sonorous siestas, as the wooden-brown grasshoppers and crickets leaped into the bright, warming air, looking like the beige dead leaves of a giant, rotting tree rattling abound within a terrible tempest; to Otis Staals, the young man who'd fired the shot, the sky became near-black for a moment, the stagecoach lost in a sea of pestilence.

Waiting to see if the stagecoach's driver would try to turn the wagon around or not, Otis watched in eager excitableness as Owen Ward, with empty gun drawn outwards into his right hand, rode up undetected from the far right-side of the stagecoach. Eyeing the scene through the long-rifle's scope, Otis could see that the driver was quite nervous, but the newly minted gunslinger noted the man made no move to grab the pistol sitting at his side on the driver's seat. Staals kept a vigilant watch.

Owen pulled back the reins of his mare horse, guiding her near to the closed door of the stagecoach.

"Gentlemen, I'm going to need both of you to surrender your firearms by throwing them into the cactus patch right over yonder; very slowly there, Dalrymple, toss your gun through the cabin's window." said Owen Ward, whose own gun was trained at Dalrymple's head through the window's opaque glass.

Slaughter was fast in chucking his pistol into the cholla, the fuzz-like pointy white spikes of the green cactus rendering human reach of the firearm to be both painful to retrieve and therefore pointless to endeavor.

"Now you, Dalrymple," commanded Owen, speaking in an easy voice, as he continued to point his gun at the pimp. "And hurry, before we waste anymore time of these lovely young ladies. When you're done, get on out here and join me."

"Do youse know who these here 'ores belong to?" asked Dalrymple, before tossing his rusted Smith and Wesson revolver into the cholla, and opening the cabin door. "Boze will hunt ya boyz down and salt yer eyez!"

"Step down from there, please, sir," Owen said to Slaughter, ignoring for the time being the Englishman's taunt. "And now I'm going to have to ask both of you gentlemen to walk about ten feet down the road from me, away from the cactus. Let's go, pimp."

"Yer a dead man!" Dalrymple snarled back.

"Indeed, now excuse me while I now address the ladies," said Owen, as he remained on his horse by the stagecoach. "Good morning, my dears. While we do hate to interrupt your journey towards your current destination, I have a proposal that you all perhaps may be interested in working for another boss, instead of for the dirty cuss at the Needle, where you have already seen the kind of fellas you'd be working for, no?"

The five women listened with great raptness, and the youngest of them, a raven-haired beauty with hazel eyes, built up the courage to ask the ex-gunslinger a question.

"Are you a pimp? Just exactly who would we be working for?" said the girl through sparkling red lips.

"Well, I suppose once we get to Redview, you can all decide for yourselves which saloon or brothel you want to work at. As for me, it really makes no difference where you ladies choose to ply your trade; that is, as long as it's *not* at the Needle, but even this request is only made from the kindly bottom of my heart."

"Yeah but even if we accept these terms, just how are we supposed to get into town now?" asked the oldest of the women, a painted lady of mixed race.

"Same way you were before, darling, only now it will be under the guidance and respectful companionship of my associate and I," nodded Owen to the woman who had not blushed for many years. "So then, what do you ladies think, do you need a moment to converse in order to make a decision?"

"Wot're youse sayin' to my 'ores, you yellow bastard?" roared Dalrymple, as he booted away at a nearby slithering snake who'd emerged from its hole to inspect the nosy intruders.

"No, stranger, the girls and I think we'd be better off going with you." winked the colored matron, as her upper body leaned out of the carriage's open window on her elbows.

"Then it's official." Owen waved the signal for Otis Staals to ride over to the stagecoach's position.

Emptying out his horse's saddlebags of the extra food, water, and blankets he'd packed for the mission, Owen got down from his horse and then walked over to the wagon driver and souteneur.

"I'm afraid we'll have to be parting ways, now. However, I'll leave you fellas with plenty of supplies and, depending on how fast you all can tread ground, you should reach Redview by early tomorrow morning."

Otis Staals then rode up to Owen's horse, grabbed the creature's harness, and headed back to the safehouse, signaling to the former shootist that he would follow through with the rest of his role to play in the master plan, by hiding all traces of evidence that could link Staals, Flores, Channing, Willis, or Ward back to the targets.

Owen Ward glanced once more at the distance to the chollas from his two hostages, where their guns now laid, and the ranch hand wagered that only the Englishman would be mad enough to make a dash for the Smith and Wesson. Strutting backwards, his eyes still upon the two men, Owen got up into the driver's seat of the stagecoach, before turning his head away from Dalrymple, and then the ex-gunslinger let the pimp see the back of his hatless head, before yawing the six horses onward towards the 'Scarlet Rose', after such an extended break from travel.

Right as Dalrymple made to dash and grab his sun-warmed revolver from amongst the poking pricks of the cholla, the white and woody points became driven into just beneath the pimp's pink fingers and gouged the soft flesh and hairy knuckles of the man from Portsmouth. Hearing the screams, Owen fired off two pellet shots from another self-made slingshot that he'd also had hidden within his saddlebags. The pieces of steel ball bearing metal hit Dalrymple in the chest, causing the thin-haired man to both lose his gun and fall backwards into the cactus patch, wounded and yelling out in severe anguish. Owen whipped the horses to trot faster.

As his former stagecoach speeded away from the two of them at a quick pace, Mr. Slaughter found his sole consolation surrounding the current predicament he was in to be in the form of a grown man crying about how much the pricks hurt.

Boze Neary sat at the bar alone, except for the presence of the younger man who stood to obtain the old Irishman's small criminal fiefdom out in the red West, Jimmy Cotton. The solitary resemblance existing between the men's physical appearance was the raging fire in their eyes.

"We gotta hit them hard, Jimmy," said Boze, as he smoked from his red clay pipe.

"The Wards' ranch will *burn*," seethed Cotton, after he took another drink from a bottle of bourbon.

"No, little bastard brother, this time we will need to beat against a new drum."

The gunslinging youth stood by with unhidden fury at the boss, but Jimmy Cotton listened to Boze's outline of attack, and then grinned.

Chapter 22- The Lovers' Decree

Twenty-two miles to the southwest of Redview, outside the sightline of the redness of the 'Scarlet Rose', Owen Ward and Emma Rabelais sat alone at a table in a dancehall located in the town of Cottonwood. The young couple had been seated for hours, not once standing up to go on to the uncrowded dance floor, because the excitable comfort of each others' eyes and the enchanted dreams of a future together were enough to both quiet the long held self-doubt within Owen's heart and salve the unseen wounds prickling the soul of Emma, a woman living for two, but on the beckoning verge of making a pleasant existence for three. The rambunctious music played by the band went unnoticed by the paramours, as they listened to the unheard notes of their own requited love song.

"How do your eyes do that?" Owen Ward asked of the blue-eyed woman.

"What do you mean, fella?" laughed Emma Rabelais, who reached back into Owen's larger hands on the table between them, drawing him closer to her, and then kissing him fast on the lips.

After the quick embrace, he pulled back a slight distance from her, and Owen brushed the red hair to the side of Emma's forehead. The ranch hand sought for words near and true to his heart. Looking once again into the shades of edged turquoise, he became inspired, and Owen revealed to his outer self the utterances to proclaim to his love.

"I see and feel the spark of life that comes from you," the man said, feeling light-headed but steady in spirit. "I have seen this fire in you ever since the very first moment I spotted you at that dive joint, not so long ago. The brightness that can be found in the world of the living is a strong part of you. I don't know if a man must be forced to walk in darkness in order to learn how to love the light, Emma, but regardless of whether I have sight or not, I will go to my dying day feeling the nursed hole in my heart that was filled by your true love, meant only, I hope, for me."

"How do I know that you're *my* true love?" she asked, not out of disbelief, but in a desire to hear more of what other sonnets he may express in her honor.

"I've gone down every street, rode every pathway, and been kissed by many girls until the money ran out, but in a lifetime of wrong, you're the one thing that's ever felt right. I'd make all of those terrible choices again, though, if it was destined by fate to be the only way that I could hold you close to me. *I am* your one true love, because these days, whenever I think of giving up on trying to obtain the distant light, and when I think I've been blinded by the perpetual darkness, I know that I can't surrender. I look into your eyes and I see the living light of love. I'm your true love, Miss Rabelais, because I love you with all of my being."

The former painted lady sat in warm silence. Emma saw his eyelashes flutter as he spoke, not because Owen might cry, but out of habit whenever he wanted to express the fullness of his feelings towards her. The noise of the band was as forgotten from the ears of the two lovers as the crackling of dawn's creation.

Emma almost laughed to herself. In a lifetime of patient loneliness and societal rejection, and long after she believed the day would never come to greet her, the mother explored the day's newest feelings of love for the man. She had decided to regret nothing.

"I have land," she said, before she leapt into the infiniteness. "That I bought with all of the money I earned back when I was whoring. Otherwise, I could never have hoped to afford it."

Emma cast her eyes downward for a second, before catching herself and gazing back into Owen's eyes again. She could see no signs of judgment in his visage or manner, so she continued divulging her last secret.

"But here's the rub. I don't have anyone to help me build a house for my boy and me, let alone a man to start a family with. What's a girl to do, Mr. Ward?"

"Welp," said the former shootist, finally at a loss for words. "I haven't built much since when I was a boy myself, on my grandmother's farm."

"I've never built anything, at any time ever, so maybe we can both learn how to do so as one being together. What say you, cowboy, do you want to help a poor mother build a ranch home out near the town of Prescott?"

"If you'll have me."

Kissing again, they took no notice of anyone noticing them.

"If that's now settled, perhaps we can actually dance!" exclaimed Emma, as she almost bounced upwards into the upper reaches of the stratosphere.

"Hey, woman, you're the one who has been jawing at me so much!" Owen said, to which the servant woman shot back a feigned shocked look of surprise. "Alright, I reckon *we both* have had much to say today, but it doesn't matter, darling. I wanna dance with you, right now, and forever after."

The two held each other for hours into the evening, long past her curfew and the woman's ignoring of the man's pleading advice for her to lay low out of Redview for a few weeks time, as Owen and company's plan had created an unknown source of unspoken friction between the town's citizens, with no one being particularly certain as to what Boze Neary would do next.

Not lost amongst the twirling red hair and grasping, sweaty hands, however, were the words said between the couple overheard by another woman, a girlfriend to a member of the Neary Gang.

Carolina Gomez had heard enough to make her feel confident to approach Boze Neary and Jimmy Cotton for what the Mexican seamstress hoped to be a sizable reward for such illuminating information about the unsuspecting enemy. Running out of the dance hall and towards the home of her brother, who owned many horses, Carolina begged her sibling for help. On understanding the non-negotiable condition that she would split part of her reward with him, Carolina's brother allowed for her to borrow one of his young and fast ponies for the night's scheme.

"But make sure to return him back to me soon, with my share of the money!" shouted the Mexican horseman, as Carolina trotted on to the trail that led into Redview.

Although the native from the Sonoran Desert had never been to the Eye of the Needle before, Carolina knew by reputation the building's location at Massie Lane, and furthermore that Boze Neary could always be found on the 2nd floor.

After arriving at the seedy saloon, and easing the mind of Jake the bartender as to the reason behind her visit, Carolina made her way up the staircase and walked down the hall to Boze's master bedroom. The door was open, so the Mexicana went inside of the smoky room.

"What do you want, dearie?" said the old Irishman, as he sat at the wooden desk near his king-sized bed; the man appeared to have been dazing off into space, mumbling incoherently to himself or some unseen entity.

"I have some information, senor, something I think you may even *pay* to hear about, if you know what I mean?" replied Carolina, who was more anxious to earn much needed greenbacks, then she was afraid of the gang leader's wrath against any insolence he may imagine her driving against him.

Boze Neary said nothing for two minutes. Carolina stood stone-faced, awaiting the outlaw's response. Although she was not losing her nerve, she kept watch through her peripheral vision for the sudden arrival at any moment of the volatile Jimmy Cotton.

Leaning over his desk with the heavy weight of his hairy arms and elbows, Boze Neary held up an index finger and bent the digit to beckon the woman closer to him. Carolina could not remember if the aged man had yet to blink at her or not.

"Information I would pay for. Is *that* so?" the man from Galway said in a rough tone.

Carolina nodded her head thrice in quick succession, but otherwise remained stoic.

Boze began rocking back and forth in his chair, while continuing to stare at the standing woman. Sensing weakness, he began to tap a large finger against the wood of his desktop. The woman blinked her dark almond eyes multiple times, but she did not run out of the bedroom and into the relative safety of the hallway.

"I'm not an unfair woman, senor. Whatever you think the information is worth, that is exactly what I will accept from you in return for it."

"Then spill it, senorita."

"The man you've been telling everybody in town to keep a watchful eye and ear out for, this 'Loco' Owen Ward or whatever, he was at a dance hall in east Cottonwood, dancing with the red-haired woman with the French name. La puta."

"Is that all you have?" snarled Boze, not breaking his deep concentration on her person.

"They *also* spoke of things, a great many things. They have big dreams. La puta owns land, somewhere near Prescott. It seems they hope to live together there."

"*Hmm*, I see." Neary said, as he started to light his red clay Pamplin pipe, inhaling the stale, left-over tobacco already emplaced in the clay holder.

"Senor Neary, I think that 'hmm' of yours has earned me some kind of reward, no?"

Carolina Gomez mouthed a thin-lipped smile, the only one she had dared to do during the course of their meeting.

Taken aback by the Mexicana's effrontery but appreciative of the now-fifth eyewitness to again confirm to him the serious nature of the relationship developing between Owen Ward and Emma Rabelais, Boze tossed a few pieces of gold on top of his desk.

Carolina leaned over the table to grab the coins, but the gang leader quickly clutched her wrist with both of his huge hands, their hairy roughness and dirty fingernails digging hot, searing pain into the woman's flesh, but still she refused to either yell out in pain for mercy or drop the money she had risked all to collect.

"Do I need to explain to you what will happen if you go spreading the news about this matter to other, shall we say, *concerned* parties?"

Almost internally breaking to the point of no longer even wanting the money, Carolina Gomez nodded her head so she could prevent herself from squealing outwards.

Boze let the seamstress go, allowing her to keep the gold pieces for all of her trouble. The woman ran out of the room without saying another word and before Neary could change his mind and decide to keep her around the Needle for his own horrifying, pleasurable devices.

The outlaw could see the scheme already mapped out in his head, but Boze also knew that Jimmy Cotton and a few other unwise associates were down the hallway, engaged in a nine hour running game of high-stakes poker. As with drinking, shooting, and raping, Neary understood how Jimmy was liable to over exert himself while gambling against exhausted opponents who, as the 2nd-in-command, would refuse to allow his underlings to cash-out of any game he was losing. When Cotton had finished with the forced marathon poker session, victorious in cheating against men who would never dare to argue, Boze sought to catch Jimmy Cotton's money-counting attention before the young gunslinger began down a new warpath of his own making.

"It's finally on, boys," said Boze Neary, addressing Jimmy and a baker's dozen worth of other cowboys who had not run out of Redview in search of greener pastures. "You need to let the Wards know who is in charge of this town. I've heard enough evidence to know what we need to do."

Hearing the plan out from beginning to end with a minimal amount of interruptions, Neary looked to end the counter strike's discussion using a direct warning to his petulant lieutenant.

"And Jimmy, remember, *do not* kick-in Doc Ward's place again. You need to hit this Owen bastard first. I'll say this only once: No out-of-town shooting convict is moving in on our game. Show him what happens when a man violates the rules of this land. *Do not* fail me."

All of the loathing that Jimmy Cotton felt for Boze Neary was soon to be expended towards a different aggravation.

Chapter 23- Dispatches: Pertaining to the Nature of the Arizona Territories

Dispatch Order #117

TO: Colonel A. P. Hayes, Colonel R. I. Irving

By order from the offices of the Secretary of War of the United States of America, we are hereby authorized and expected to take command of 100 troopers, 500 horses, 50 wagons, 200 rifles, and 5,000 rounds of ammunition for said rifles, concerning a reinforcement mission to be led into the central and northern Arizona territories to re-fortify the United States Army's defensive position at Camp Verde, a town of some 100 souls.

Colonel Hayes, you will leave Washington, D.C. headquarters take command of the leading vanguard unit that will be composed of 25 troopers and be deployed to enter the territories first, and your unit will serve as the scouts to guide Colonel Irving's larger force of 75 troopers, the main body of horse, and most of the supply wagons through the high desert land. As of this past spring hunting season, the local Apache tribes have been preoccupied with tracking deer and wild game, but several towns in the central regions have noted larger Indian gatherings, and these growing bands of tribes are not simple hunting parties; or so the local settlers claim.

More dispatches will be forthcoming.

General Buford Thomas Morris

4th Response Letter to Dispatches

TO: General B. T. Morris

No hostile Indians have been found in the western New Mexico or eastern Arizona border lands. All resistance was minimal and pacified, or bought off with outdated firearms, diluted whiskey and subpar cornmeal.

News from certain central Arizona town officials, territory judges, and concerned private citizens reporting illegal operations and or outlaw banditry. Considering the current nature of our engagement with the local Red Men, it is my intuition that the earlier prescribed orders assigned to Colonel Irving's bulk unit should not be altered to assist any of these provincial settlers, who are untrustworthy in most assessments, as these are petty local trifles that do NOT concern the Federal Army; however, sir, many personal letters from citizens are starting to accumulate in my forward base camp, as immigrants drift towards the troopers for assistance in their individual matters.

As always, I await your further instructions, General.

Colonel A. P. Hayes

P.S.~ My unit is in dire need of medical expertise. Doc Adams and his assistant, Mr. Burnett, have both succumbed to debilitating illnesses which we believe to be of the cholera variety. New medical officers are of the utmost urgency!

Dispatch Order #139

TO: Colonel A. P. Hayes, Colonel R. I. Irving

Command Headquarters have received reports of small uprisings being conducted by several Apache tribes in northern Mexico, within 25 miles of the United States of America's sovereign soil. For now, the Secretary of War's administration has asked for our specific unit of troopers to maintain cautious awareness but defensive distance away from any and all Mexican Army-Tribal disputes and warfare.

As per the need for new medical personnel, please, gentlemen, neither one of you officers should forget that, as cited by provisional orders decreed by President Lincoln during the Civil War, when entering into the territories, the Federal Army possesses at its disposal the legal ability to draft and conscript ANY doctor deemed medically necessary to keep and maintain our troopers' health, for up to a time period of no longer than six months. Use your discretion, Colonels, but please do try to avoid upsetting the local citizenry when drafting a medical man into helping the Army, as we would hate to anger the provincials while completing construction of new forts within the territories.

Concerning local complaints about banditry, Colonel Hayes, again, use your own judgment but certainly by the time that Colonel Irving's bulk force of the troopers arrive, new citizen complaints about outlaw activity sent to Command Headquarters are warranted enough to investigate. Some of the men in the region linked to criminal activity are wanted in multiple States, bandits such as Boze 'The Dirty Irishman' Neary, James 'The Whip' Cotton, William 'Curly' Brocious, etc., and are presumed leaders of cowboy outfits near the central territories, in towns like Redview; these men SHOULD be dealt with AFTER we have secured and fortified our defensive position at Camp Verde, 27 miles due south from Redview.

More dispatches will be forthcoming.

General Buford Thomas Morris

13th Response Letter to Dispatches

TO: General B. T. Morris

Due to the dying of approximately 40% of our available horses, the main command of my unit's troopers will now be compelled to requisition animals and other war materiels from nearby farms and towns.

The bulk force will therefore be delayed entering Camp Verde by some weeks.

I have also received word from a certain Judge Graves and a Dr. Ward about the urgently needed assistance of the Federal Army's troopers. They have been QUITE forward in their requests for help. I have not written back to them or any other of the residents of the close-by towns who've passed their letters to our soldiers asking for favorable aid. What shall I do, sir?

Much slow going.

Colonel R. I. Irving

Dispatch Order #156

TO: Colonel A. P. Hayes

Reports are coming into Command Headquarters in Washington, D.C. describing the wreckage of the fort in Camp Verde inflicted upon by the late summer monsoon winds and rains.

Updated vanguard unit orders are to rapidly proceed to the damaged fort, so as to allow for the Army Corps of Engineers assigned to your unit to assess the damage and begin initial emergency repairs to the structures, as they are needed.

Also, if this Doctor Ward person, who we've all received letters from in the nearby town of Redview, is so vocally insistent on the premise that justice be served to the local criminal element, then perhaps you may just have found your troop's new medical officer? I feel that six month's service to the Federal Army isn't an unfair exchange for the United States' Government's assistance in eliminating any cowboy threat, now wouldn't you agree, Colonel Hayes?

More dispatches will be forthcoming.

General Buford Thomas Morris

Chapter 24- The End of My World

Dr. Taig Ward and Judge Eugene Graves walked in the low evening, disappearing sunlight, their boots kicking up whirls of the crimson dust behind them. Taig had been reluctant to leave his wife and four children without his presence at their home, but after the doctor had armed both his family and hired six more armed ranch hands to maintain a constant watch over his property, he'd hoped to attempt to end the feud with the Neary Gang by words, even if he was called to deal with other unsavory businessmen to accomplish that goal's ends.

Near the front entrance of the darkened 'old' courthouse in Redview, Taig stopped walking and turned to look at the much older man, who'd been his friend for almost 15 years.

"I just wanted to say that I appreciate you doing this, Judge," sighed Taig, as he quickly glanced into Graves' aged, pale blue eyes. "I really do despise the man, but I would do anything to protect my family."

"I hear ya, Doc, but don't let it get you down. I can assure you that while *I also* would prefer not to have to deal with the make-believe 'colonel', he owns a lot of firepower and enough money to finance what may need to be done to save this town." said Judge Graves.

"The federal troopers will never be here. Even if they do ever make it out to Camp Verde, they don't care a damn for us up here in town."

"Bah," said the judge, as he double-stamped the bottom of his cane onto the ground, before he straightened his back. "Enough of that, young man. Have some faith. Now, let's go inside and talk over matters with Ridge."

Seated at the main long-table positioned near the center of the near-empty courtroom was two men. Although Taig was sure he could see from a distance the hated Ridge sitting in a chair nearest to them, the doctor had difficulty discerning the face of the other man seated next to the 'colonel'.

"I thought you said there would only be the three of us, Eugene?" asked Taig in breathless manner.

The two friends walked nearer to the long-table, and Taig was stunned to see his cousin, the hatless Owen Ward, stand up to greet the newcomers.

"What is this man doing here? It was enough just to meet the foolish Ridge, but Owen's counter-actions have put my family in stark mortal danger!" Taig said in a heated tone, but he kept himself from yelling.

"Taig, please listen," said Judge Graves, putting a hand onto the back of his young friend. "I understand that this may not be easy, but I also further desire for you to comprehend the danger we are *all* in, and that you recognize that your cousin saved the very lives of your loved ones last week. Is that not correct?"

Taig refused to look at the judge, while staring at Owen with daggers in his pupils.

"Yes, and?" snorted Taig after a moment.

"Then perhaps a man should be more grateful to those who helped the people he holds most closest to his heart. We are in a *war*, Taig!" the judge slammed his cane onto the wooden floor one time, almost chipping part of the floor into splinters with his force. "The sooner we unite together, the sooner it will become more difficult for Neary and his ilk to tear apart our community. Will you at least allow the man his say?"

The doctor looked from the judge, to the emotionless Owen, and then back to his friend's visage again.

"At 6 pm, I'm going back home to protect my family," said Taig. "Let us begin."

Every man feeling reassured to an extent, the three standing men sat down to join 'Colonel' Ridge at the table.

"I just wanted to add something, gentlemen," said Ridge, as sweat began to pour down his face in the soft, yellowing light projected by the green-glass lamp. "I feel it is incumbent upon me to offer both an apology and a firm truce. How does that sound to you all? Especially for you, Dr. Ward?"

"I have conditions, as I have not forgotten that you are the dirty cuss who put the whole ball into motion, years ago, when you hired these men to be your muscle." said Taig.

"And what might those conditions be?" the 'colonel' smiled back at him, like the crowned jack in a deck of playing cards.

"I need more rifles and ammunition. The word on the street is that you're completely on the outs with Boze and his boys, so I figured any man not looking to shoot you would be your natural ally."

"And you're not looking to take a shot at me? Kidding, my friend!" Ridge laughed an unnatural laugh. "Okay, done. That was simple."

"But I'm *not done*," Taig cracked a smile for the first time in many weeks. "No more arguments, Ridge, as far as my land goes. You need to drop all of your hounding pursuit and let things lie. Judge, here, has made it all legal for me, now."

"Okay, okay, that's fine, Ward." Ridge uttered in a less friendly voice.

"I've *also* got something that *I want*, for the town's sake," interjected Judge Graves.

"Let me guess. To have me re-start the construction of your precious new courthouse, eh?" crinkled Ridge in response.

"That seems fair, too, Ridge." added Taig.

"Indeed." said the non-military man more to himself than to anyone else, before raising his eyebrows to bring forth a question that had been burning within him for the past week. "And what about Sheriff Daggs? I, personally, have no problem having him gone, along with the Neary Gang."

"That's risky, Ridge!" Judge Graves raised his voice.

"We'll have to see about the sheriff." said Taig, who had been considering that obstacle, as well.

"Then what in the hell am *I* getting out of all of these arrangements here, if I may ask, gentlemen? I'm the fool funding everybody else's enterprises, letting good land deals go by the wayside, *and* building a bloody new courthouse just for the town's judge to further work me over, legally! Madness, I say! Why should I not just walk away, I ask you?" exhorted Ridge.

"I can answer that, Mr. Ridge," began Owen Ward, whose eyes had been closely following the meeting at hand, biding his time for such an opening as this. "We know about the ranch hands that were killed on your botched orders. Sure, I can buy you didn't intend to have them boys killed, nor have my kin's servants raped and property partially burnt down, but we can see what a federal judge might have to say about *all* of the doings carried out by your business empire out here in the bloody West. And finally, but most importantly, we intend to do the actual fighting and dying. Can we expect you to join us in a firefight and risk being murdered by Neary and Cotton?"

Ridge winced his eyes shut for a second before shaking his head and responding to the ranch hand.

"Do you mean to tell me it is your intention to rid that damn Neary stain from off of this land? To finish it, forever?" asked Ridge.

"The man's remaining hours on Earth are numbered and his gang these days consists mainly of drunkards and paid mercenaries. You fellas are fighting for your homes," Owen winked at Taig, before adding. "Of course, with the added advantage of having a little help from my gunslinging friends and I. What say you, 'colonel', do we have a gentlemen's agreement on all of these matters that we've discussed this late afternoon?"

"I can agree to these terms. I will have my assistant, Samuel, draw up a contract later tonight for all four of us to sign, in good faith, mind you," Ridge stood up from the table. "Until next time, gentlemen. I will leave you to consider how best to relieve Redview of all these damn cowboys."

The non-military man stood alone, and then he walked down the corridor to exit the building.

The three remaining men took their time in leaving the 'old' courthouse, as they discussed how best to eliminate the Neary clan.

"We need more gunslingers, not just cow-punchers and horse rustlers. Don't you know anyone else who might be able to help us, Owen?" asked the judge, who looked every minute and day of his 62 years of age.

"Right now I got Flores, Bob Channing, and a couple of other fellows that know how to use the sharpshooter's scope, target shoot, and burn down safe houses. That won't be enough to hit Boze and company when they're at full strength, but if we can hire another practiced gunman or two, and maybe catch the gang in a weak position, then we could finish off Neary and Jimmy Cotton. The cowboys in this town are finished without them holding the reins." said the ex-gunslinger.

"I don't know how to shoot all that well, but I will do what I can to help." said Taig, in his truthful way.

Owen looked at his cousin with half-closed eyelids, measuring his words with careful consideration for the tender moment, withholding any sign of his typical wry smile.

"That's a burden, Taig, that I wouldn't want you to destroy your soul over. Shoot a man once, and you shoot him for the rest of your eternal, sleepless nights. Your family needs you to stay alive, too."

Owen patted Taig on the shoulder, as the judge looked to move on to other personal business.

"Well, Dr. Ward and Mr. Ward, let's say we meet two days henceforth from now, without the detestable presence of old Ridgey, no?" said Judge Graves, as he lit up a cigar and used his cane to push open the unshut courthouse door. "I'm sure you boys have some things to discuss on your own. And do stay safe, gentlemen."

While the Ward cousins started to rein-in their own corralled horses, the tall serial rapist and another crony of the Neary Gang sauntered by ten feet away from where the Wards stood.

Owen and Taig did not move from their position, not breathing in the dusty red air which suffocated the 'Scarlet Rose's' petals and lungs to the point of the town's submission to evil. They could guess that the two cowboys were semi-drunk, as their walking appeared off-center and the shorter man's gait was shifty and unbalanced, and the smaller man was close to falling down into the dirt, without the assistance of the tall man's gripping hands on his shirt's collar.

The serial rapist then saw the eyes of Owen Ward, and he started to point a derisive finger at the ranch hand, laughing to his much inebriated companion. After a quick exchange of mocking gibberish, the tall man stared deep into Owen's countenance as a duelist challenging another.

"Is he looking at me?" asked Taig, his blood starting to curdle and rise out from his veins.

"No, he's looking at me." replied Owen, his eyes wide to the moment.

The tall man made a pouting, kissing face at Owen, laughed in a scratchy baritone, and then wrapped his arm around his fellow gang member, compelling the man to now help carry the larger cowboy further down the street, where they entered into a saloon to continue their roaring drunk.

"Something's wrong, Taig," whispered Owen. "I need to go check on someone!"

"I'm going with you!"

"No, you have your family and home to consider, man; only I need to do this."

"The hell with that. I have nine armed men roaming my property and watching my people. You don't even have a gun of your own, I can see, but *I* have one!"

Dr. Ward revealed a loaded revolver underneath his jacket.

"Alright, then. Follow me!" yelled Owen, jumping onto his horse, and racing into the red wind.

Before getting onto his own gray mare, Taig double-checked his gun, said a prayer to the Lord, and then he followed his cousin into the unknown lion's den.

Emma and Tom Rabelais turned around a wet creek bend in the paralleling dirt road. The pathway was a shortcut and nice reprieve from the end of summer's monsoon heat and humidity, although the recent arrival of ravenous mosquitos had almost caused the servant woman to avoid taking the back roads today on her way to work at Mr. and Mrs. Jonathan Napier's home. She cleaned there on the first and third Tuesdays and Thursdays of every month. Rare was the event she would encounter even a single man down near the creek out this way, in the wilderness, let alone an entire group of men.

Hoping to God that her son would not be seen, Emma lied to the boy, saying she wanted him to go back home, and that she did not really need his help at the Napier house today, like she had said earlier in the morning to Tom. At the command of his mother, the ten-year-old ran like the snared jackrabbit that he was.

Unseen by the mother, two wolves bearing the appearance of mortal men followed after the boy on foot, on the double and cackling.

Emma thought of blue skies when she was a little girl playing with her giggling friends, the sunshine smile on her son's handsome face, and just how happy she may have been in another life, if only the ranch hand were allowed to be her man and build a home together.

'I love you, Tommy. And I would've loved you so much, Owen.' was the woman's final conscious grace.

Owen and Taig Ward rode on their horses in near-dark, the sun falling into the night. The road was becoming fainter and hazy to their eyes, but Owen kept yawing his beast of burden to gallop faster, as his fears outraced his understanding.

Off the reddish-brown trail, near a dry, rocky bed of the wet creek, Taig shouted and pointed towards a small clearing. Owen came to a full stop and peered over to the flat, sand-pebbled beach, where a body lay on the ground. The paleness stood out amongst the gray, water-smoothed stones of the dead river stream. Taig knew the body had to be female, because of the long, red hair.

The doctor slowed his mare down to a crawling pace, watching as his cousin sprinted forward to the woman he loved. Owen got onto the ground next to Emma, whispering into her ear.

On his closing approach, Taig could read the serrated word cut across into the skin and red muscle tissue of her left side, thigh, and down along her back: WHORE.

Taig looked down at the woman, recognizing no sign of movement from her. Lost for words, Taig placed a soft hand on his crying kinsman's brawny shoulder.

"I don't want to breathe anymore," Owen cried through his tears. "Take the air from my lungs, cousin. I no longer care to breathe!"

Taig took off the jacket he was wearing and covered-up the nude Emma Rabelais, and he tried to guide Owen away from her corpse. After the doctor believed Owen was calmed, the former shootist became even more frantic than before.

"The boy! Where is the boy?" yelled Owen to the silent skies. "Come on, let's head south down the creek!"

The two men placed Emma's lifeless body onto the back of Owen's horse in great haste, during which time Owen had taken Taig's gun unbeknownst to the doctor and then they rode in fury upon the red, rockless road.

From off the main dusty trail, Owen Ward spotted a long-abandoned cabin and horse-staging corral. Two of Neary's men were toying with their prey. Although the cowboys' guns were still in their holsters, Tom laid atop the cabin's roof upon his stomach, the sling-shot Owen had given him for his birthday leveled at both men as they circled back and forth around the cabin on the ground, taunting the boy to come down from there before they would climb up to grab and gut him. Tom perspired salty sweat and tears out his fear of the wolves.

"Come now, kid!" yelled a bearded cowboy. "We just want to play with ya!"

Taking advantage of the hirsute man's unguarded position, Owen Ward shot him twice in the middle of his back and once just below his brain stem. The bearded man expired during his dead-fall to the ground.

Anticipating the other Neary gang member about to jump out from behind the cabin's corner and fire in his direction, Owen crouched down onto his knees, stopped his breathing and all thoughts of aching memory, and then waited.

The man came into Owen's gun sight after the cowboy had shot two wild, blind bullets nowhere near Owen's vicinity, before the 'Mad' Ward targeted the man thrice in his face, shattering apart the cowboy's cheekbones and forehead, his visage disappearing into red mists of marrow and bone.

Owen ran up to the man and felt for a pulse. Feeling none, he nodded his head back towards Taig. The doctor decided to jog in a circular direction around their position; scouting for another of Neary's wolves, and Taig was able to pick up one of the dead cowboys' revolver, prepared to fire if necessary.

"Who's there?" screamed Tom from his hiding spot on the roof of the dilapidated cabin.

"It's Owen!" the tired man shouted back. "Please come down, Tom!"

The boy climbed down the side of the cabin and walked into the open arms of Owen, who grabbed Tom close into his bosom, squeezing the child with all of his might.

Taig watched them weep in hushed stillness, as his scattered mind thought about what must be done to quell the madness.

Chapter 25- A Promise

The cheeks of Tom Rabelais's face were wet, but the boy had at last stopped crying. The morning light coming down through the open windows of the Ward ranch home hurt his eyes, while he tried to be a man in front of the adults. He wanted to use words to communicate his internal thoughts, but instead he had discovered a desolate feeling, one so overwhelming, at times, which exuded fuller control over his actions, as the emotions were like waves in the sea, compelling his body to act as a boat adrift in the world, lost to any hope for reason and no chance for an answer to the eternally universal question of 'why'; the idiom of desolation remained wordless for the ten-year-old boy.

All Tom knew with adult certainty was that his mother was gone forever, and the pain of her mortal extinguishment would never fully be healed. The sun could only remind the child of the missing light in his new life. But still he kept himself from crying further in front of his hero, and the other grown-ups.

Owen and Taig Ward glanced at one another, and then the doctor looked to his wife, nodding his head after a shared moment of understanding had passed between the husband and spouse.

"Tom, what say we bring you into one of the guest bedrooms we have near Michael and Stephen's room? I think it would do you good to lie down and rest for a while, young man. You need to try to get some sleep." said Nelcy Ward in a soothing tone.

"Yes, ma'am," responded the boy, and in trying to sound masculine, he succeeded only in tendering the woman's heart all the more to just how vulnerable the child really was, as to be expected. "I suppose you are right, Mrs. Ward."

Tom Rabelais stood up from the couch, realizing the physical exhaustion had now grown to first match and then nearly exceed the mental and spiritual fatigue he'd been experiencing since yesterday afternoon. The motherless son started to follow Nelcy out of the parlor room, leaving the men behind in their pillowed, wooden chairs.

However, before Tom could leave the room, Owen Ward walked over to the boy and stuck out his right hand. Tom gazed into the man's eyes and shook the outstretched hand with depleted force.

"You're a good man, Tom 'Sawyer', and you take care to get some rest, now, you hear me?"

"Yes, sir." said Tom, as he turned his head away before Owen could see him cry and swipe the tears away.

Nelcy led the child down the hallway and into his new room; the other children were still asleep, and he kept his feet quiet, so as not to disturb them. As he sat down upon the twin bed, the lady of the house could just prevent the welling tears from pouring down her own cheeks and crying in front of the damaged boy, as an unstated fear started to grow across young Tom's countenance.

"Your mother was a true angel, Tom." said Nelcy, as she looked out of the small bedroom's window.

Tom nodded his head back in agreement, but he continued to look scared. Nelcy waited in thoughts of concern for the boy, as she detected a new panic. Not wanting to goad him, Nelcy allowed time enough for Tom to decide to give words to his growing frightful panic.

"Mrs. Ward," Tom said in a quiet voice, determined to speak his conscience. "Are the men who killed my mother coming back for me?"

No longer wanting to have the boy feel as if he were alone in the numbing world, Nelcy sat down on the bed beside him, and then hugged Tom, who was again near to tears himself.

"No, dear, those men are never gonna harm you again. Dr. Ward and Mr. Ward will not allow that to happen," said the woman, with great firmness. "I *myself* would not let them do anything to you, not now or ever. Do you believe me, Tom?"

Nodding his head yes, the boy seemed to have calmed himself, as he allowed his welting eyelids to close, while the woman rubbed his back and shoulders in a wide arching motion.

Not wanting to cloud the child's mind, but afraid to leave him cast away to his drowning thoughts, Nelcy rushed into the notion she'd been thinking about all night, and had already expressed to her husband.

"You know, Tom, I would be very happy if you'd stay with my family in our home here for a while; my children can always use another playmate. What would you say about that idea?"

Smiling at each other in renewed hope for a peaceful future, neither the boy nor the woman could hear Owen and Taig exiting through the Ward's ranch home's front entryway, which had been repaired after the damage inflicted upon the portal by the Neary wolves the prior week.

Not looking at each other's faces, the two men made their way over to Owen's secured and heavily packed horse. The doctor watched with a weighted conscience as his hatless cousin jumped atop of the brown and white-spotted creature.

"I was never meant to be a husband or a father. This is all just further proof of that. But you, Taig, you're already a great dad and a good man to your wife, as well, possessing a big and tender heart. I know that if I leave Tom with Nelcy and yourself, he'll grow to be a fine man some day. I could never give him that," Owen stopped looking outwards into the distant, vacant redness, and cast reproving eyes at his cousin. "But I want you to promise me something. I want you to let him be free, while still teaching him that there are consequences for pure freedom in this life."

Taig nodded his head in silent agreement.

"Adios, then, friend." said Owen, as he pulled on the reins of his horse to start heading away from the ranch home.

Taig suddenly then ran and stood in front of Owen's horse, snatching the reins from out of his cousin's leathered grip.

"And where are you going to run to, Owen? If both prison and Redview can be said to have taught you anything, I suppose their lessons should have been that a man faces his problems head on, and he charges into the blowing wind. I'm not a gunfighter like you are, but I *know* that together we can rid this town of those damn, rotten bastards for good!" yelled the doctor, but to no avail.

"All my life I've been on the wrong side of the fight. I no longer care to be a part of this morality play we call life. I only long to be left alone, forevermore. Things are as they should be, no?" said Owen Ward, dead eyes set deep in his skull. "Again, *goodbye*, Taig."

Standing a few steps from out of the horse's way, Taig let his kinsman pass him on by.

"Goodbye, Owen."

Taig continued to watch as Owen wade into the distant craggy mountains, as the horse and rider became just another part of the browned crimson landscape, before prevailing upon himself to go back inside of his home to talk with his wife.

Gone astray in his distorted mind, Owen Ward thought of a question he did not have a ready response to.

'How does any man *know how* to live?'

The shootist rode on without answers.

Chapter 26- Where Does a Man Go to Die?

Owen Ward hacked a hard cough, bringing up sputum and yellowed-brown snot; the jolting power elicited by the rasp ruptured more capillaries, and his nose-bleed continued unabated. He ignored this in favor of a great sensation of stabbing pain reaching down his throat when he tried to swallow, as though giant invisible fingers were choking him to death. The hardness of his head felt like a wagon wheel pressed upon the front end of the skull, with a bullet to Owen's brain being preferable to the man when faced with the choice of living in ache or dying to escape the pain.

Coming awake to the sound of mumbled, soft-spoken Spanish, Owen discovered that he was still seated inside of the same stiflingly hot cantina he'd been drinking in the entire day and night before. The alcohol sweats both reminded him of wanting to die and needing to have another drink, the vicious cycle of the drunkard on a long binge of excess.

Owen believed he was in a tiny Mexican village south of Tucson, but he did not care enough to know the pueblo's name by asking the bartender, who in his own turn slowly eyed the white man up and down, wondering if the gringo had any more money to pay for his tequila. The shootist took no notice of the aged man's hesitancy.

"Another drink, senor." Owen muttered through dry, grimy teeth, and his throat experienced another tingling feeling that throbbed harsher each time he tried to swallow in air.

"Dame mas dinero." said the ancient Sonoran man, who was also the owner of the small cantina and therefore much interested in obtaining any customer's money before they continued to imbibe in his establishment.

Not wanting to engage in a heated argument that would cause his headache to inflict any further pain upon his soul, Owen planted down the last of his rumpled greenbacks onto the frayed bartop, before demanding another bottle of tequila. After achieving his request, he stayed seated for another half-hour, drinking the blue agave-derived spirits to steady his nerves, as the tremoring of his hands started to cease at last, and the hot sweat on his forehead no longer bothered him and his heartbeat was no longer jouncing frenetic.

The bartender stood nearby to Owen behind the bar, washing dirty translucent, glass cups. Watching the old man watch him, Owen nodded to the Mexican that he could speak to him.

"Te gustaría alguna comida? Mi esposa es una buena cocinera." said the cantina owner, indicating to the American that perhaps he should eat something, as his wife was a willing cook.

"No esta bien. No me gusta. Gracias." Owen responded in haste, standing up for the first time in ten hours and ready to move on from the dirty barroom and head on further down the nameless road of the unknown pueblo.

Taking the three-quarters full tequila bottle outside of the cantina in his dirty hands, Owen moved as a man trying to cross a deep, free-flowing river at mid-stream. The audio hallucinations of the delirium tremors were kept just at bay; her voice was drowned out, and the ardent spirits helped to hush her presence in his mind. All reality and incumbent sounds had become warped and, being lost and unaware of his own present existence, he failed to hear the definite approach of a living stranger on a horse.

"Haven't you had enough yet?" asked the searing bright light, as Owen turned around into the face of the morning sun; its radiance failed to cleanse the broken man.

Owen drank again from the tequila bottle in response to the beaming accusations of questioning noise. Taking another few steps, the former ranch hand was unsure whether the utterance was in his head or not; he slowly became aware that the voice *did* come from a man on a horse. Feeling emboldened by the alcohol, Owen jaunted past the rider, ignoring his own raw conscience, as all curiosity had died within him.

The strange rider leapt down from his horse and walked after the drunkard in the small desert town built upon rocky Mexican soil, the white clay enveloping his boots in an ivory-colored soot, the result of massive burnings occurring near to the pueblo. The rising sun started to bake both men.

"Will drinking your pain do you any further good?" said the living dream, who was now a foot behind Owen, following him. "It's been four weeks since Emma died, Owen; you need to quit this and come home."

Taking another sip from his dwindling supply of booze, Owen hiccupped hot rancid breath, but steadied himself as he started to fall down sideways into the white dirt.

"I'm not allowed back in Texas!" belched Owen, coming to an abrupt stop, as Mexican villagers wearing straw hats took breaks from their work, standing at attention to watch the angry gringos argue with each other in the middle of the road.

"No, I don't want to take you back to south Texas. I'm talking about your new home, in Arizona, close to me and my family."

"The mezcal and agave fields are my new home, cousin."

"Oh, so *you're not* so blotted out by drink as to not recognize a fellow man in dire need of help, then, are you?" asked Taig Ward, whom Owen could now place within the dawn's clear brightness.

Catching the doctor off guard, Owen suddenly wound back his arm in a fierce motion, and then he tossed the near-empty glass bottle at Taig's head, pulling back just at the last second so he would not strike his kinsman, before he spat mucus onto the ground and continued walking down the white road.

"Do you really want to die as a drunken fool drowning in a shallow puddle of water, the same way our grandfather Ward killed himself with drink? Not able to have enough sense to lift his head above two feet of muddy rainwater?" said Taig, just able to lower his voice down from a scream.

Owen turned around to face Taig. To his cousin, the shootist appeared as the beggar in a dying city, aged far beyond his 37-years, and the doctor could see the browned-blood matted into the stubbled, unkempt beard Owen had not bothered to clean in many days, and the grime covering his shirt and pants.

"There's nothing left for me to do. What use am I to you or anyone else? I thought I had finally started to do some good in this here life, but I was *wrong*," Owen said, with a vast darkness in his eyes, before spitting out once more the foul taste that would not leave him. "Any man who can honestly say that he's found peace with himself should count himself most fortunate. Blessed, even."

Seeing an opening, Taig took another cautious couple of steps closer to his kinsman, unsure if his cousin had another object to throw at him or not.

"Flores and Bob Channing got that tall bastard the other week, the Neary Gang's head rapist of many women," said Taig in an even tone, which seemed to have been met with great approval from Owen. "Well, now he's known as 'R.I.P.'. We finished him, as we have a couple of the other smaller wolves in Neary's wolfpack. A few other of Boze's cowboys, semi-professional types even, have turned cowards and fled from Redview, on account of all the rumors concerning the presence of Federal troopers being in the territories now."

"Have the soldiers gone after Neary or Cotton?" Owen asked in a false sense of seeming not to care about Taig's answer.

"No, they're too busy reconstructing the fort at Camp Verde, and pacifying some outlander Apache bands that have been stirring up a little bit of trouble near the borderlands. Maybe the troopers will someday come to our aid, or maybe they won't, but either way their being around the area works to our advantage; Boze and Jimmy Cotton have been mostly holed up at the Needle these past weeks, not taking any chances leaving the saloon. They're *afraid now*, can't you see?"

Owen stared back at his cousin, but made no response., as his vision still saw double.

"Alright then, man, must I *beg* you?" said the doctor. "Will you come back with me, please? These are desperate men, and I don't know for how long they will hide out before striking again. Probably against my own family. You understand the great risk I took coming down here to find you?"

The shootist saw the beautiful face of Emma Rabelais in the distant sun, her red hair flowing downwards in the rays of light, causing his heart to beat to the point of bursting. Her disappointed visage almost forced Owen to cry out in pain, the disappointment in her fiery eyes almost too much for his soul to bear.

"I don't know, Taig." Owen mumbled.

"We *need you*, Owen. The Neary Gang will ultimately destroy all of the hope which exists in the town of Redview, unless you ride back with me and we stop them. Together."

Owen stared at the sky for several more moments, listening to the sound of his heart. When Taig was afraid that the shootist was refusing to help, the drunken man then appeared to have become more sober and present in mind.

"Do you remember how to shoot, cousin?" Owen smiled in his wry way, for the first time in the course of their conversation.

"Maybe as we ride through the northern countryside, you can show me again the techniques you and your father taught me all those years ago, on grandmother's farm."

Owen Ward nodded his aching head in agreement.

"However," said Taig, taking stock of what was still to come. "We're gonna need one more skilled shooter, though, and I think we can find him on our way home to Redview. I've encountered him out in the wastelands before."

No longer possessing his own horse, as he had sold the animal for drinking money, Owen Ward joined Taig on the back of his cousin's old gray mare.

"We will *also* need to get you your own horse, boy," grinned Taig, as he looked back to face Owen. "Because you stink to high heaven!"

The two men laughed as they rode into the rising sun.

Chapter 27- Will You Fight?

The young Indian followed the slow approach of the white men through the sandy wash with his elongated telescope, and he laughed in petulant giddiness to spite the sky gods. The divine creators had told him that they would not come, but he had been waiting for the pale riders' arrival.

"I know more than all of you combined into one spirit," said the half-Apache to the unseen world, which refused to listen to mortal rationality. "Let them come. It will save me another trip into the white man's village to find them."

Sams unloaded his Springfield Model 1880 trapdoor long-rifle, and then he tied the gun to the back-end of his black stallion's leather saddle. Not wanting to alarm the white men, the Indian did not get down from his horse, so he could remain visible to both the newcomers from far away, and the sky gods who taunted him with thunderous insults.

"Silence comes from all divinity which cares." was all that Sams would say to the creators' raging impudence, as they rained down invisible bolts of lightning from the imperceptible heavens above, missing him in the sands and rocks and juniper bushes all around him.

The two cousins had closed the gap in distance between them and their searching destination. While the doctor was certain in his intellectual aspirations, the shootist, being a man of action, started to doubt the plan.

"How do you really know he'll even be out here?" Owen Ward asked Taig Ward, who was riding beside him.

They guided their horses away from the dry sandy wash and up a small hill covered in fir-green juniper bushes that smelled of rotten mint, the plants' crushed berries laying desiccated throughout the ascending ground; scrawny ravens picked at the remains, while watching the horsemen ride by.

"I was lucky once before; or rather, *unlucky* to run into him out here."

Taig yawed at his gray mare to move faster; she whinnied her displeased objections back in response but followed his command.

Owen spurred the sides of his own horse in order to keep pace with the doctor.

"But what I don't know," said Taig, in a lower voice. "Is if he's willing to help us. Ridge has told me that he's had his men already make contact with the 'Apache Kid', but you know just how much the so-called 'colonel' is good for, and that ain't much."

"We need another real gunslinger, and not just more men that can serve as bodies for target practice. I know he's a sharpshooter, but how quick is he with a six-gun?"

"I don't know, but let's find where he went and get him on our side, cousin."

The men rode in silence the rest of the way as they scanned the red land's horizons.

Riding another hour without finding him and on the verge of turning back in defeat, Sams suddenly appeared around a broken boulder next to a patch of dead junipers.

"I see that you have come back to speak with me again, white medicine man," said Sams, his hands motionless on his reins, as he continued to speak, while sniffing loudly. "And this time you have brought a man who has given himself over to the demonic ways of the white man's devil-water, if I can guess by the smell and look of him."

"What's the bounty on your head, red man?" Owen teased the much younger gunfighter.

"Worth more than yours, old 'Mad' man." Sams shot back at his elder.

The two shootists tapped their middle fingers across the butts of their holstered revolvers. Eyeing one another, both men watched for who would blink first. The doctor did his best to remain breathless.

After sixty seconds of staring each other down, Owen glanced over to Taig, and then laughed out in a loud burst, taking his hand off from his revolver.

Taig took advantage of the broken tension, and made his way closer to the Indian.

"You operate outside of the law," said Taig, as he grabbed his small, metallic flask filled with water and drank for a few seconds. "But neither do we represent the law, either, but simply our own particular interests. After we take out Boze Neary, Jimmy Cotton, and any other vermin who gets in our way, Judge Graves and I can make arrangements to ensure that any surviving men that fights for us will be looked after, one way or another."

Sams looked into the deep blue sky; he had almost appeared as if he had forgotten that Owen and Taig were there, waiting to hear from other persons on what they thought.

"What say you, 'Kid'?" asked Owen, as he remembered his own visions from earlier in the week. "Will you fight? How much will it cost?"

Sams then, in a single motion with his right hand, unholstered his gun, grabbed the revolver, and shot a jackrabbit through the neck as the critter poked his inquisitive head from out of his hole. The Ward men were shocked into awe.

"Life is a fight," Sams looked back at the men with obsidian eyes that were as dark as the endless inky night. "And now you know whether I can shoot, 'Mad' Owen."

Owen Ward nodded back with a wry smile etched into his wearied face.

"It was white men like Neary who killed my family, and this is all I will ever say about that to people such as you. But fighting with you allows me to kill a white man legally, and this brings me much more than mere green paper could provide."

Sams hopped off from his horse, took out a Bowie knife, and picked the dead jackrabbit up in a quick stabbing motion. After depositing the animal into his knapsack, he returned to being on top of his black stallion.

"Does that mean that you will fight with us for free?" asked Taig, with a tinge of desperate hope in his voice.

The 'Apache Kid' laughed and shook his head no.

"The gods be cursed for such an arrangement," said Sams, his eyes back to facing skyward. "Nothing is free in the white man's world; a rich white man such as you should know this more than anyone else, *Doc*."

"Ha! Only a fool would ever doubt the intelligence of an Indian like you, Sams! Pay the man, Taig." Owen guffawed, in spite of his better judgment.

"What is it worth to you, 'Kid'?" asked Taig.

"After the fight's over, give me the same amount as the price of my scalp's bounty in Redview. I'm curious to see if my reputation has grown or not."

"Any man still alive at the end of the shooting can get *whatever* he so desires." Owen nodded to their new companion.

"No, this is not true, 'Mad' man; some of us can never get back that which we have lost," Sams said, as he looked back to face Owen, before he started to laugh. "But for now, at least, when do we get to kill the white men?"

Owen and Taig detected no absolution in the Indian's constitution, and they had no notion towards mercy to grant to the snarling wolves howling in the distance, ready to gnash at their throats.

The three men rode down from the small hill, prepared for death.

Chapter 28- Boze Neary's Testament of Revelations

Boze Neary smoked from his red clay Pamplin pipe, allowing the Virginian tobacco to cloud his lungs to near oblivion; the 'Dirty Irishman' hungered to be choked by the noxious fumes of his own vices, if only for a blissful moment of release. The vaporous tendrils from the Pamplin pipe singed his eyes and irritated his esophagus with slicing pain, and the gang leader appreciated that, too.

The anniversary date of when his mother abandoned him alone in the family mudhut was still three months away, the only day Boze Neary allowed himself to imbibe spirits; he refrained from drinking now, but this did not prevent the outlaw from boiling in the poisonous vespers which clouded his mind. After he had finished his thankless tryst with one of the regular girls at the Eye of the Needle, a young painted lady who had been disallowed from running off with a few coward cowboys like most of the other prostitutes, Neary had sent her to find Jimmy Cotton to tell the youthful gunfighter that he wanted to speak with him.

The man from Galway had not left the Needle in weeks, and his paranoia had grown elevated to new levels of distracted caution; but this did not stop Neary from scheming about his control over Redview, as he still wondered if the odds were in his favor.

Jimmy Cotton, dazed from many nights' collective lack of sleep, opened the door to Neary's upstairs master bedroom without knocking, the young man daring a look of scalding impropriety at his employer.

"Alright, Boze," said Jimmy, as he carried a brown bottle with him into the room. "Norma said ya wanted to talk."

"Sit down," Neary demanded, pointing to the empty chair in front of his small wooden desk.

Electing to do as he was told in a slow manner, Cotton offered Boze a drink from his whiskey bottle.

"Drink to your health, boss man?" snarled Cotton. "Oh, no, what is it again? Is it only on the day your mother was *born* or the day that *she died* that ya drink like a true Irishman? I always forget."

"Listen well, boy, as I have just a few things to explain to you, and I don't have much time left to tell you how things need to be."

Boze suddenly dropped his burning Pamplin pipe onto his desk, sending gray and black and orange ashes into the air and onto the floor, before he snatched the bottle of alcohol from his insubordinate lieutenant and slammed the glass container down in front of him.

"But before we get into long-term strategy, I want to know if there's been any further word as to the whereabouts of the ranch hand, Owen Ward? Is he still glued to the liquor bottle himself down south, even as we speak?"

"Oh, ya, we've had one spy sighting him near Tucson, and another that says he's like a fish at sea somewhere in northern Mexico, or elsewhere thereabouts along the border lands," said

Cotton, as he tapped the top of his holstered gun with itchy fingertips. "The bloody bastard *still* ain't got no gun on 'em; just his drink, to hear the snitches jaw it."

"Good, but don't lose eyes on the man, as he's dangerous to our business. And don't forget to keep a look out for Doc Ward, either."

"Then why don't we hit back against the Ward's place again, huh?" Cotton asked in loud defiance. "What we waitin' for, anyhow? For them to take out a couple more of our boys?"

Boze picked up his red clay pipe and crushed up a stick of tobacco in his hands, tearing apart small pieces between thumbs and forefingers, before placing the dried leaves into the Pamplin's holder bowl. Scratching a match along the rough leg of his chair, the Irishman then placed the burning wood to the holder, breathing in the fumes.

"In time, man, in good time. The odds are not in our favor, but that can always change," Boze blew out the smoke in Cotton's direction, causing the gunslinger to lower the brim of his hat. "We first need to see what those damn troopers stationed at Camp Verde intend on doing after they rebuild the fort."

"Wait and see, wait and see," Jimmy Cotton said, while he lit a cigarette. "The game that's been mastered by old men, after a lifetime of practice. Ya ever notice that only weak men die old?"

Boze Neary laughed with great gruffness, as the smoke wafted above their heads, swirling like a snowflake that never touches the ground. Jimmy Cotton's eyes started to narrow, and he could just keep himself from unholstering his pistol, using the way of the gun to end his chief irritant in life.

"You said it yourself, Jimmy. We're losing too many cowboys and too much money to risk losing a shooting war with Doc Ward and his rogues. And you know as well as I do that after killing the doctor and his hired guns, we'd then need to execute any and all breathing witnesses, no matter the age or sex. There's too many lawmen nearby to tempt such a risky fate, and the odds much too long. So, we wait."

"Alright, then, Mr. Sports Bookmaker, but if greenbacks continue to be an issue," said Cotton, before swiping his whiskey bottle back from off the table. "I say we knock around Ridge some more, or maybe take him out *for good*, and that'll give us all the loot we need to pay out for the boys, whores, rats, and turned lawmen."

"No! Don't you see what that plastic 'colonel' represents and provides for our syndicate here in this county?" said Neary, his voice rising. "We have a legal businessman who acts as both our benefactor and front against the straight world. We don't want to kill our last remaining viable source of money. We can always expect some job from him; just can't trust him for right now, is all."

Near the end of his ranting, Neary started to cough with an uncontrollable force that elicited a painful contortion on the aged Irishman's face. He brought from out of his coat pocket a handkerchief already soiled with yellow and brown sputum, but now dark, ruby-red blood poured down his nose and the crinkled sides of his mouth.

Jimmy Cotton half-smiled in a vindictive way, with his cigarette dangling low between clenched lips, as he appreciated the sight of the man who'd been his employer for the past decade finally starting to meet Mother Nature's call to be hellbound in a season's time.

"What is it?" asked Cotton, as he stamped out his cigarette and took a long drag from his whiskey bottle; his teeth clattered together several times to punctuate his enjoyment.

"Five docs and counting have said it's cancer of the throat, cancer of the tongue, the esophagus, fucking goddamn cancer of *every part* of my body! I didn't know the odds of smoking, kid."

"Am I supposed to care?"

"No, not at all, lad. It's only that if a man finds himself to be in a station above God, then he needs to be aware of the angels and devils that he creates for himself."

Boze took another small puff from his Pamplin pipe, but he was unable to blow out any smoke, as his stomach acids continued to eat away at the linings of his intestines, and the pain was too much for him to sustain. Cotton finished the rest of his whiskey bottle in a last swallow.

"I've lived for a spell, Jimmy, but my time may be near its completion," said the gang leader, as he dropped his red clay pipe onto the table again, forgetting the Pamplin. "When I was young, there was an older boy with pale blue-white eyes, and he could look right through anybody that dared to grant him a view. Some of the scrawnier pathetic kids said that he had the very peepers of Lucifer. Remembering back now, I can still recall how the teenage vandal could put even *my* 12-year-old mind at unease, whenever he chose to single me out from the crowd with his glaring stare."

Boze stopped talking, and he looked away from his lieutenant; to Jimmy Cotton, Neary appeared to have seen the shadow of the man who intended on murdering him, before the gang leader looked back at the younger man with dead eyes.

"Well? What ever happened to old devil orbs?" Jimmy smirked, in spite of his lack of caring about the old man's tired stories.

"Hmm. Do you know that there are savage tribes and island nations who believe that it's possible to gain the strength and power of your enemy through either actual cannibalistic practices or by staged, ritual mimicry of the consumption of one's adversaries?" Boze leaned over the table on his elbows to get closer to Cotton. "You ever look into my eyes for long, Jimmy?"

The young gunslinger kept his mouth shut but his own eyes firm in their hatred. Instead of gunning Boze down, Jimmy Cotton instead lit another cigarette, and resigned himself to the words of his nemesis.

"In the New Testament, the Book of Revelation, the prophet speaks of an angel of the abyss. I believe all angels to be evil, but there is one in particular, in the end times, who leads forth armies out of the bottomless pit. Abaddon is his name, and he causes epic destruction throughout the entirety of creation. Do you know of this?"

"Naw, boss man, I weren't much for Sunday school." said Cotton, smoking in slow movements.

"You are *my* Abaddon. Few men are able to create their own designed 'Angel of Death', but that's exactly what you are to me," said Boze, as he steadied his upper body by planting the palms of both his hands onto the wooden desk's smooth corners. "You're a weapon in the flesh, afraid of no mortal sin. I have formed you in my own image, but I know you will also bring destruction to all that I have built in this land of the free, far from my homeland. However, as long as the red that flows out from me and onto this jagged ground may one day be replaced by a world of obscene green, then I die the way I came in."

"All this talk of them, do you really believe in angels?" asked Cotton.

"I believe in the powers which lend themselves to natural destruction of the universal order. It's all meant to be broken, you can see that, can't you, boy?"

Jimmy Cotton finished his last cigarette, and then he stood up, pushing away from his boss's table.

"I can oblige towards crashing the party, if that's what you mean."

Before the gunslinger could exit the master bedroom, Boze Neary offered a last testament to his angel.

"If we are already broken men, then all a man can choose to do is be broken apart forever from this wholeness."

"I'm the fellar who breaks men, old timer. I'll keep a lookout myself tonight. Most of the other boys are too jittered up; and they'll be worse for wear, if they hear you talking this nonsense." said Jimmy Cotton, before vanishing down the hall, gun already drawn for any creature who aimed for his downfall.

The exhausted Irishman closed his eyes for many hours that night, but sleep would not find him.

Chapter 29- The Shootist

The men gathered in the hide-out home's parlor room remained as silent as the dead. They shined the wooden and metallic handles of their revolvers, checking and rechecking the bullet chambers; the 'Apache Kid' was alone in readying his long-rifle with tallow, as the beef animal fat provided the appropriate lubrication for the spring-roll mechanism on his Springfield Model 1880 to properly function, but the others sought only to be armed with pistols, of which Sams had already polished all three of his own to a bright and blinding shine; not one of the seven fellows looked another man into his eye, as they practiced the final steps of their individual calming and idiosyncratic rituals. Not a man was heard to pray out loud, in front of the others' ears and judgments.

The word had been planted amongst the bartenders and painted ladies of the 'Scarlet Rose', and then spread by the rats and snitches of Redview, that Judge Graves and Dr. Taig Ward were determined this morning to head out to Prescott, capitol city of of the Arizona Territories, in order to garner a group of government support to fight the Neary Gang, although the town's men and firepower were quite limited by what could be spared; the rumor told it that the judge and doctor were growing despondent and desperate to end the shooting war. Instead, however, while Judge Graves and a large-hatted imposter disguised as Taig rode southwest in the direction of Prescott, they had no intention of reaching their stated destination, and were to siphon away several of Neary's cowboys from the Eye of the Needle and into the wooded valleys of thin trees. Judge Graves and a ranch hand would then lay low at the judge's home, awaiting news about the outcome of the planned gunfight. The two men ensured that they were followed by several of Neary's outlaws, before setting off to the Arizona capitol.

At the twenty minute warning from Owen Ward, the men at last looked away from their weapons. Tex Willis played poker hands against himself on the carpeted floor of the parlor room, peeved as a spoiled child each time he lost against one's self. Sams, the 'Apache Kid', and Flores, the 'King of Flowers', rested their eyes, and the Mexican had his hat hung downwards, shielding his countenance from the world. Their grizzled hands laid motionless atop their guns that were set upon their laps. Neither man dreamt of anything. Bob Channing had started to imbibe a little from the whiskey bottle, but after having just enough to straighten his shaking hands, Owen glared at the drunkard, causing Bob to walk outside to pour the remaining liquor onto the ground, before coming back indoors. Owen then looked to the young Otis Staals, who did his best to continue in his youthful attempts to hide his petrified emotions, but the shootist saw and knew all around him. Owen caught Staal's attention and then he demonstrated to the would-be gunslinger how to inhale and exhale in deep breaths. The veteran winked at the rookie, before 'Mad' Owen Ward walked over to his isolated cousin.

Taig Ward sat in a tattered cushioned chair, his back to the rest of the men, as he looked out of a small window of the parlor room; the clouds of the early morning's daylight appeared as the faces of his wife and children. The doctor had already prayed the night before, and he could only have faith that the Lord had listened.

"Don't think of 'em," said Owen, breaking the concentration of his kinsman. "That's the worst thing you could ever do before a gunfight, Taig. Clear your mind and conscience. Thoughts of your family will cause your will to be weakened, and your shooting time to be off kilter. Just think about each moment's responsibility, and the task at hand."

Owen placed a soft hand upon Taig's shoulder, drawing the doctor's head away from the brightness of the window.

"We can beat them, can't we, Owen?" asked Taig Ward in the voice of a child.

"I don't know," said the shootist in an honest manner. "But a good man is one who is committed to doing the right thing, even if doing so causes him great harm; the action itself will justify us, brother."

Taig nodded his head in silence, while Owen patted the doctor's shoulder for a final time.

"It's time," said Owen Ward, the usual wry smile long since vanished from his face. "You're sure that about a half-dozen boys were seen riding after the Judge?"

Dr. Ward nodded his head, while he unbuttoned his gun's holster, as he desired to be quick on the draw.

"Then, based on your watch, Tex," Owen said loud enough so all desperate men present in the parlor room could hear him. "And the word of the girl we have inside the Needle, just how many cowboys are we going up against, one more time, for clarity's sake?"

"About six altogether, including Boze, Jimmy Cotton, and that rat fool Sheriff Daggs, who's taken to living at the saloon out of fear for his own worthless hide," said Tex, as he puffed on his corn pipe. "A fair fight if ever there was such a deal."

Owen said nothing in response as he placed his revolver into his side-holster, and then he buttoned the firearm securely within the tanned leather belt, confident in his mind as to his own quickness.

"Let's go, gentlemen." said Taig, as he walked out of the hide-out house.

The rest of the men followed him and gathered their horses together.

"We drive up to the front entrance of the Needle, right there in the street, so that the whole town can see the challenge. The right move would be for them to bunker and wait for the other cowboys to return from tailing Judge Graves," said Owen Ward, as he swiveled his head to face each of the men, while they started to ride, and the words poured out from his racing mind. "But Boze and Cotton won't stand for that, not being called out on their own turf. They'll come out blazing, but don't nobody shoot until I signal you fellas to do so. We kill the heads of the Neary Gang snake, then the rest of those yellow bastards will break and run away. Any questions?"

The seven men galloped through the redness towards town, without making a human sound.

The hour was near 10:30 am, and a few mothers and their very young children window shopped along the streets of Redview, glorying in what could be, if they only had the money. Townsmen with red dust encrusted into the black and brown fabrics of their hats watched in fear as the modest seven thundered into town, the floating gritty crimson particles looking akin to red tears falling out from the ominous blue sky. A hatless man led the other six riders, and the people of town could guess as to where they were headed.

Outside the Eye of the Needle on Massie Lane, warehouse men unloaded a shipment of alcohol purchased by Jake, the bartender of Neary Gang's saloon. The workmen had moved 20 boxed cases of booze from the horse-drawn carts, and they set down the last of the boxes onto the dusty ground with a gruffness that caused a couple of the glass liquor bottles to shatter apart. The quick approach of Owen Ward and company excited the workers enough to jump back into their carts so they could speed away from the inevitable gunfight bound to occur, payment for the whiskey delivery be damned.

A few interested souls watched from out of the security of second floor windows, putting down their coffees and newspapers long enough to witness the eruption of the town around them.

None of the members of the Neary Gang took any initial notice of the gathering commotion in the blood-colored street in front of their headquarters, as wild horses galloped to and fro; the eager seven were quick to spread out, leaving open space between them.

Upon Owen's signal for the men to get off from their horses, Otis Staals ran in great haste to tie-up every man's animal to a hitching post just down the street from the Needle, so the creatures would not be struck by gunfire.

Taig and Owen Ward stood next to each other, about twenty paces away from the liquor boxes in front of the saloon's left side, with Flores to Owen's right side, seven feet away. To the right shoulder of Flores spread out some distance was Bob Channing, Tex Willis, and then the young Otis Staals, returned from his task of securing the horses. At the furthest right end of the Needle, alone, stood Sams, his tallowed-up trapdoor long-rifle loaded, aimed, and at the ready.

Owen Ward took two steps forward and fired his gun into the skies above.

At first, no noise came from within the saloon. After a long moment, though, the brave townsfolk who dared to watch and the seven gunfighters heard a rumbling of feet, and three cowboys, Sheriff Daggs, and Boze Neary ran out of the front entrance of the Needle, their guns shooting live rounds, as they dove for the protection of the containers holding the liquor.

Sheriff Daggs scrambled his way to the far right end of the saloon, in front of Sams' position, with a young cowboy next to the corrupt lawman, who mostly desired to save his own life rather than protect the surly sheriff.

Boze Neary crouched behind several boxes, hidden near the center of the fray, with two of his gang members armed and shooting to his immediate right-hand side.

Missing all of their shots except for the target of fear which existed in the hearts of every man present in the gun battle, the Neary Gang then took cover and paused to reload their weapons. Boze was handed a sawed-off shotgun by a ducking cowboy, but the gang leader kept the weapon at an arm's length distance from his person, waiting instead to use the shotgun at a vital moment.

The other side had been waiting for Owen's signal, as the shootist raised a thumb's up, before returning back a barrage of their own gunfire. After the shootist dropped his left hand, the 'Apache Kid's' first rifle shot came within inches of hitting Sheriff Daggs in the face, causing the lawman to lose his nerves, and he proceeded to get up and run from the fight. Sams steadied his long-rifle and took aim again, while Flores and Bob Channing followed the Indian's sightline with gunshots of their own.

The sheriff was struck twice, one bullet in the back of his head, and another shot ricocheting from off the wooden side-panel of the saloon, hitting Daggs on the bottom of his neck; neither shot had been fired by either the 'King of Flowers' or the drunkard Channing. While the two men celebrated their untrue aims, Sams remained calm and moored his heart rate, not wanting to risk an opportunity to take another killshot if Daggs was to rise up from the ground. The lawman ceased to move from his bloodied, face down position.

In a quick moment, three new cowboys from around the left back-side of the Needle appeared, as Flores was whooping and hollering to himself. While Owen and Taig continued shooting at those already present in the fight, pinning down Boze and those gang members nearest to him, the three new gunmen shot their revolvers in wild motions in Flores's direction, causing many successive shots to ring out and burst forth much gray smoke, with one of the bullets hitting the Mexican in the temple, and he was dead in mere seconds after the fired projectile made impact with his skull.

The soul of the man deep withinside the body of Dr. Taig Ward felt a visceral hatred for another human being for the first time in an entire lifespan, one where he had taken an oath to preserve all those he came across; the doctor zeroed in on a clean-shaven cowboy and then he pulled the trigger. Taig thought of all the dead bodies he'd seen as both a man and as a doctor, but none of them had ever been caused by the deliberate mis-actions crafted by his own hands. Shuddering at the idea of his destructive power for a slight instance, Taig was fortunate that Owen was able to level two shots at the two remaining surprise cowboys, and the shootist killed the man on the right, while he ruptured the pink-sinewy bicep muscle of the other man's shooting arm, rendering him incapacitated and weeling away in pain, before the man bled to death.

A sudden roar came from above the heads of the fighters, as a second floor window of the Needle was broken, and Jimmy Cotton jutted the upper half of his body through the remaining jagged pieces of the window's glass, as he fanned the trigger of his aimed pistol at Bob Channing, using the palm of his fast left hand to pull the trigger down repeatedly, dropping Channing dead into the dirt. His bullet chamber emptied into Channing, Cotton ducked back into the room to reload his revolver.

Taking charge of their forward momentum, Boze Neary's pistol shot Tex Willis through his upper left thigh, rendering the man a screaming and bleeding mess, and the Texan crawled away to his horse, where he hobbled on to the animal's back, and yawed his way out of Redview.

The old Irishman then took a careful aim at Otis Staals, firing though missing the target, but putting enough fear into the scared young man to cause him to get up and run down the dusty red street, in the hopes of saving his life; not caring much about ending Staals' existence, Neary bent down to grab the sawed-off shotgun, and then he waited for the opposition's next move.

Owen Ward saw his men starting to break; knowing he needed to rally them to the cause, the shootist shouted up to the still hidden Jimmy Cotton.

"Come down here and fight me, you damned coward, Cotton! You're just a scared little boy, afraid to battle without his daddy around."

Jimmy Cotton vented his rage as he ran down the inside stairwell of the Needle, before bursting through the front entrance. He fanned the back of his gun's trigger four times, missing each shot.

Owen inhaled once and kept the hot air inside of his lungs and mind, and then he fired twice, missing the first shot just wide of Cotton's hat, as the second bullet fired hit Jimmy near the center of his heart, and the young warrior's feet left the ground beneath them, and he was launched dead onto his side, his gun misfiring in his departed hand.

Alerted by the movement of a sawed-off shotgun behind a liquor box being pointed at Taig, Owen fired his last remaining chambered bullet, and Boze Neary's left cheekbone suffered a grazing flesh wound, just enough to draw blood. Dropping his now empty revolver to the earth, Owen pushed Taig a few feet away from Boze's shotgun blast, and the backtail of Dr. Ward's jacket was pierced by the shotgun's shrapnel, although Taig was unwounded by the shot. Owen bore the brunt of the scattered bullets; the torso of the shootist's body was riddled with holes, and his right forearm remained attached at the elbow by only exposed ligaments and tendons. Owen laid on his back, bloody tears trickling down his face, as he fought to gargle viscous air into his damaged lungs.

Taig hunched over to Owen, forgetting about Boze Neary for a moment, but the doctor kept a firm hand remaining upon his pistol. Once Taig arrived at Owen's side, he could see the man's body shaking with each wheezing gasp of breath.

"I'm sorry for failing you, Taig," Owen spat out solid red matter in a weak voice. "I just want to sleep now…and see her again."

"You will, Owen, you will. Just go to sleep now, and when you wake up, you'll see her face."

Taig took Owen's left hand and pressed it hard; for a while the shootist's fingers held tight to his kin, before he let go and released himself from the running gun battle.

As Boze attempted to reload his shotgun, Sams had positioned himself for a clearer shot, and now the Indian aimed his long-rifle at Neary, shooting him below his right breast, which caused the gang leader to drop his weapon.

Seeing the devil who had killed his cousin become wounded served to awaken Taig back into the fight, and the doctor stood up and fired at Boze, striking him in the nose, where half of the man's face disappeared into red nothingness.

The last remaining cowboy threw his gun away from his person, and then took off running. Both Taig and Sams watched as the man became a distant black speck down the road from them.

Before the fog of war could be lifted, the sound of fifty horses clamored into Redview. As the front of the massive blue bulk of the Federal Army of the United States of America came into view, Taig spotted Judge Graves and several officers leading the charge.

The judge arrived out of breath and in shock at the sight of the gore in the street around his horse's feet.

The crimson-faced colonel and his equally red lieutenants stared daggers through the white medicine man and the 'Apache Kid'.

"You're too late, Graves. Neary and Cotton are both dead. The last fellow took off north, maybe heading towards Flagstaff. What happened to the fellas chasing you to Prescott? And how in hell did you get the troopers here?" said the exhausted Taig Ward.

"Going through the valley, we bumped into these boys on a scouting expedition," said Judge Graves. "They arrested the cowboys."

"Yeah, just like we are going to arrest that bloody savage!" roared one of the Army's lieutenants who recognized the 'Apache Kid', and he directed a contingent of troopers to cuff Sams, who made no move to defend himself.

The boys in soldier blue beat the half-Apache with swift boot-kicks before the iron cuffs were placed around Sams's skinny brown wrists.

"Hey, this man helped to kill Boze Neary and a few of the other cowboys. What are you doing?" yelled Taig, as he cast cold countenance upward to the head officer.

The mustachioed colonel gave Taig a half-smile, before smirking at his lieutenants.

"Bring the savage in with the rest of the trash," said the colonel.

"Wait, here, colonel," demanded Judge Graves, as he stood near Sams. "This here is my jurisdiction, and the Apache is still needed to be questioned by myself for past crimes committed in this county. It is my right to detain the man for at least the night."

"You want to argue who's in the right?" said a lieutenant. "We know that *we are*, Graves. Sams is wanted all over, and we got 'em now, fair and square."

Graves looked at the silent Sams, and then back to the officers in blue.

"I suppose you gentlemen are correct, but could I then perhaps make a simple request?' asked the judge.

"Depends." said the colonel.

"You already have all of those cowboys we captured earlier today. I say you split up your forces, sending some of your troopers to bring in the surviving Neary gang members to the jail at Camp Verde, not counting Sams, of course, because I do want to question him about what happened here. The other half of your force can chase down this final, escaped cowboy. I could keep the 'Apache Kid' locked up here, in Redview's jail, just until the morning."

"You trying to tell the Army what its business should be, sir?" asked the colonel.

"Not at all, Colonel Irving," said Judge Graves, as he searched for his words. "I'd just assume that the more men you capture associated with the Neary Gang, the more reward money you boys are liable to collect from Washington, no?"

Seeing no harm in prolonging bringing Sams into Camp Verde, the colonel split his men into two groups, all either going further north to Flagstaff, or back south to the fort, except two privates.

"I'll leave behind two of my men to help ensure the prisoner is kept safe from any and all danger." said Colonel Irving.

Judge Graves nodded his head in concurrence, and the soldiers of blue glory left the town of red ill repute in a beehive of activity.

The judge winked at Taig, and then told the Federal troopers to gather up as much of the unbroken whiskey bottles as they could carry, as the liquor had been owned by the outlaw Boze Neary and his band of renegades, thereby designating the full bottles as contraband, which they were required by law to repossess. The blue soldiers were quick to oblige in their eagerness, as they carried bottle after bottle into the town jail, the first few sips of the opened liquor warming the two fellow's minds before rendering the men to seek further drink. Within an hour's time, while the men roared out in laughter, drunk to the world around them, Sams, Graves, and Taig walked down the street, and the Indian's dark horse following close behind them

Arriving at the edge of Redview, Judge Graves uncuffed the Indian. None of the men said anything, while Taig removed twenty crisp greenbacks from his wallet.

"Here, Sams, as we promised you," said the doctor. "That's $200, the price on your head for capturing you alive."

"What's the bounty for bringing me in dead?" asked the Indian.

"$500." stated the judge in easy nonchalance.

Sams spun around twice and then proceeded to ululate a laugh mixed with accepting grief, dancing a short jig upon the tips of his toes.

"Isn't it funny how a man is worth more dead than alive in this country of yours?" Sams said in passing mirth.

Rubbing his raw wrists, the 'Apache Kid' gazed into the two white men's eyes a final time, before he strapped his long-rifle to the side of the black stallion, and jumped up onto the great creature's back. Waving goodbye, the horse's whinnying carried Sams out into the western wilderness.

"What will we tell Colonel Irving?" asked Taig.

"That his soldiers are good for nothing drunks," replied Judge Graves. "Now, come on, we gotta go find the gravedigger, and try to put this town back together again."

Chapter 30- There Are No Heroes Anymore, Kid

Eight months had passed since Owen Ward's body had been laid to rest in Taig Ward's family plot on his ranch property, right next to Emma Rabelais. No birth year or death date were cut into their stone markers, and the grass sodded around the ground had grown brown; the soil would not allow life to be fostered there, no matter the tenderness of the harvester's hands. Nearby trees of heaven dominated the surrounding area, and Doctor Ward's pleading with the local arborist to rid his land of the poisonous plants went for-not, and the invasive tall, skinny trees had prevented other vegetation from growing; the tree of paradise's toxins riddle the earth its roots grow in, resulting in the death of all greenery it comes into contact with. No man can fight the heavens' long reach.

Peering down at their graves, the ten-year-old boy had made his decision just then, after weeks and weeks of close-mouthed consideration, and he now looked to the medical man for his blessing.

"If you would allow for it, sir, perhaps my name could be changed to Thomas Rabelais…Ward?" said Tom, firm in his conviction, but respectful in his persuasion. "I want my name to be related to the man who would have been my father, if the hand of providence had not intervened."

Taig Ward steadied himself by leaning onto his hickory cane, considering the question for a moment, while choosing the correct words to say to the boy. The doctor's right upper thigh elicited stabbing pain whenever he stood still for too long.

When Colonel Irving had discovered the disappearance of Sams, the 'Apache Kid', from the town of Redview's jail, the military man's wrath had been quick to induce Taig to join the forces of the Federal Army, as a medical officer. By orders decreed from the Secretary of War in Washington, D.C., any doctor in the territories could be conscripted by the troopers for a period of six months, when the health of the Army was at stake. In return for not facing any legal charges over the irregularities related to the vanishing of Sams from Judge Graves's custody, Taig had allowed himself to be drafted into the military.

In addition to the hours and days of loneliness and solitude inflicted upon him over the course of his dreaded term of service, as desolate camps and undermanned forts left little opportunities for social discourse, a surprise raid by a renegade band of Apaches in Cochise County, just outside of the mining town of Bisbee, had resulted in not only the deaths of the two murdered soldiers he had failed to save the lives of, but also an arrow wound just below his groin area. The missile had missed the lower parts of his intestines, thus avoiding his own painful demise, but the injury had produced a lesion that seeped with smelly, yellow pus, and the doctor feared he would never again be able to walk without the use of a cane. Taig did not blame the Red Man in his heart, but his soul burned in hatred for the Blue Officer, as the Federal Army suffered no abuse towards its collective conscience while continuing the vigilant march towards Progress. After the completion of his required six months in the Army, Taig was released without ceremony, while still waiting to be paid for his time and lost wages in serving his country. The doctor did not hold his breath waiting on any forthcoming letter to be sent by Washington.

Rubbing the injured thigh, and detecting no foul odor over the salve he had rubbed on the gash earlier in the day, Taig Ward thought Tom was old enough to make his own decision on the matter, and he further knew that the boy would be forced to become a man in the next few years anyways, so he decided to let the child do what was in his heart.

"Is this what you really want?" asked Taig, looking from his cousin's gravestone and then to the side of Tom's face.

"Yes, Dr. Ward," said Tom, as he turned to face his guardian. "But it is your name, too, and I would hate to be forward, sir."

"Never be afraid, my boy," said Taig, as he patted Tom once upon the shoulder. "Your father would have disapproved of such a notion. If you would like to have your name legally changed to become Thomas Rabelais *Ward*, then so it is done."

Delighted beyond belief and words, and in spite of his sadness for what could have been, the boy tempered his pain over the loss of his sadness by desiring to tempt fate further by risking another request of the medical man.

"Can I go see him, sir?" asked Tom, who looked out into the direction of the ruddy wilderness, not daring to say the man's name. "Don't you think he would still be out there, where my father and you once discovered him to be? I want to go through the wash areas and up the juniper hills, if you would allow it."

Taig Ward had no more laughs to give to the world, but he could recall a time before life had beaten the unbridled joy out of him. The man foresaw no harm in the request, as he believed the boy would not be able to find the Indian.

"Only on the condition that you are back and washed before supper this evening," said Taig, as he gazed back down at the graves. "Mind me, boy, because Mrs. Ward abides by no soul being late to say grace before we have supper. Don't be late!"

"Yes, sir!" exclaimed the petite boy, before he squatted down to kiss his hands and then touch the gravestones of his mother and father, before turning to run out into the desert.

"And Tom, make sure to bring your slingshot," Taig said in a stern voice. "Those rattlers are starting to come out to warm themselves in the spring sunshine. They don't like being disturbed by a lad out on a lark, so best to be armed."

Tom nodded and was off again, running to load his brown pony and race around the creek bend.

Taig looked for a moment longer at the headstones, and then made his way in contemplation back into his home, hoping that Neley would understand that not all of his decisions were really his to make.

After searching for hours in the prospect of seeing the 'Apache Kid' in the flesh, and as the time to turn around for home was almost reached, Tom happened along a horse trail that consisted of a single track, one which must have been made by a gigantic horse. Going further along the trailway, the boy spotted a black stallion chewing the cud around a juniper bush in the short distance ahead, and Tom knew the horse to be the signature animal of choice for the wanted half-breed outlaw.

Tying his pony to a dead branch, Tom walked in careful consideration towards the dark creature, and he hoped to see the Indian nearby. Holding a flat hand, palm down, just above his eyebrows to prevent the sun from burning his eyes, the boy scanned the horizon. Sitting alone on a round, flat boulder, Tom could see his man, shirtless and with an object in his lap. Approaching closer, he could see that Sams's eyes were wide open and unseeing, and the smell of smoke became stronger as he drew nearer to the man. Vespers of twirling clouds floated from out of the end of an elongated wooden pipe sitting on the man's lap, and the mists became like small tornadoes, as the steam drifted into the outer ether.

The boy could not contain his emotion, and he wanted to speak with the Indian about many things.

"Sams! Hey, Sams!" said Tom, startling the black stallion, who had roamed nearer to his master, and the horse looked to the boy as a sphinx. "Good afternoon, my name is Tom Rabelais Ward; I'm Owen Ward's boy! My friends call me 'Tom Sawyer', like the Mark Twain character."

The Apache gave the child no acknowledgement of hello, nor any recognition of his presence. Sams continued to stare off into the distant redness, and the pupils of his eyes were dilated a half-inch larger than their normal positions, his breathing quickened and interrupted by small gulps of air.

Not knowing what to do next, Tom got within touching distance of the gunfighter, the smoke singing his nostrils, and he realized the smell was not of tobacco alone. He reached out to touch the Indian, but then thought the wiser, pulling back his hand. The boy did not like the 'peace' pipe or its constant bellowing.

"You boys all did it, Sams," said Tom, his voice breaking in high pitch. "You are all my heroes! Better than any Wyatt Earp story they publish in them penny novels, I tell you."

His excitement overwhelming his prudent judgment, Tom tapped Sams on his naked, tanned shoulder, but the young man remained stoic in his terrible tranquility, the sweat covering his entire body glistening in the dying sunshine of the day.

"What he was, that's what you *are*," said Tom, growing more fervent in his hope to gain the Indian's attention. "I mean, Dr. Ward is a good man and all, but he was forced by life's circumstances to fight against mortal evil. But you, Sams, you're a *shootist*, just like Owen!"

In a remote, droning voice, the 'Apache Kid' opened his mouth at last, but he refrained from looking at the boy.

"There are no heroes anymore, kid. I'm just a living dead man," said Sams, as he ignored the vengeful words of the sky gods. "Next time, it could be my turn. Listen to your white medicine man, and he will help you to see the reason of your society."

Tom closed his mouth for the first time, at a loss of what to say. Sams still did not look at the youth.

"But, for now, 'Tom Sawyer', would you care to sit and watch the talking mountains and opinionated skies with me? I must leave this place in the morning."

Tom sat down in front of the man before the Indian had finished asking the question, and Mrs. Ward was very angry upon his eventual late return home that night.

Dr. Taig Ward and Judge Eugene Graves drank out of sharp snifter glasses shipped from the Irish port city of Wexford, and each cup contained three-fingers of French brandy that did not burn either man's throat; the occasion marked the first time Graves had socialized at his old friend's ranch home property since their falling out last year. Although the judge suffered no repercussions for the escape of Sams, Graves wrote a letter every week demanding for the release of Taig Ward from his conscription into the Federal Army, crafting legal arguments to end the terms of his friend's service; all of his ornery hopes had fallen upon deaf ears, but the doctor appreciated the aged man's valiant efforts to help him.

Holding up his snifter, Judge Graves proposed a mocking toast.

"To the 'Dirty Irishman'," said the judge. "May the angels decide his fate as kindly as the man lived."

Taig raised his own Wexford glass in turn, but he did not sip long on the smooth brandy.

After drinking their first glass, Taig poured them both another tall brandy, while Judge Graves cut off the butt ends of the Carolina cigars he had been saving for when his daughter was to be married; as the girl now approached forty years of age, the father accepted that she never would grant him an occasion to light them anyways, so the judge brought them over for his friend to enjoy them with instead.

"Have there been any volunteers for the job at all?" asked Taig, as he took a first puff from his cigar, stifling a harried cough.

The judge held his own cigar between his thumb and index finger, as he inhaled for a long moment, the light brightening his face in the evening's darkness.

"No, none as of yet," said Judge Graves, as he rushed to blow the hot smoke out of his lungs. "But I will reach out to some lawmen friends of mine that are based in Prescott. Perhaps we may be able to scour up another county's deputy to come here to be our sheriff in Redview."

"Yeah, sounds real promising, Judge." said Taig, taking a long sip from his snifter.

"Hey, now, we're bound to find a man who intends on keeping the peace throughout this area," said Judge Graves, as he dipped two fingers into his glass, and then licked them like a kitten. "Have some faith. I just hope he's half-ways honest, whoever the man happens to be."

Taig nodded several times and then he finished his second brandy, debating whether to have a third drink or not. His fear of Nelcy won out, and he accepted no more enticement to have any more alcohol for the rest of the night, no matter the quantity of his old friend's good-natured abuse.

After a long moment's silence, the doctor looked over to his friend.

"Yes, perhaps you're right, Judge. Maybe one day we will have law throughout the red lands, but until then, I aim to keep shooting."

"Amen to that," said the judge, nodding his head in concurrence. "But perhaps one day, Doc."

The tired men smoked their cigars until the orange embers glowing in the night turned a pitch black and ashy gray.

Made in the USA
Monee, IL
10 January 2024